Acclaim for *Gimme Shelter*

'*Gimme Shelter* is an uncompromisingly traumatic book whose
body count and tension incline steeply upwards from the
outset… Throughout, Gittins confounds and surprises with
tectonic shifts of allegiances and motivations in both the cloying
corruptions and rivalries within the police service and among the
criminal characters… corrosive psychological consequences which
match those in the best Nicci French thrillers… this disturbing and
exhilarating novel should quickly establish its author as a
fiction writer of universal note.'

Morning Star

'… full of intrigue and narrative twists… powerfully written and
uncompromising in its style, the author makes use of various games,
such as squash and chess, as a metaphorical sub-plot that registers the
various psychological manoeuvres of the characters as they negotiate
a world in which no-one is as they seem – inadequate police,
psychopaths – inadequate police who are psychopaths –
sexual deviants and torture junkies.'

Dufour Editions

'No one could guess that *Gimme Shelter* is Rob Gittins's first novel
because his hand is so sure in developing characters as complex as
they are convincing, in managing a plot chock full of surprising
twists and in maintaining a tension that keeps the reader totally
absorbed… Gittins's gritty story introduces the reader to a dangerous
and troubled part of society, and his murky, damaged and at
times violent characters are as vividly (and disturbingly)
portrayed as those of Elmore Leonard.'

Susanna Gregory

'Rob Gittins is a highly acclaimed dramatist whose work has been enjoyed by millions in TV and radio dramas. In *Gimme Shelter*, his first novel, he has advanced his skills in a compelling story of modern times. He takes us into the violent and murky criminal world of witness protection where boundaries between good and evil are ill-defined. *Gimme Shelter* is an extraordinary achievement.'

Nicholas Rhea

'An unflinching debut… as vicious and full of twists as a tiger in a trap.'

Russell James

'A major new crime writer has given us the definitive interpretation of 'page turnability' and created characters that step effortlessly off the page and into the memory. This is a book that will haunt the reader long after the covers are closed.'

Katherine John

'TV writer Rob Gittins's ultra-violent crime debut hits hard from the start.'

Iain McDowall

'Visceral realism doesn't come much better than in this taut, superbly plotted debut, where no-one in its snake pit of lies and betrayals is as they seem. Brilliant.'

Sally Spedding

'An unflinching spotlight on the lesser-known corners of police work… noir at its most shocking.'

Rebecca Tope

'Terrifying and suspenseful, non-stop jeopardy. Just be glad you're only reading it and not in it.'

Tony Garnett

Gimme Shelter

For Dani and Zain

Gimme Shelter

ROB GITTINS

The characters in this book are entirely
fictional and are not intended to bear any
resemblance to anyone living or dead.

First impression: 2013

The publishers wish to acknowledge the support of
Cyngor Llyfrau Cymru

Cover design: Matthew Tyson

Paperback ISBN: 978 0 95601 258 6
Hardback ISBN: 978 1 84771 762 7

FSC

Published and printed in Wales
on paper from well maintained forests by
Y Lolfa Cyf., Talybont, Ceredigion SY24 5HE
e-mail ylolfa@ylolfa.com
website www.ylolfa.com
tel 01970 832 304
fax 832 782

NIGHTMARES ARE SUPPOSED to end. This one didn't.

It all started in such an ordinary way. She was walking down the path that led from the rear of her home. The sun was shining, traffic could be heard from the nearby streets as could the distant sound of children playing in the park. Everything seemed so normal, so everyday.

As she reached the front of the house she looked sideways at their small front garden, then stopped. If she had not, then she'd have fallen to her certain death because the front garden wasn't there. Nothing was. There was a gaping chasm where once there'd been solid ground.

What looked like the sea thrashed at the bottom of that deep chasm and – a detail that still particularly terrified her for some reason – drainage pipes bucked to and fro in the raging water, surfacing, then sinking, before surfacing again. She stood there, unable to take a step back, knowing it was also impossible to take a step forward, suspended in some sort of purgatory and – unlike most nightmares when they reached this most terrifying of points – she didn't immediately wake from it.

That's what she also remembered and all-too keenly. Once a nightmare peaked like that it was normally the moment the sleeper would awake. But she knew she'd remained staring down at the chasm that had suddenly opened before her, at that raging water and those thrashing pipes, for what seemed like an eternity.

Now it was back. That same nightmare and she was in the middle of it and she knew what she was going to see but she couldn't do anything about it, couldn't even turn back because there was nothing behind her, only a blackness even more terrifying somehow than all that lay ahead.

But there was a twist as there was always – now – a twist. She looked down again at the chasm that was waiting to swallow her, to see faces there now too. She couldn't see their bodies, they were submerged, but the faces were looking up at her, beseeching her for help; the faces of adults, of children, of terrified infants, all staring at her, appealing to her to do something.

Some of the faces she recognised. Some indeed were all-too familiar. Some would always be with her. But there were other faces too, the faces of people she'd never seen although they were connected to her as surely as if they were tied by some kind of eternal, invisible, umbilical cord.

The faces of those who should have been there.

The lost offspring of faces she'd previously failed to keep safe.

I

ELSHA HADN'T EXACTLY approved of what she'd termed the whirlwind romance and wedding although, as her daughter had pointed out, it was hardly that. Divone, better known to all in the family as Di, had known the man who was now her husband for the best part of a year. This hadn't been some drink or drug-fuelled impulse on a wild night out in Vegas.

They'd met, they'd talked, shared meals, done everything Elsha herself had done all those years earlier with Di's father. But all that had been in the company of both their families of course. She'd met his parents fairly early on in their relationship, he'd done the same.

Seminal moments.

Rites of passage.

The rites denied to her, somewhat typically, by her middle daughter.

Moments missed.

Elsha opened the fridge, checked the well-stocked shelves for roughly the fifteenth time in as many minutes. With the exception of a couple of ingredients for the salad dressing, ingredients Di herself had volunteered to fetch from the local convenience store – which doubled as a garage and which trebled as a post office – everything was in place for the family meal that evening; the meal where they'd finally get to know a man who was already part of their family.

First impressions, she had to concede, had been favourable. All right, there had only been a fleeting introduction as he dropped Di off on his way from the airport to some meeting he had to attend. But his handshake seemed strong and manly, his smile warm and genuine as were the quick kisses he'd exchanged, Continental-style, first with Di's sister, Braith and then with Cara, their youngest, not yet five years old but clearly not immune, even at that age, to male attention if the pleased flush that had illuminated her face was anything to go by.

There was still Di's father, Macklyn, to contend with. Emmanuel wouldn't be able to win him over with a simple handshake and a warm and seemingly genuine smile. Macklyn had spent the best part of thirty years assessing people in his line of work and Emmanuel was going to be well and truly assessed and in some forensic detail later on.

Macklyn certainly wouldn't be influenced by the one other factor about Emmanuel that was also immediately obvious to Elsha, to Braith and even to the young Cara; that Di's new husband, Elsha's new son-in-law and Braith and Cara's new brother-in-law, was definitely and undeniably hot.

Elsha smiled as she closed the fridge, listened to the delighted peals of laughter from Cara as she tried on some make-up upstairs, heard drawers opening and closing and cupboard doors banging as she and Braith also tried on a succession of clothes, the two girls already preparing themselves for the evening ahead. Di may have bagged something of a prize in the shape of an exotic beau from some distant land across the sea, but clearly neither Braith nor Cara intended to be put in the shade by their newly-arrived sibling. Tonight, everyone intended to look their best.

Elsha ducked slightly, an instinctive reaction perhaps, checked her own hair in the polished glass-like surface of the chest-high oven, then turned as a ring sounded on the doorbell outside.

For a moment some small shadow appeared on the very edge of her vision, a trick of the light most probably, the sun going behind a passing cloud perhaps.

But later, much later, she'd replay that moment, pore over it obsessively, wondering if it had been something else, some instinct stirring, punishing herself with the same question again and again; what would have happened had she acted on it?

Braith was already moving down the hall, Cara clattering down the stairs behind her. All she could hear were the same words chanted by them both as they headed for the door – 'Ditzy' – 'Ditzy Di'.

'Ditzy Di' was the family nickname for the middle daughter who was perennially forgetful; scatterbrained to use another well-worn family phrase. How many times could Elsha remember them turning back as they set off on some family outing and Di would suddenly remember she hadn't brought along some book, some crayons, a favourite soft toy?

Braith and Cara were placing bets as they made for the door, trying to second-guess what it was that had brought her back this time. She'd already returned twice, the first time for her purse, the second for her phone. A giggling Cara was placing her bet on shoes but Braith doubted even Di could have walked out of the door without footwear.

Was it again some instinct at work? For a moment Elsha held her breath, almost as if she knew that she wanted to preserve those moments, those simple ordinary family snapshots, freeze them in time somehow, freeze her daughters in that same moment, keep them as they were right there and then, suspended in that instant forever.

A second later she heard it. It was as if a clap of thunder had sounded outside, which was impossible she knew, but what else could it be? How else to explain the deafening explosion that suddenly seemed to blast through the house?

But as she looked towards the window she could see that the sun was shining as brightly as it had done just a moment earlier and even the slight shadow she'd sensed previously seemed now to have lifted.

Everything looked exactly the same, but it wasn't.

She knew, in that instant, that everything had changed forever.

Cara was a few feet behind her sister. It had become a race as to who would reach the door first, who'd be the first to taunt Di with her nickname.

Braith won the race. Later, Cara would wonder whether it would have made any difference, whether what happened a moment later wouldn't have happened at all if a little girl had opened the door as opposed to her grown-up sister.

A man stared back at Braith, a man who looked quite ordinary. Certainly Cara could recall no particular distinguishing features in the days and months that followed. She'd be asked the same questions over and over again; how old was he, what was the colour of his hair, how tall was he, was he muscular like her father or thin like their next-door neighbour and Cara tried to answer all their questions as honestly as she could but it was difficult when all she could think of was the gun in his hand.

As Cara stared down the hall it was all she could focus on. Everything else seemed to melt into the background.

Braith would have been of more use to the subsequent inquiry. In the single second before a blinding white light seemed to bleach the whole world, bleeding all colour from everything before her, she looked straight into the man's eyes. Braith didn't look at the gun at all. All she saw was his eyes staring at her, pausing just a moment as he seemed to check her features.

Then he gave the slightest nod, seemingly satisfied now.

Then the nozzle of the gun kicked upwards and Braith, acting on some compulsion to protect her younger sister, moved to shield Cara who was hovering just a few feet behind.

As she half-turned, the bullet exploded from the short barrel of the gun, smashing into her face, her brains exploding out of the back of her skull. Braith was propelled back by the impact, arms flailing, her body instinctively attempting to break the fall, to protect what had already been destroyed.

Cara looked down at her sister, only the face that stared back at her belonged to no-one she now recognised. In fact it didn't even seem to belong to a human being at all. The nose and eyes had been replaced by what looked to be a second mouth which was not a mouth at all of course, but a large and gaping wound inside which everything seemed to be dancing; veins, bits of skin tissue, bones.

And coursing through it all, spewing out from that second, open, mouth was blood, running down over her neck, staining the dress Braith had picked out for the party that night.

Cara looked up and saw the man still standing in the doorway, not even seeming to see the young girl, the man checking now, making sure, but there could be little doubt. The face that had once belonged to her sister had been totally destroyed, bits of her brain were staining the stairs and while her body might still be twitching, horribly, she had to be dead. How could she not be, how could anyone survive something like that?

Then the gunman was gone. Cara looked down at Braith who'd now rolled onto her side. Cara turned, the will to survive kicking in perhaps, the little girl knowing she had to get away.

Which was when she saw another figure appear in the doorway behind her. She didn't hold a gun but she was still a stranger, which was the second totally bewildering realisation in almost as many seconds because how could her mother suddenly appear to be a stranger? It didn't make sense, but she did.

For that moment it was like looking at some caricature of a woman Cara had once known as her mother as Elsha looked down the hallway at the twitching body of her eldest daughter and at parts of her brain now beginning to slide, snail-like, down the wallpaper leading up to the first-floor landing.

For that moment too there was silence, but that didn't last.

Then her mother started to scream.

2

THE CORRIDOR WAS grimy. Generations of handprints stained the walls, paint peeled from the cracked ceiling, old scene-of-crime posters peeked out from behind new, destined themselves to be plastered over in turn.

Ros looked up as a hand came into view. She focused briefly as Conor, some two years her junior and recently seconded from this very unit, handed her a cup of foul-smelling coffee in a stained mug. The crest of Cardiff City Football Club, a local favourite, the ground just a few miles away, was wrapped round the side. Someone had tried to scratch something on it, presumably derogatory, but the enamel had defeated the attempt and all that remained were splinters and scratches.

Ros looked round. This place always had been fiercely territorial and that wasn't just in its choice of football teams. As far as this place was concerned, you were either in or you were out. You were part of the team or you were the opposition even if, technically, everyone was supposed to be on the same side.

Us against them.

The world out there against everyone in here.

There was an unspoken justification for that which Ros sensed every time she paid one of her largely-unwelcome visits. Murder Squad had always dealt with human depravity in its most extreme forms. Those sorts of experiences forged a special type of team spirit, bonded fellow officers in a way few other crimes could.

Or twisted the spirit of everyone who ever passed through these doors, corrupting anything resembling a normal world-view and forever guaranteeing that everyone in here would look at a world out there with eyes that had not only seen the worst but now expected the worst – and not just from those they called by all manner of names but who, in Ros's department, were still called clients.

No wonder the divorce rate in this department was twice the average for the whole of the force and that, given the statistics for marital disintegration in policing, was saying something.

'The machine was bust, I popped into the kitchen.'

Conor nodded at the mug in Ros's hand.

'Not the Swans are you, Ma'am?'

Ros wasn't even listening. She didn't even register the deliberate hesitation before the final address, the habitual mark of respect that was anything but.

She knew what Conor was saying. I know this place. I know my way around, I know what to do when a vending machine gives up the ghost, vandalised in all probability by one of the low-life villains I used to nick.

Because this used to be my world. A world where real police officers do real policing, not the glorified babysitting I'm now doing thanks to some procedural screw-up Ros hadn't even bothered investigating too deeply because she knew she'd only be told half the truth anyway.

It didn't matter where Conor used to work. He was an extra body, an extra pair of eyes and an extra pair of hands and for now that was all that mattered.

Then Ros looked up as, from inside a nearby room, she heard voices raised in volume; one voice in particular – a female voice – sounding louder than the rest.

Conor hadn't exactly enjoyed too much in the way of conversation from his new DS on the way over to his old stomping ground. From the little he'd been able to glean since his recent arrival, no-one did get too much in the way of idle chit-chat from her. Conor had met some strange individuals in his time in Murder Squad but there was still something unsettling about Ros. She was a cold fish, he'd been warned of that, but there was something else going on inside her too.

Anyway, being cold at heart didn't really square with the demands of the unit she'd elected to join immediately after her initial training. That unit – Witness Protection – now his unit too, had traditionally been seen as little more than a support service, staffed by jumped-up care assistants who, more often than not, wore their bleeding hearts on their sleeves.

Did Ros even have a heart? There was precious little evidence of that either. She lived alone, didn't mix with anyone from the department socially, was occasionally seen in the company of some male or other in one of the local bars or restaurants so that answered one question, the dyke angle at least; but that aside there was literally nothing to report.

Perhaps because there was nothing. Perhaps because she was an open book, a loser, an inadequate, a twenty-something woman who couldn't cut it in either normal policing or normal life, who'd elected to spend her life in this backwater, picking up the pieces after everyone else, mopping up the mess.

Conor didn't even hear the raised voices from inside the nearby room. He was used to it. He just looked round at a place that was now his past. Then he looked back at Ros, hoping – as fervently as he'd ever hoped for anything in his life – that he wasn't looking at his future too.

'Looked like vandals at first, guv.'

Half an hour earlier, Donovan Banks, late twenties, still single, no significant other as yet, had kept step along the stained corridor with Kayne Masters, early forties, marital status unknown, at least so far as Banks was concerned.

'A neighbour had called the fire boys. Said there was smoke coming out of this disused shop down the street.'

'What sort of shop?'

'Butcher's.'

Masters nodded, grimly. It seemed to fit.

Masters and Banks barely paused as another officer, Keiran Scott, a contemporary of Banks, part of the same year's intake, handed his current senior officer a mug of coffee before handing Masters his usual mug of tea, strong, just a dash of milk.

Masters did proffer Scott the courtesy of a nod by way of thanks but Banks had other priorities on his mind right now and delighted in letting Scott know that by hardly even seeming to see him.

'There was a storage room in the back. It still had some of the old hooks in the ceiling. There wasn't anything else in there apart from an old chair, not an office chair but an armchair, great big thing it must have been too. That's what had been set alight.'

Banks paused.

'Then they realised there was something else in there too.'

Masters moved ahead of Banks into the interview room, seated himself on a hard chair, Banks taking the seat next to him. Opposite was Tyra Rhea, early twenties, slim, mixed-race – although what races had been mixed to create that stunning face Masters couldn't decide. Her face, currently framed by a shock of dyed blue hair, had been her passport to what must have seemed like heaven to a girl in her late teens but which now, just a few years later, looked as if it had been a one-way ticket to some particularly twisted version of hell.

And that's what interested Masters rather more at present.

What particular hell had she witnessed in that old storage room in that disused butcher's shop?

What demons and ogres had she kept company with in there?

And what sort of deal could they now do to make sure those demons and ogres – whatever and whoever they were – would never visit on anyone else the horror they'd inflicted that day?

'I want a smoke.'

'Not possible.'

Tyra hadn't even looked at Banks as he answered her. She'd clearly already developed a sixth sense for those who held the real reins of power.

Masters reached in his pocket and, in strict contravention of procedure and good practice, pushed a pack of cigarettes and a lighter across the desk to the young woman. It wouldn't be the first breach of protocol or the last.

Tyra lit a cigarette, inhaled, then exhaled a cloud of smoke that enveloped Banks as he leant forward to check the interview tape was working.

Tyra eyed him coolly for a moment.

Then she'd begun.

'He'd started getting whispers a year or so ago. This new face had opened up somewhere close by. There were a couple of adverts in some of the free sheets, girls wanted for escort work, that kind of thing.'

Masters studied the young girl before him. Her age must have been one of her biggest attractions for her new boyfriend. She would have been useful. New girls arriving in a city, any city – London, Nottingham, Manchester or in their case the melting pot of old and new, race and creed, that was modern-day Cardiff – were always going to gravitate towards someone like her, towards one of their own. Or at least a girl who appeared to be one of their own rather than the overweight Ukrainian that Tyra had been living with for the last six months.

But all roads still led back to the Ukrainian – Yaroslav – in the end.

'It wasn't that big a problem, at least not at the start. It's not as if he expected any kind of monopoly or nothing. And it's not as if there's not enough business to go round either, let's face it, you lot and sex.'

Tyra nodded at the middle-aged copper and his youthful companion, seeing one thing and one thing only; inexhaustible demand for which her boyfriend promised limitless supply.

'So what changed?'

Tyra paused and Masters could understand why. Even at this late stage in what had already been quite a journey, all this was clearly still something of a trial to her. She'd never in her wildest imaginings dreamt she'd be sitting on one side of a police interview desk, of her own volition, volunteering chapter and verse on the activities of a man she'd seen as a boyfriend and protector, possibly for years to come.

But what had happened in that butcher's shop had scared her badly – as the slight shake of her hand as she raised her half-finished cigarette to her mouth attested.

'A couple of our girls went over. The usual thing, they reckoned they could get a better deal with someone else, maybe got tired of their regulars, I don't know, I never get involved in that sort of stuff myself.'

Banks nodded, sour.

'Just open the door for others.'

'Who's he, Snow White?'

Masters stepped in, defusing the sudden tension, diverting her hostile stare and raised voice away from the younger officer and his somewhat ill-timed intervention.

'One of his girls is now with us.'

'Kirino.'

Tyra nodded.

'I know.'

'And Yaroslav knows too?'

'Of course he knows.'

'And?'

'And what do you think? He's spitting fucking blood.'

Tyra paused.

'That's one of the reasons for what happened. He never said nothing, he wouldn't, he's never exactly been the confiding type but I reckon he started to feel things were slipping out of his control. New face on the manor. Then an old face suddenly switches sides and starts talking to you.'

Tyra shrugged.

'It upset him.'

Masters reviewed the mental arithmetic.

Yaroslav's office housed twelve landlines all with different numbers. A small workforce manned the phones answering each with the name of a different agency: Studio 7, Best Choice, 18 & New. To service the twelve landlines Yaroslav had more than a hundred and twenty women on his books, all ages, shapes, sizes and nationalities. He saw himself as a one-stop shop. No need to go anywhere else, whatever your preference, Yaroslav always had the product and that product didn't now just service the capital city which had become its base. Yaroslav's sphere of influence and operation was expanding almost daily.

The minimum outcall charge was £200, often more once travelling and optional extras such as uniforms and specialist services were added on. The clients paid Yaroslav, he paid half to the girls on what he called the platinum band, the highest; followed by a third to girls on the gold band and a quarter to those starting out who were placed on the trainee tier or 'his new angels' as he sometimes referred to them.

Out of that little lot Masters estimated that the Ukrainian raked in somewhere in the region of a million, maybe a million and a half per year. Throw in various associated activities such as sex-trafficking and drug distribution, often using those very same girls and that same clientele and that figure had to be doubled, if not trebled.

No wonder, to paraphrase the young woman sitting opposite right now, Yaroslav had become a little upset.

'Then this girl came over to us. It had been pretty well one-way traffic up to then, but it seemed this new face was getting greedy.'

'Wojike.'

Banks had broken in again.

'That was his name. Wojike.'

Tyra didn't reply, just exhaled again, the smoke curling till it hit the ceiling where it vapourised.

'The girl had gone on an all-nighter. Some art critic or somebody, he was supposed to be really well-known. He paid her two grand to sit and have dinner with him in some fancy restaurant somewhere down in the bay, then go back to his place. They agreed on the money up front. The punter paid by credit card, all usual enough.'

Tyra paused.

'This girl was a bit out of the ordinary too. Name was Alison something and she was temporary and yeah, I know they all say that but she was different. She'd been in Uni, had run up a few debts, the usual, drugs and stuff, didn't want to go back to Surrey and explain all that to Daddy and Mummy so she'd decided to turn a few tricks, pay it off that way, then get out. She probably would have done too, she had her head screwed on.'

Tyra paused again.

'Not that it stopped her getting right royally screwed over by – .'

Tyra inclined her head towards Banks. She was now in charge of this story and was well and truly calling all the shots too.

Banks hesitated, but Masters was now looking at him too.

'Wojike.'

Tyra nodded, then ground out her cigarette on the interview table, flicked the dead stub on the floor.

'The next morning, Wojike tells her there's been a problem with the card. The transaction didn't go through. Leave it to him, he'll get on the case, come back to her. He does a day or so later, tells her the bloke had got himself maxed out, what can he do, he can't exactly go to the police, looks like they'll have to write it off, he's as upset as she is about this, he's down a grand himself but that's what happens sometimes.'

Tyra shrugged.

'Hadn't happened at all of course and she knew it. A couple of the other girls had been done over in the same way on the really big jobs. They didn't compare notes, he made sure they had next to no contact with each other, but he did use the same drivers to get them to the marks. The girls talked to the drivers, the drivers told the girls what some of the others had said, it didn't take long for them to get the full SP.'

Tyra paused.

'Yaroslav decides this was his chance. OK, he'd scored himself a nice little meal ticket with Alison thanks to this Wojike getting greedy, but he wanted more. What he was doing was giving them all a bad name, girls were getting suspicious, punters were beginning to get a bit antsy too because the girls were starting to ask all sorts of awkward questions, so he decided to teach this new man on the manor a bit of a lesson.'

Tyra paused, let the last word hang in the air much as her cigarette smoke a few moments earlier.

'Yaroslav gets Alison to call him. She tells him she's tried going solo but it's not working out. Maybe she was a bit hasty walking out on him like that. Maybe they could talk about things. And

Wojike, he's delighted. He'd heard whispers that she'd gone over to some other outfit, so maybe he wasn't only going to get one of his star performers back, maybe he's going to get some tasty little info about one of his main rivals too. So when she says can they meet, he's only too willing.'

'And they met in a disused butcher's shop?'

Tyra looked at Masters for a moment, hesitated. Suddenly she wasn't in that room, sitting at that interview table, talking to two cops. She was in a place she never wanted to be again, seeing sights she never wanted to witness, sights she'd never eradicate from behind her eyes no matter how hard she tried.

'Yaroslav used this cheap hotel, out on the link road heading over towards Newport. Alison told Wojike that's where she'd been staying while she tried to set up by herself, he could meet her there. Yaroslav and a couple of his faces were waiting in the bathroom. It was all over in a second or two. He came in, Yaroslav stuck a taser in his balls, pulled the trigger.'

Across the table, Banks tensed instinctively.

'I'd seen him pull the same trick before. Sometimes, if they're lucky, they pass out, sometimes they just go into some sort of shock, whatever, they're never exactly in any sort of state to do much about it. Yaroslav bundled him into a laundry cart they'd found at the end of one of the corridors, wheeled him out and drove him round to the shop. By the time he came round he was tied to this armchair they'd found in a skip round the back.'

Tyra paused.

'By then he was naked too. Legs apart, crown jewels on show. Arms tied behind his back.'

Tyra paused again.

'Me and Yaroslav had watched this film once. It was all about this bloke who'd gone up against some gang or other. He wasted pretty well all of them but he kept one alive. He'd picked him out right from the start, made sure he saw the lot, watched as every one of his friends and family got taken out, the girls raped, the men tortured, as if he was saving him for last, as if there was something really tasty in store for this one. When it came to his turn he was last man standing, only he couldn't stand by then, couldn't sit either, it was like someone had taken out his spine or something, he just flopped all over the place, like he was made out of jelly.'

Tyra continued, images from the film now flashing before her eyes.

'But then he let him go. Didn't touch a hair on his head, just told him to get out. That way he could tell everyone of course. He could tell everyone what had happened which was always going to be a lot better than relying on a few dead bodies to do it instead.'

Masters kept his face impassive. From the scene of crime report he had a pretty shrewd idea what was coming next, but that didn't mean he actually wanted to hear it. In the scales of justice stakes, what had been meted out to Wojike was undeniably harsh but not anything anyone was going to lose too much sleep over.

What also happened in that room was something else entirely.

'They'd brought that Alison along too. She didn't want to come, she'd done what she was supposed to do, what was the point, but she didn't know the half of it, did she?'

Tyra paused again.

And all of a sudden she looked scared.

'No-one knew what he had in mind. Maybe he didn't have it in mind, maybe something happened inside that weird head of his once he got in the room, I don't know. All I do know is now it wasn't Wojike he was looking at all of a sudden, now it was the posh bit, only doing it to clear the student loan before moving back to Surrey, say hello to her horse, marry a solicitor, only she wasn't going to be doing that in a hurry was she, not unless she met a seriously twisted brief who got off on freaks.'

She was talking too much and she knew it and so did Masters. Maybe it was some kind of defence mechanism but they usually did one or the other; babbled away ten to the dozen or retreated into a silence so complete it was catatonic.

'We didn't even know he had it with him. He hardly needed it let's face it, a knife, a shooter OK, cut him up a bit, stick the shooter in his gob, threaten to pull the trigger, even pull the fucking trigger if he wanted, wouldn't be the first from everything I'd heard, probably wouldn't be the last neither, but that was his business.'

She was doing it again, trying to fill the space inside her head that was currently filled with everything that was venal and evil.

Tyra took another deep breath, regained some sort of control.

'She thought it was water at first. Couldn't work out why he'd suddenly emptied a whole bottle of water all over her head mind you, but maybe it was some sort of game or something. There was about a second or two when she looked at me, when the rest of us looked back at her and thought, what the fuck? Even Wojike was staring at her now too and with everything else he had on his mind right now that really was something.'

Tyra paused again.

'After a second or two we saw this smoke coming off her head. She had really thick hair, tied up in a sort of bob so it must have taken that amount of time to start eating its way through it all. But once it reached her scalp, it must have reacted or something, I don't know, I'm not any sort of chemist or nothing, don't want to be neither, I don't want to be anywhere near any of that stuff ever again, not after seeing what it did.'

Outside, in the corridor, a silent Ros was reading the case notes at the same time.

Yaroslav had emptied a two-litre bottle of acid over the young girl's scalp. There was nothing particularly exotic in the choice of acid, just the usual sulphuric variety you could find in any common or garden industrial laboratory or chemical store, even a school classroom. Easy to acquire, devastating in its impact and the really clever part, for the likes of Yaroslav at least, was the high survival rate among the victims of those sorts of attacks.

Sure, that victim's going to need an intensive period of corrective surgery, reconstruction of the gullet where they've most likely inhaled or even drunk some of the poison not to mention dozens, if not hundreds, of skin grafts but the body keeps going even when the brain is willing it to close down, to give up, to stop fighting the unendurable agony that's going on seemingly forever. The organs can still function; and do.

So the victim becomes one of the living dead, as Alison, even at this early stage of what was being euphemistically called her recovery, was already discovering by all accounts.

Ros looked up, stared down the corridor, taking in nothing, seeing only a face distorted into a silent scream, a living testament to the evil one human being can do to another.

Back in the interview room, Tyra was now hunched forward over the table, staring at the tape.

'She reached out, screaming, holding out her arms and he took hold of them, but that was just to stop her holding them over her face and now her eyes were smoking too and her eyeballs, it was like they were melting or something, all this white and yellow stuff was coming out but he just dragged her over to Wojike who was staring at her like we all were and now she couldn't even scream no more, now it was like she was trying, but nothing was coming out or maybe the stuff had already got into her mouth, was already starting to burn away her voice.'

Banks checked the tape, a reflex action, but in reality he was looking away from all this, turning away from everything he was hearing, from the involuntary images now forcing their way into his head.

Masters just stared at her, betraying nothing, knowing how close she was to giving way right now, how even the slightest sign of weakness on his part would probably be enough to make her crack, how young she was despite everything she'd done, how thin the veneer she hid behind.

Masters also knew she'd tell this story once and once only – the true story anyway in its each and every detail – and he knew it was a story she'd been wanting to tell for days as if somehow she might purge herself of it all, release it in some great cathartic outpouring that would rid her of it forever. But once she'd told the story, once she realised it could never be purged, once she'd understood the futility of the confessional, she'd lose interest, would retreat. So they had to get this story, here and now, get it committed to record, preserved.

Tyra paused and Masters allowed his concentration to wander just for a moment, his mind's eye flickering briefly over the figure he'd seen waiting in the corridor as they'd arrived, the figure who would now play as large a part as anyone in the eventual success or otherwise of the court case to come.

Ros Gilet. The surname wasn't pronounced like the well-known razor, the last 't' was silent apparently. Which, in a curious way, complemented the woman herself. She was one of the best in the business in delivering witnesses in one piece and in something approximating the right state of mind to the witness box.

His ever-present niggle was his complete inability to even begin to get to know her despite at least six years of liaising on at least five times that number of cases. Ros was a closed book to Masters. So much of her remained hidden, silent indeed; and Masters didn't like that. In his line of work he liked everything out in the open. Maybe that was an occupational hazard. Maybe it was something else.

Tyra started again.

'Yaroslav didn't even seem to see her. He was just holding her in front of Wojike, pushing her face as close as he could to his, even pushing her face into his so part of his cheek started to smoke where the acid touched him, but then he held her back because he didn't want him damaged, not yet, not like that anyway, he didn't want his eyes burning out or nothing, he wanted him to see everything that was going to happen to him because what he'd done so far, that was just the start.'

Tyra took a quick, deep breath.

'He took the girl back towards the door, the rear one that led onto an alleyway and the yard. And just pushed her out. He didn't bother doing anything else with her, what was the point, she couldn't see as it was, couldn't even speak. But he wanted her to be seen and he wanted her to be taken into hospital because he knew that way she might recover. It might take weeks, might take months, but then the crazy fuck would have done what that bloke in the movie did, he was going to have her telling people what had happened to her, what he'd done and he wanted that story to go round, he wanted everyone to hear it, everyone who mattered anyway so then everyone'd know what happened to girls who work for someone else and as for you lot getting involved – .'

Tyra shot Masters and Banks a contemptuous glance.

'Don't even think about it. If he could do something like that to some kid who'd hardly even crossed him what the fuck could he do to someone who seriously pissed him off?'

Tyra paused again.

'So. That was the warm-up and I really didn't fancy hanging round for the rest and even the two goons Yaroslav had brought along with him were looking a bit wary now. They weren't the sharpest tools in the box but even they could work out we were going to be in for something extra-special tasty and as for Wojike, he was just staring at him almost like he'd gone beyond fear, like his head was somewhere else completely.'

Tyra unscrewed the top off one of the bottles of water that had been provided for the interview but didn't drink. She just stared at the opened bottle for a moment, then everything came out again in another great rush.

'Yaroslav went for his balls first. He must still have been in agony from the taser or thought he was, but he didn't know what agony was, did he? Not till he felt the acid eating into them, dissolving them I suppose and it was like with Alison, the screams that were coming out of his gob were so high-pitched you couldn't hear them. Then Yaroslav yanked his head back and I thought he was going to do what he did with the girl, that he was going for the hair but he wasn't, not yet. He opened his mouth first instead, poured some of the acid inside and now Wojike was trying to breathe out, trying his hardest not to swallow, not to take any of it in and all you could see was something that looked like flames coming out from behind his teeth, like he was a fire-eater in a circus or something. Then Yaroslav went for his ears and we all just stood there watching while they melted, shrivelling like they were pieces of bacon, all the folds of skin collapsing in on themselves. And I think Yaroslav knew the end was coming now because Wojike's skin had gone all clammy and you could almost see his heart coming out of his ribcage it was hammering away so much.'

Tyra paused once more.

'So then he yanked his head back one last time, stuck his finger into his eyeball, under his eyelid so he was staring straight up at him, couldn't blink, couldn't do nothing and then he started dripping acid into his eyes, one drop at a time, he even splashed his own fingers with some of the stuff but he didn't care, probably thought it was good PR, every time he shook someone's hand from then on it was going to be there, his hand, all scarred and if they'd heard the story about how he'd got them scars they could see straightaway it was true and if they hadn't he could hold his hands out in front of their face and tell them.'

Banks reached out and took one of the bottles of water. He needed a drink now even if Tyra didn't.

'One of the goons had already been sick in the corner. Yaroslav didn't even seem to see him, didn't even seem to realise any of us were still in the same room. I made for the door, I couldn't take any more, this wasn't a lesson like he'd meted out before, this was something else. I started to open it when I felt his hand on my shoulder. He spun me round and for a moment I thought I was going to get same treatment as the posh bit, he was that far gone, his eyes were looking at me but I didn't know who he was seeing.'

Tyra stood up and for a moment Banks thought the interview was done, that all she'd just re-lived had proved too much and relief washed over him that it was over, at least for now. But it wasn't.

Masters didn't move, just kept staring as impassively as he was able as Tyra turned, lifted up her T-shirt, revealed her naked back adorned by a single crude cross burnt into the skin by a finger dipped in burning acid.

Tyra had been branded. A mark scored into her skin. As if she was cattle, something to be traded, bought and sold.

Meaning another lesson had been meted out in the old storage room of that disused butcher's shop.

Another signal dispatched.

C ARA COULDN'T WORK out what her mother was doing at first. What she was yelling, over and over again at her, was clear enough –

– 999! –

– 999! –

And she was gesturing, all the time, at the phone on the hall table too, the table which was still standing, which hadn't been knocked over in the mayhem that had just been visited, Armageddon-style, on them all.

Cara moved to the phone but her eyes didn't leave her mother who was bent over the still-twitching body, her hands scrabbling towards her daughter before reaching out, then moving back towards her again.

The young girl kept staring as a voice on the other end of the line asked what service she wanted and then she heard another voice also on the same line repeating their home number, recording it and matching it, she'd later discover, against an address in case the caller was too traumatised or injured to speak or if this was a hoax.

'Ambulance, ambulance.'

That was her mother again and Cara didn't need to repeat it. The operator, who was clearly well-trained, had picked it up and had already punched through the call.

Then another voice came on the line, asking for details, wanting to know what had happened, pausing, shocked despite all she must hear in the course of all her working days, when a clearly-small child told her that her sister had been shot.

As Cara said it, her mother moaned, her hands now still and all of a sudden Cara realised what she'd been doing.

Years later again, she'd see some old newsreel footage of the shooting of a President, and his wife, soon to be his widow, had done exactly the same thing, had scrabbled with her hands in just the same way. Her mother had been trying to retrieve parts of her daughter's brain and force them back inside her open skull.

4

HALF AN HOUR later and the gladiators were facing each other in the arena which, in this instance, comprised Masters and Banks on one side of the room, Ros and an increasingly uneasy, ever more monosyllabic Conor on the other; Conor making it painfully obvious, despite his silence, which side of the room he really wanted to be on right now.

'Who else is with this Yaroslav? Is he a lone operator or is he connected?'

Masters knew exactly why Ros was asking the question but chose to ignore it for now.

'Yaroslav's enough so far as Tyra's concerned. Up to now it's been sweet and he's been keeping her sweet because she's been useful to him and not just in maintaining the supply chain, keeping it supplied with runaways and addicts. Up to now he's liked having a girl like that by his side, it would have been good for the image, good in lots of other ways too probably, just look at her, little twat must fuck like a rattlesnake.'

Ros just kept looking at Masters as beside her Conor snorted in response along with Banks.

What was she ever going to do with this one?

Why should she even try?

'The upside is she's had six months on easy street. Taken wherever she wanted, living in some very nice penthouse down the bay, nights out in some of the more upmarket clubs. The downside and she's probably only just realised there is a downside, is that she's seen too much and so now she knows too much, she's seen who comes to that very nice penthouse, who he parties with in those upmarket clubs.'

Masters shrugged.

'Again, that's not been such a problem up to now, these two have been pretty well joined at the hip from even the little we've been able to find out, but that stuff with the acid changed all that. She spoke out, didn't she? Tried to tell him what to do, how to conduct his business and look what happened, look at her back. And she's not stupid, she knows what happens once he starts down that road. Now all of a sudden it's not so sweet, now all of a sudden she's wondering what happened to all the other girls that came before her and now she's starting to worry. It's a bit like that shit old country song about that hotel where you can check out but never leave.'

Masters rolled on, giving Ros more background she didn't need, forestalling more questions she needed to ask.

'A couple of traffic cops picked her up speeding, heading for the bridge. She gave them a fair old chase too, it may only have been one of the smaller Ferraris she was driving, but they can still shift.'

Conor opened his mouth to ask which model, he'd always been something of a petrolhead, but then choked back the question. When he'd been one of them, standing by Masters's side just like Banks was standing there now, he wouldn't have thought twice about it, but something told him the ballbreaker standing next to him wouldn't exactly appreciate an intervention like that right now.

'Then she pulls into this service station. At first they thought she's giving herself up but all of a sudden she turns round, points the motor straight at them and tests the nought to sixty right there and then. They thought they were about to get broadsided or something.'

Banks, happier now he was out of that interview room, took it up, taking a sip of coffee from another of the station stock of football mugs at the same time.

'What she hits turns out to be the plate glass window in the front of the service station and she goes straight through it too, glass smashing down behind her before she comes to rest in the middle of a whole pile of one-armed bandits, which weirdly enough all start paying out.'

Masters took over. Banks was obviously beginning to play to the audience just that little bit too much now.

'So that was that. Mission accomplished. Our clever little lady had just guaranteed herself a little bit more than a ticking-off and a ticket. Once they managed to clear all the glass from the little red number she was taken into the local nick where she asked for us. We picked her up a few hours ago and she's been singing ever since. At the moment she's our best chance to put away one of the most seriously twisted maniacs we're ever going to come across and that's saying something in these days of hands-across-the-Channel and send us all your low-life scum.'

Ros stepped in, moving this back to what she regarded as the matter of the moment even if Masters quite clearly did not.

'And if you take Yaroslav out that's it, everything collapses, his girls move on, other outfits move in to take over whatever else he might be running right now?'

Masters just looked at her. Ros wasn't about to give up on this line of questioning and he knew it.

'Or has he got other people working with him? People who won't just move on, who won't just roll over if any other outfit starts sniffing round?'

'We don't know, how can we?'

That was Banks.

'Take an educated guess.'

'No.'

That was Masters.

'No, as in you won't take an educated guess or no, as in his people won't just roll over?'

'The second.'

'So if all this goes as well as we all want it to go, if Tyra sticks to her story, if she doesn't try and do another runner in some borrowed sports job, if she finally has her day in court and Yaroslav's sent down for the rest of his natural that isn't the end of it, she's still going to be in line for some seriously heavy-duty retribution from whoever's left behind?'

Banks stepped in again.

'So go back in there. Tell her that. Tell her we can't run to a Ferrari but we've got a couple of hot little hatchbacks out in the pound if she fancies another dash down the motorway.'

Ros looked at Banks. Masters was calm but his face was mottled, frustration clearly building inside. It was an expression she'd seen a hundred times before.

The hunters were moving in for the kill and it was the best kind of kill too, a justified kill, an honourable kill indeed and now they were staring at a sudden complication, an obstacle standing before them and they were willing it to disappear, already perhaps wondering about other ways of removing that obstacle if it obstinately refused to do so.

'I have to explain the risks to her.'

'For fuck's sake!'

And now Banks all but exploded, Masters making no move to restrain him, he was still just staring at Ros, cool and level, as she, cool and level in turn, ignored his volatile subordinate and rolled on.

'If this isn't going to be over when those cell doors close behind her old boyfriend then she needs to know and I need to know, we need to work out what she does afterwards, where she goes, how long we offer her support, who else we offer support to, is there anyone else who's going to get caught up in all this, any family we need to know about that we can pick up and that's as in right now?'

Across the room Banks started fantasising about gags and handcuffs.

Ros rolled on.

'Not leave it till the day before the trial when she finds out her Mum and Dad have been wasted in some drive-by and she decides that maybe she won't stand up in that dock after all just in case she comes out of it to find her little sister's been mowed down in her school playground as well.'

'Her old man's in a nursing home. Completely out of it, wouldn't know her if he fell over her. She hasn't visited him for over a year. Her Mum died a few years back. And she hasn't got any sisters or brothers.'

Ros held his stare.

'Whatever.'

Half an hour later again and Ros was driving away. The exchange with Banks and Masters had concluded with Banks storming out after letting her know that in his opinion she was a tight-arsed apology for a copper and why didn't she just give them all a fucking break?

Masters didn't say too much himself but he didn't exactly contradict him either.

Conor just kept his head down, eyes averted from Ros, his body language once again making it crystal clear where his loyalties lay in this all-too familiar exchange.

It was the old, old story. Two departments, two very different ends in view.

For Masters and his merry band of brothers and the occasional sister it was simple. Get a villain into court, get a conviction, then get wasted round the corner in the nearest boozer, then move on, get another villain into court, get another conviction, kick off another session in some other local boozer, the cycle of life in Murder Squad.

But there was an inconvenient truth, a necessary pre-requisite to it all. They had to get the villain into court. They had to persuade twelve good and mainly fair souls that the villain in question should be sent down. And for that they needed the witness.

Sometimes there was just the one, sometimes more than one. But however many there were, however complicated or dangerous the case, they always needed the person or persons who would stand up, often in full view of their former colleague, partner or employer and tell their story, simply, honestly and, hopefully, effectively – meaning Masters and his merry band could get even more merry in just a few hours' time around the corner.

Ros never got involved in the actual cases themselves. She tried on most occasions not to even know anything about them but that usually proved impossible. She simply had to assess the risk to her client and then work out how best to minimise that risk, a process that to Murder Squad usually meant one thing and one thing only; spooking their mark, queering their pitch, running the risk that their much-cherished witness would turn tail and run from it all.

It didn't help that, in the vast majority of cases, the vast majority of those clients weren't exactly innocent victims themselves. Some had been seriously heavyweight criminals in their own right, most only turning Queen's evidence to secure themselves a lighter plea. Which meant, more often than not, that Ros was then keeping low-life safe. Turning a blind eye to all they'd done, sometimes to all they would do as well.

A few years earlier, relations between those who used witnesses to put villains away and those who tried to make sure those witnesses lived long enough to do so, deteriorated almost to the point of open warfare. Then the decision was made to make the whole protection procedure more open and inclusive, to encourage officers from other departments to apply for secondments, to try to promote a new understanding about this often-mysterious unit, give other units in the same force an understanding of the pressures they were under, the conflicting claims and counter-claims they continually had to juggle.

It would have been better not to have even tried. It was chalk and cheese time. For the vast majority of the force, witnesses were a means to an end. They were plugged into a system at a certain point, discarded when that system had no further use for them. The problem being that those witnesses were also people with hopes and dreams and fears.

Masters and Murder Squad saw them as the former, Ros had to deal with them as the latter.

Chalk and cheese.

No point in even trying to heal the unbridgeable divide.

Ros swung her car down the street that led to her apartment, a fleeting glimpse of water on one side, a converted warehouse on the other. Between them was the office of an old dredging company now converted into a restaurant, part of a chain. She paused by the security gates, held up her pass to the electronic reader, then drove into a courtyard.

Heading for a small underground parking area underneath a three-storey building at the far end of the courtyard she saw him. Not the nervy supergrass who'd just come into her mind for some reason, the supergrass who was calling her at least once a week at the moment, sometimes more, with fresh fears and new concerns. So far he hadn't come to any particular harm although the first of the men he'd helped send down weren't due for parole for another two years or so.

Ros saw Oskar instead. Sitting on a low wall outside the door that led up to her second-floor, single bedroom apartment. He wouldn't have been let in by the security guard which meant he'd probably slipped in along with another of the cars that had either entered or exited earlier that day. Ros had no idea how long he'd been waiting but guessed, shrewdly as it turned out, that he didn't much care. Oskar looked as if he had a score to settle and all the time in the world to do so.

Ros took a deep breath, struggled a smile through the windscreen at the watching Swede. He was over six feet tall, blond and muscular and very definitely a cut above the usual collection of human flotsam and jetsam she'd collect during the course of a nocturnal trawl around her usual haunts. But he was still destined, as she already knew, to share the same fate as the rest.

Only he clearly didn't know that. More to the point he didn't expect it and, even more to the point, he obviously didn't like it either.

What did he expect in a place like that? Did he really expect to find it stuffed to the wall with serial monogamists?

'Oskar.'

Ros nodded at him, cautious, as she exited her badly-parked car. She'd read somewhere about a car that parked itself using sensors or cameras or something. Forget the seven wonders of the world, that sounded like the ultimate to her, all her Christmases and birthdays rolled into one and tied up with a big pink bow.

As Oskar just eyed her back, didn't respond for a moment, she wondered why she was thinking about parallel parking for Christ's sake, why she could take on the likes of Masters without a second thought and he was one mad, bad and seriously dangerous bastard, but wouldn't now even meet her former boyfriend's eyes.

'Been to work?'

Ros nodded. She hadn't told him, initially at least, what she did for a living. She didn't tell most of the people she met in places like that. Not that anything they were doing was particularly illegal, although some of the ways of intensifying the experiences on offer might be deemed to be so. But most would still have run a mile at the revelation of her way of earning her daily crust or, at the very least, suspected some sort of undercover sting.

But over the course of the following few months she had let a few details slip.

'So how was your day?'

'I'm not supposed to talk about it, you know that.'

'So what shall we talk about? You not returning my calls, not replying to my texts, throwing away the note I left on your windscreen the other night, I found it over there by the way.'

Oskar nodded towards the small garden.

'You might at least have had the decency to put it in a bin.'

A couple of days previously, tears streaming down her face as she read the clearly-heartfelt words before throwing it out of the window and driving away, hardly seeing the road ahead through a windscreen she thought was being pounded by a rainstorm of almost Biblical proportions, realising within a few moments of putting on her wipers that the world outside was currently being filtered through those self-same tears.

But standing before him now, seeing herself reflected in his eyes, she was hard and closed and cold, nothing getting in, letting nothing out.

'Do you think I want to stop you doing what you want, is that it? Do you think I'm going to get all heavy, play the jealous boyfriend? What did you think I was doing in there in the first place, looking for an unspoilt soul to take home to my parents in Stockholm, someone I could live with happily ever after with our children and dogs?'

She was doing it again and she hated herself for it, taking refuge in silence, wanting to say something, but how could she even begin to explain the inexplicable?

'OK, it's never going to be like it is for most people. You get off on it, so do I. I'm not some evangelist looking to convert you,

you can do it all, anything you want, anywhere you want to go, with me, without me, so why put me out of the frame, why just kill it?'

Ros finally felt impelled to meet his eyes.

'When you don't want to?'

'How do you know I don't want to?'

'Because I know you.'

And he'd done it. If she'd even momentarily weakened, even fractionally felt her will unbend, all of a sudden she rebuilt herself, strengthened all that inner resolve. And he must have sensed it too because all of a sudden the fight seemed to ebb out of him, defeat beginning to replace appeal.

'You left some clothes. I found them in the dryer.'

Her tone was mild, non-confrontational. She used it a lot. It normally defused difficult situations, calmed volatile clients. It did neither for Oskar but he didn't make too much of a protest either as he followed her up the stairs, took possession of the shorts and the shirt she'd folded neatly into a carrier bag, intending to post them onto him.

Oskar, bag in hand, turned to the door, pausing as she knew he would, but instead of one last entreaty, his tone was mild now, non-confrontational too. Maybe he'd picked up some of the tricks of the trade.

'All those people you look out for. Watch over. All those lives.'

He nodded at her.

'What happens to yours, Ros? When are you ever going to let anyone look out for you?'

One hour later, a tissue box beside her, its contents snot-stained and strewn over the sofa and that voice, always that voice, inside her head, conducting now the conversation she'd never allow herself to have, telling him he was wrong, that the problem was exactly the opposite. It wasn't letting him in, she'd done that, without realising it maybe, but she'd done it. If she hadn't he'd still be here, sitting on her sofa eating her doomed attempt at some latest pasta recipe, before they both plunged again out into the night.

But somehow he'd inveigled himself well and truly into her life and that was why he now had to be out of it.

The voice was quiet. It had to be. Walls may not have ears, but there were plenty of other ears passing outside on the corridor, all going about their own business, perhaps, but all-too ready to make someone else's business their own.

'They're using the usual hotel.'

The usual hotel was a favourite haunt of corporate businessmen, the occasional sightseer, even a football team who used it for pre-match briefings. It was mid-table, a little like the football team, nothing too showy, but nothing too downmarket either. Nothing out of the ordinary, meaning perfect for purpose.

The voice paused, listened.

'No, just for a night or so.'

The voice paused again, listening some more.

'They'll definitely head out of the city, maybe go down to the coast, but that's not been decided yet. One of the houses was compromised down there a couple of months ago, it could have been a one-off but they might decide not to take any chances.'

This time there was a longer pause as options were computed, strategies silently debated.

'I don't know. They're always more edgy in the first couple of days till things settle down a bit. The hotel's easier to get to but even so – .'

Again, another silence.

'Let's talk again in the morning. But just in case any opportunity presents itself.'

There was a rustling of paper, the voice dipping in volume again, reducing to almost a whisper. Now it was even more vital that none of this should be overheard.

'She's on the fifth floor. On the left as you come out of the lifts, at the end of the corridor. There's a fire escape next door, stairs leading down to the car park.'

The voice paused again.

'Room 512.'

5

D I, DITZY DI, walked back from the convenience store, bag in hand, every item on the list she'd been given inside, not a single item forgotten nor, as had happened on more than one occasion as she was forever being reminded, mislaid on the short walk home.

Maybe she was getting less forgetful with age. Or maybe she was becoming more aware of everything around her, more alive in some way. And if so there were no prizes for guessing why that might be. For not the first time that day, that week, that year, she flushed as she thought of Emmanuel.

Di turned the corner into her street, pausing as she saw a hire car pulling up outside her house, their hire car, the car they'd collected from the airport that very morning. The meeting Emmanuel had to attend had obviously concluded quicker than expected and he'd wasted no time in returning to the family home.

Briefly, as she saw Emmanuel himself exit the car a hundred or so metres ahead of her, her mind drifted to the evening ahead and the meeting to come. He'd made a good impression on her mother and on her sisters, that was obvious enough; but what about Dad, how easily would he fall for Emmanuel's undeniable charm?

Later, she was to realise that in one respect she still very much deserved her childhood nickname. Because while she might have remembered every item from the local store for the family meal that evening, she'd somehow missed the fact that there was a police car parked in front of the hire car, parked outside her own home in fact.

And as she registered that suddenly-disturbing realisation, she now heard the distant siren of a fast-approaching ambulance too.

Two policemen from the local station were first on the scene. Elsha vaguely recognised them. It wasn't surprising they were the first to arrive, they only had to come a mile or so down the road while the ambulance HQ was some distance away. It used to be nearer but a round of spending cuts had amalgamated three stations into one. The old ambulance station was now a gastro-pub, Elsha had been there with Macklyn a couple of times.

As the first of the policemen stood in the doorway, momentarily ambushed by all he was witnessing – the pieces of human brain all over the walls, the slumped figure at the foot of the stairs, the scared young child hovering in the kitchen doorway at the far end of the hall – Elsha found herself trying to remember what she'd had for her main course on her last visit. She'd talked to the waitress about it, hoping to replicate it at home sometime – doing anything in fact but deal with all the policeman was currently finding equally difficult to handle right now.

The policeman didn't approach Braith, or rather the splayed figure that used to be Braith but now more resembled a carcass in an abbatoir, he just spoke into his radio, checking on the progress of the ambulance.

Even in her currently-distracted state, Elsha could see that was more for want of anything else to do than some attempt at purposeful action. Like everyone else in that hallway right now, the officer was way outside his comfort zone.

But then, all of a sudden, Emmanuel appeared in front of her, said something to the officer. Elsha didn't catch what it was, but the next instant Cara had been ushered by him into the kitchen, out of sight of all that had unfolded before her too-young eyes.

Had she been thinking more clearly Elsha should have done that herself, but then Emmanuel was back again, was kneeling next to Braith, his hands moving along what remained of her neck, checking her wrists, trying to find any evidence of life so Elsha assumed.

Elsha looked down at her own hands, at parts of her daughter's brain staining her fingers, testament to her own futile attempts to prolong what was clearly already beyond saving.

Emmanuel moved back to the door to meet the paramedics who were now pulling up behind the police car. Behind them another figure was approaching. It was Di she'd later realise, but she was being stopped by the officer at the car, protecting what was clearly – even if they could be certain of nothing else right now – the scene of a crime.

And one thought kept hammering away inside Elsha's head and it wasn't about Braith or about the now-absent Cara and it wasn't even about Di, whose panicky voice she could now hear outside asking what was happening, what was all this, what was going on? And she wasn't even thinking about Macklyn, still in work, still blissfully unaware of all that had happened in the last few moments and how she already envied him that unaware state.

All Elsha could think was, he doesn't look surprised. Emmanuel's eyes had widened as he'd taken in the body on the floor, the blood and skin tissue sprayed all over the walls, but there was almost a resignation in the way he'd looked on the scene rather than anything else.

Not that he'd expected it, that would be overstating the case. He just didn't seem surprised by it either.

A PPROACHING HER CAR the next morning Ros slowed as she saw the note on the windscreen. For a moment she tensed, preparing herself for yet another injured imprecation from Oskar.

Or maybe he'd moved on from that. Maybe she was in for a torrent of abuse instead. Maybe they were about to move from the lovesick puppy stage. No wonder, Ros silently reflected, she didn't do relationships.

Ros flicked the note out from behind the wipers, pausing as she felt a stiff piece of card inside the open envelope. Ros, now rather more puzzled and a little wary too, extracted what was indeed a business card from inside, a slow smile then spreading across her lips as she saw a logo on the top with numbers, both landline and mobile, underneath.

The business was local, as was the landline number. It was a business she'd seen advertised in some of the local free sheets from time to time. The company offered lessons for drivers who might have been abroad for some time and who felt the need for some sort of refresher course or those who simply fancied brushing up their technique in some way.

Ros looked at her car, the front slewed across one parking space, half the rear end slewed across another. Then she looked at the cars parked to her left, all thrown out of line by just her one rogue vehicle. Ros had been about to throw the business card in a nearby bin but now she put it in her shoulder bag instead. Maybe her mystery messenger had a point.

As she moved past the concierge on the gate and negotiated the slightly tricky left-hand turn out onto the main road she could see him in her rear-view mirror giving a silent, ironic, round of applause.

Three miles later she was moving along a series of newly-constructed roads with open wasteland on all sides punctuated by the occasional budget chain hotel.

Swinging off the main carriageway onto a small retail estate, Ros pulled up outside an anonymous unit in the middle of a whole row of similar units, a sign outside advertising the business seemingly conducted within; Mega Bed Sale.

When she first arrived at her new posting, Ros assumed it was some sort of veiled reference to their activities. Part of their brief after all was providing accommodation for those dispossessed of their own. She was told later that the sign belonged to the previous occupant and no-one had bothered taking it down.

Ros let herself in through a small steel door set into some larger up-and-over shutter roller doors, walked across the empty ground floor, home to just a couple of pool cars, before heading up a steel stairway to a door still marked 'Showroom' where she punched in an access code which changed weekly.

On the other side of the door, waiting to see if she'd remembered it perhaps, she could see Conor.

Then the door swung open and he nodded at her, grim.

'Problem.'

Five minutes later, Ros and Conor were on the opposite side of his desk from Jukes – or DCI Jukes to give the forty-something career cop his full title. A file was open on the desk in front of him. From the very start Jukes had told all who would listen that he really wasn't sure about this one and it seemed he might have had a point.

'She started kicking off last night. Some problem with the room service order or something.'

Jukes waved a couple of receipts at them.

'The only problem was how much she ordered, you could have fed a medium-size family for a week on what she was planning to put away. And as for the booze.'

Jukes studied another receipt.

'I reckon she just read the menu right to left, picked out the most expensive and decided to have that.'

This was already creating uncomfortable echoes. A year earlier a young boy had been stabbed on a badlands estate on the outskirts of the city heading up into the Valleys. Murder Squad had taken in a thirteen-year-old girl as witness, putting her up in the nearest hotel while Jukes and his hard-pressed cohorts negotiated with the rest of her family as to who'd join her. She'd set the record so far when it came to extravagant demands, well over a thousand pounds in room service orders in less than twenty-four hours. Tyra wasn't threatening that eye-watering total yet, but there was still time.

Conor took up the tale, a copy of the duty officer's report also on the desk in front of him.

'Then this morning she looks out of the window and sees the hotel's got a health club so she heads down there, without telling anyone where she's going of course. Once she's in there she sees a Spa and now she's thinking she's well and truly died and gone to heaven – .'

Ros interrupted, not interested in the florid embellishments.

'In other words?'

'In other words she's nearly blown this at least four times in the last twelve hours. And we're hoping she'll keep her head down for the next twelve weeks?'

Conor shook his head.

'This one wouldn't know how.'

Jukes looked across at Ros who paused.

'Let me talk to her.'

Conor checked his watch.

'You'll have to give it at least a couple of hours, she won't be out from under the detoxifying facial till then.'

Ros ignored him.

'See what I can do.'

'And if she can't be delivered?'

Ros didn't hesitate.

'We cut her loose.'

The thirteen-year-old also couldn't be delivered, department-speak for ensuring a witness appears at a trial. They cut her loose too. Only Murder Squad decided they needed her and dug their heels in, announcing that they could look after her themselves.

After going AWOL five times in the next five days and letting all and sundry on her old home patch know how important she now was, the girl who would always be thirteen forever was found at the bottom of a council skip. Or at least parts of her were. No-one ever actually found the head.

OK, she was always going to be a risk no matter whether she was taken in or not and no fingers were pointed and no blame apportioned. It just brought home the unalterable fact that decisions like that, to take a client in or to cut them loose, were never neutral, that there were always consequences; which was probably why those sort of decisions were always wrapped up in phrases such as, can't deliver. As if they were talking about a parcel of some description, a household delivery. It distanced the decision from the human being.

'And if she can be delivered, if we don't cut her loose?'

Conor was looking at Jukes, unaware of the subtext, unable to decode the half-glance now exchanged between the DCI and his DS.

But Ros knew exactly what he was thinking about, the faces that were now swimming through his mind, the same faces she'd think about first thing in the morning and last thing at night, sometimes all through the night when those faces would appear unbidden in dreams that then lurched into nightmares.

And Ros knew what else Jukes was thinking about right now too, the supplementary question hanging in the air between them.

Cutting Tyra loose would certainly pose a risk to the case as well as posing a risk to Tyra herself.

But sometimes that was absolutely nothing compared to the risks involved in keeping her inside, in delivering her to trial, in securing the conviction, in spiriting her away as the first of the champagne was opened by Masters and his band of brothers and occasional sister in the pub around the corner from the courtroom, in watching her as she took her first faltering steps into a world that might seem everyday and ordinary but which was always going to seem as alien to the client in question as if they'd just landed on Mars.

Sometimes, if they'd known previously all they'd learnt by then, they'd have run a million miles away from the small, slight officer who'd guided them through the early stages of it all.

Just ask the Kincaids.

OK, he might as well admit it, he was jealous.

Scott hunched down in the driver's seat of the pool car, a takeaway coffee from some nearby chain outlet in the cup holder, a burger from another chain outlet on the seat beside him.

On the floor of the passenger compartment was an empty bottle, plastic, screw-top and, half-an-hour previously in a grimly comical endeavour, he'd had to make use of it; holding it up against his crotch, praying no-one would pass in the next few moments, trying to direct his urine inside, managing to do so with roughly eighty per cent accuracy, using some paper towels also provided by one or other of the nearby chain outlets to mop up the rest.

It wasn't quite the life he'd imagined for himself in the first few weeks of his training. He'd imagined the sort of life Donovan seemed to be inhabiting right now or, to give him his proper title, DS Donovan Banks, soon to be DI Donovan Banks if station rumour was even halfway accurate – and it usually proved to be almost one hundred per cent accurate as Scott knew to his cost.

That same station rumour machine had predicted with equally devastating accuracy that he himself would be passed over in the most recent round of promotions as indeed he was.

Scott shifted in his seat, glanced over at the fairly ordinary-looking office block that housed, or was rumoured to house, at least one of the businesses run by their Ukrainian quarry. There was little on the outside to advertise the fact but that didn't count for much. The national affairs of the UK were determined inside a small terraced house in a London side street as Masters had pointed out in many a team briefing in the past.

Never go on appearances was the lesson.

Always look below the surface.

But before they could do that they had to keep tabs on the mark. They had to know where he or she was at any given moment of the day or night, see where they went, who they met. Scott was in a team of four who were attempting to do just that, but it really didn't matter how many times Masters, with a smugly nodding Banks at his side, told him this was every bit as vital as the more sophisticated surveillance taking place back in the nick, that they all played their part; they all knew what this really was in truth.

The way Banks looked at him, almost pityingly, confirmed it only too clearly. This was donkey work. Carried out by donkeys. While the big boys got on with the real stuff, the important work.

Scott shifted again in his seat, wondered whether he should even tell Bel about the latest setback to his career plans. She'd made all the right noises the last time, but he could still see the disappointment in her eyes.

He could also see the silent question there too. The night they'd met in that club she'd had a choice. In fact she had more than the one choice if truth be known. She could have gone home with any one of a handful of wannabe police officers who'd chatted her up through a succession of coke-fuelled dances, including Banks.

Bel, the beautiful Bel, had never said it, would never say it – or so he hoped – but had she made the wrong choice? Had she backed a loser? Was she destined for a lifetime of disappointment, watching a husband becoming gradually embittered, trying and probably failing as the years passed by, to hide her own creeping sense of disappointment and bitterness too?

Scott didn't have any answers to questions that hadn't even yet been asked. But part of him, and for not entirely selfless reasons, thanked his lucky stars that his beautiful wife was now six months pregnant with their first child. It was always, surely, going to be more difficult to give up on a family than giving up on just a husband who wasn't quite delivering all he'd once promised.

Then all thoughts of Bel, of Banks, of promotions that might or might not come his way were wiped as the rear door of the unmarked police saloon suddenly opened.

Scott wheeled round, his half-open mouth framing a question but it was another question destined never to be asked, never mind answered. Everything simply happened too quickly.

Half an hour later and Ros was walking through the doors of the new-build hotel overlooking the river, before taking a right past the reception desk and heading for a mirrored lift.

In her bag she was carrying the department bible, the various criteria for admission to the protection programme, listing the different boxes she now needed to tick, the specific agreements she now had to secure.

It was all standard procedure. She'd memorised it in her first few days in the department and it had all sounded so easy back then, so eminently reasonable and achievable.

Before admitting a witness to a protection programme, an assessment needs to be conducted to enable the authority to make an informed decision.

Just before the lift doors closed a twenty-something track-suited man carrying a clutch bag, got in. He was heading up to the same floor as Ros, as his quick glance across at the illuminated button on the side of the lift made clear.

More pearls of wisdom from the primer swam before Ros's eyes.

The most important elements of that assessment are:

– the level of threat to a client's life –

– the importance of a client's trial testimony –

– the role of the testimony in dismantling a criminal organisation –

Ros paused as the doors opened at the fifth floor and the track-suited young man stepped out, taking a left down the corridor.

Heading for a room at the end of the corridor.

Room 512.

Tyra's room.

Holding his clutch bag even tighter.

– witnesses must also be under the most serious threat –

Moving more quickly now, his steps increasing in pace all the while, not even looking back at the young woman who'd emerged from the lift behind him; a man seemingly on a mission.

– the threat should not involve the witnesses property, the threat must be against the witnesses life –

Stopping outside a door three doors down from Room 512,

the man tapped, quickly. A stifled giggle was heard from inside, the door opening as Ros appeared at the young man's shoulder.

No-one was actually standing in the doorway itself, they never did, Ros knew that, it didn't matter if they were knocking out a half-hour quickie in a cheap hotel in some motorway services somewhere or, as in this case, offering a rather more upmarket experience, the tactic was always the same; hookers never stand on view.

Partly it was so the punter actually had to move inside the room itself before he could take his first look at the delights on offer. It was always going to be so much more difficult to leave with a closed, and usually locked, door barring the exit behind.

But partly it was also down to simple security. Hotel corridors were busy places, maids, waiters, front-of-house staff, all passing several times a day. As far as guests were concerned, discretion was usually the matter of the moment but how many times could those same maids, waiters, front of house staff turn a blind eye to that one open door, that same woman standing inside, greeting all those different men?

The young man with the clutch bag moved quickly inside the room as Ros passed by, the door closing equally quickly behind him. Briefly, Ros caught a glimpse of an unmade bed.

Then Ros moved on down the corridor, tapped, lightly, on the door of Room 512.

All Scott had felt was a stabbing pain in his lower back as if something had exploded against his spine.

For a moment he arched upwards, his head smashing against the roof of the unmarked police pool car, then he looked down into a pair of dispassionately observing eyes which seemed to be counting –

– one –

– two –

– three –

Then everything went black, his body flopping as the disabling drug, more commonly used on small to medium-size animals in abattoirs, but quite obviously equally effective on medium-size human beings, took hold.

The owner of those dispassionately observing eyes went round to the driver's door, ignored the takeaway coffee in the cup holder, the half-eaten burger on the passenger seat and averted his eyes from the bottle of yellowing piss he could see on the floor of the passenger footwell. He'd always had something of a weak stomach when it came to bodily functions. Then he unclipped the seat belt around the now-prone driver.

By that time a small van had pulled up alongside and it was the work of a moment to transfer the limp weight from the front seat of the car into the rear of the windowless van.

Then the van drove away leaving the man with the dispassionate eyes to drive the pool car away in turn. As he turned the first of the succession of corners ahead, the bottle of piss rolled against the side walls of the footwell, its contents sloshing around inside.

The man with the dispassionate eyes kept his eyes firmly on the road ahead and tried to ignore it. He knew he'd gag the moment he glanced, even momentarily, its way. He really did have a delicate stomach and so thanked his lucky stars that his role in the day's proceedings was now over and that he wasn't going to be called on to play any part in what was to follow.

'Fancies you, doesn't he?'

Ros looked from Tyra across to the elderly custodian of the crumbling snooker hall, wondering if she'd heard right. Jocus was not only eighty and half-blind but one of the more obviously gay inhabitants of the old Tiger Bay.

'That copper back in your nick, the older one, Masters?'

Ros battled an inner smile which was nothing to do with Masters, she'd have been the same if there'd been any similar reference to anyone. It was always nice, after all, to be noticed. At least that's what she told herself.

'It's not my nick. It's Murder Squad. And if Masters really does fancy me he's got a weird way of showing it, I'm still wiping the spit off my face from our last meeting.'

Ros bent to the table, cannoned the white into the triangle of reds, the balls scattering to the middle and top pockets, one hovering tantalisingly over the top right before wobbling to a halt on the cushion, an easy slice into the pocket now for her opponent.

Tyra leant down, casual, too casual. Already Ros could see she might be on for something of a hiding here as Tyra duly sliced in the first of the reds.

'It's obvious.'

Tyra looked over the table, eyeing up and then selecting the black. They'd been out of the hotel room in five minutes. Tyra was going stir-crazy anyway and had already seriously pissed off most of the staff with her endless demands. They needed a change of scene, somewhere they could talk, somewhere Ros could outline the deal on offer and Tyra could say yes or no.

A yes meant a whole apparatus of officialdom would then crank into action. A no meant Ros could go home and practise her parallel parking.

An old snooker hall in a run-down club might not have seemed the most obvious choice for such a summit but Ros had used it several times in the past and always found it more than fit for purpose. The fact it was round the corner from one of the biggest nicks in the capital helped. The uniformed copper summoned from that self-same nick and currently manning the entrance helped too.

The first item on what might be called the agenda, although this was carefully designed to seem more like a fairly casual chat, was the simplest one of all. It was called protecting the life of the witness and Ros had first to establish if that was indeed what Tyra wanted.

Did she feel her life was at such sufficient risk that she needed that level of protection and was she prepared for the measures that might have to be employed to achieve that?

Tyra, now clearing the reds, looked at Ros as if she was a child with special needs. If she didn't want protection, if she didn't feel her life was at risk then what did Ros think she was doing here, with her, in some shitty snooker hall as she, not altogether unreasonably, pointed out?

And why had she just spent the last few hours with those two missing links back in that nick?

Ros took that as a yes.

Next item on the agenda:

Witnesses need financial support to help them adapt to their new circumstances. Financial support may be temporary or last the duration of the programme.

'So I get a house or a flat?'

'You get a house or a flat.'

'And I won't have to work down the local check-out?'

'You'll be provided with food and an allowance.'

'And once the trial's done and dusted, once Yaroslav's put away, what happens then?'

A participant should be encouraged to become financially independent through the provision of education, professional training and skills development.

Ros didn't read out that bit. She had a feeling it wouldn't exactly go down too well.

'We'll cross that bridge when we come to it.'

Help may also be given to start a new business.

Or that bit either.

So far it was simple. This is what the witness wants; protection. These are some of the safety nets, including money and a home that the system provides. But the next matter of the moment was always going to be one of the most problematic; the not-so-simple question of family and friends.

There must be no direct communication between the witness and relatives who are not included in the programme.

'Masters mentioned your father was still alive.'

Tyra snorted, uncharacteristically fluffing a yellow as she did so, the ball cannoning back off the cushion and coming to a rest behind the blue.

'Call that living? Sitting in some home somewhere, can't speak, can't hear, can't feed himself, doesn't even know when he's shit himself, give me a gun and look the other way, I'd finish the old fucker off myself.'

'No other relatives?'

'None that I ever want to see again. Definitely none that want to see me.'

'Can any of them be traced?'

'Only if Yaroslav found out my real name and where I actually come from.'

'And how easy would that be?'

'You tell me.'

Ros looked at her.

'You lot haven't managed it. So why should he?'

Ros kept looking at her.

So now she knew she wasn't even being told the real identity of the witness she was attempting to protect. Strictly speaking she didn't need to know of course. That identity would be changing within a matter of days if not indeed the next few hours, wiping everything that had existed previously. But still Ros felt uneasy. At least at the start of a programme she liked to begin on something approximating to sure ground.

It also, slightly at least, compromised the next item on the list; conduct of the witness.

Upon entering the programme, the witness is required to cooperate fully and to fully disclose all personal history.

But what was Ros supposed to do? She could push this now for the sake of a point of procedure, but how was she to know she wouldn't simply be fed another selection of carefully constructed evasions?

The past wasn't really the issue. And the present was always going to be a lie from this point on too. All that really mattered was the future and one moment in that future in particular – when a client stood in a dock and delivered a carefully rehearsed speech, unleashing what was hoped would be devastating evidence.

Who they were, where they came from, who they used to be, all that would already have been erased. In the ever-shifting battleground between the rules of good practice and effective policing this was one of those instances where the latter well and truly won out.

Ros experienced a rare moment of victory, rolling the white down the cushion to come to a rest behind the black, forcing Tyra into a grudging nod of respect. Now she had to negotiate a tricky snooker off the top cushion to come back down for the green.

As Tyra bent to examine the line she needed to take, Ros contemplated, all-too briefly, the next item on the checklist: discharge of debts and other legal obligations.

Admission to a protection programme may seriously affect the rights of third parties to collect debts or other outstanding legal obligations.

But Ros dismissed that along with the now-redundant matter

of actual identity. If Tyra had debts and obligations to anyone she had them no longer. So far as any creditors out there were concerned it was already tough shit.

Ros should also have run through the various procedures involved in any termination of the programme, such termination either initiated by the programme itself or forced upon them by the actions of the witness. There was also the issue of termination arising because the witness simply couldn't hack it any more, but she decided, at this stage anyway, to pass over that one too.

Tyra extricated herself from the snooker easily enough but she'd left Ros with an easy pot and she seemed to realise that too. Ros bent down, assessing the line to the pocket, calculating the force she'd need to employ to return the white ball halfway down the table to pick up the black after she'd potted the green. And sure enough the green ball dropped into the pocket, the white ball returning to the spot Ros had mentally allotted in her head, halfway down the table, nestling just behind the black again. If she could now pot that black and run the ball round for the brown then Ros might be on for a clearance.

As she bent for her next shot, Ros reviewed the next item on the checklist, the one that really sent the life of the client into something approaching fantasy-land, at least at the start of proceedings and sometimes forever.

Identity change – hiding the original identity of the witness, creating a new name, resettling them in a new area and creating an alternative life history.

Even though they tried their best to mirror the previous history of that self-same witness – because the fewer lies there were to memorise the more convincing any consequent story might sound – it was all still deeply strange.

What's your name? One of the first questions you're asked

when you make a new friend, meet a new lover, start a new job and the answer is usually instinctive. That was one of the first lessons to be learnt. All the old instincts from that point on had to be unlearnt.

'Have you any old documents?'

'How do you mean?'

'Passport, medical or national insurance cards, driver's licence, birth certificate, anything with your actual name or even any name on it.'

Tyra just looked at her, pityingly, again.

'What happens when you want to go on holiday, you'd need a passport then?'

Tyra shrugged.

'I'd buy one.'

Something told Ros this case was going to prove easier than most when it came to the covering of tracks. It sounded like Tyra had been doing it for some time anyway.

The brown had now been swallowed by the left middle pocket, the blue was travelling down to the bottom left, the white coming back up the table for the pink. Potting that would put Ros within one score of Tyra.

'Do I get any sort of say in this?'

'In what way?'

'Who I am, what I do, what my name is, where I've been all my life.'

'We try and keep as much of your old life as we can.'

'So my story's going to be that I dropped out of school, served time for some youth offending, then fell in with a heavyweight psycho.'

Tyra paused. The pink had now joined the blue in the pocket. Just the one ball to go.

'We'll probably need to be a bit more creative than that.'

As Ros bent for the final shot Tyra picked up the black. For a moment Ros thought it was some gesture of surrender, the kind chess players sometimes make when they see an inevitable checkmate ahead.

But Tyra had a rather larger matter in mind.

'I want out.'

'What?'

'This is fucking stupid, all of it, I'm not doing it.'

Ros stared at her.

What was this, what had she said, what had spooked her?

'I said, I want fucking out!'

And then Tyra turned and hurled the ball, past the elderly custodian of the single-table snooker hall, Jocus ducking as the ball smashed into the few bottles and optics clinging onto existence behind his bar. A bottle of whisky exploded as the black ball scored a direct hit.

Then Tyra sat down on the floor, encircled her arms around herself, comforting, self-protective; and for a moment Ros saw the young girl beneath the shell.

And in that moment too Ros knew that, despite all she was saying right now, all she would probably say on similar days on similar occasions in the future, Tyra was staying inside the programme and she was doing that because she had no choice.

Tyra was staying because she was terrified. Terrified of the Ukrainian, terrified of her memories, terrified of everything that had happened in her life up to that point and even more terrified of what might now be around the corner.

Ros walked past the reception desk, glanced instinctively at the bank of monitors all focused on different parts of the club. It was early evening, there were a few people dotted around the bar, a couple of single males in a large room to the rear of the bar, reading magazines, watching the adult content on the constant

DVD feed, but there was no-one, she was pleased to note, in the large Jacuzzi as yet.

Ros moved into the changing room, which was the only one and communal – this was no place to be coy – slipped out of her clothes and secured them in the locker. Putting on the robe provided inside, she moved into the bar, keeping her eyes averted from the silent invitations already wafting her way, moved past the cubicles, one of which seemed to be occupied at present, but whoever was in there quite obviously did not want anyone joining them.

The door, in two parts, was closed along its bottom length. Club etiquette was simple. If any part of the door was closed then the occupants wanted privacy and, aside from Friday nights when the doors were thrown open to more casual customers, house rules were respected.

Ros didn't even look at any of the other cubicles. She slipped out of her robe, hung it on a hook next to the Jacuzzi, before slipping, naked, inside.

Then she closed her eyes.

Dimly, she felt another presence enter the same Jacuzzi a moment or so later but she didn't open her eyes and he or she didn't make any sort of approach. Ros just stretched out in the water. Later, a lot later, she might check out the rest of the guests but she'd probably just remain on her own on this visit. It had been a stressful day but not the kind of stress she had to work out of her system in one of those cubicles as she'd done on countless nights in the past with partners, sometimes men, sometimes women, who were probably doing the same.

Whoever had joined her in the Jacuzzi left a few moments later meaning the silent message had been received, understood and respected.

Ros kept her eyes closed, her mind blank, letting the jets

play over every inch of her body, blotting out everyone and everything.

It would only be a matter of moments now, Scott knew that. Oddly enough he'd gone beyond pain. Maybe, having endured so much, the body reached a plateau where nerves gave up, when signals to the brain stopped functioning, perhaps because some sort of overload had taken place.

Or maybe he was just closing down. Maybe the reason he was feeling less and less these last few moments was simple; there was less and less of his body that was capable of feeling anything. Like a victim of a creeping gangrene, he was simply dying alive.

But two things didn't add up. Actually, a lot about this abduction, enforced imprisonment, torture and imminent murder didn't add up, but two questions still dominated.

What was the point of all this, was the first? He hadn't been asked anything his Ukrainian torturer didn't already know. Yaroslav was well aware that first one of his girls and then another had defected across to them. He was also well aware, as he made crystal clear as the flame thrower was waved in front of Scott's terrified eyes, branding first one cheek and then another, that both those self-same girls were chirping more sweetly than a chorus of canaries right now, giving their hosts chapter and verse on all his activities.

OK, Yaroslav didn't know exactly where they were being held but neither, genuinely, did Scott and he could see that the Ukrainian believed him. So that was the first puzzle. Torture without a point. Horrifying pain inflicted for no purpose. And no end in sight aside from the inevitable death of the victim.

The second question had been prompted by the latest branding. A full-length mirror dominated the far wall, testament to the building's former use as some sort of dance or rehearsal studio. Yaroslav had taken it over after the former tenants had decamped to a new purpose-built unit near to the site of the new Sports Village.

The building itself was run-down and the facilities hardly state of the art but that paled into insignificance compared to the major attraction on offer, at least to one in the Ukrainian's line of work. The whole place was soundproofed. It had been designed to allow the various dance companies, bands and theatre groups to rehearse without fear of disturbing any immediate neighbours. Now it performed the same function for torture victims too.

Courtesy of that full-length wall mirror, Scott could not only feel but could now see the large, ragged cross that had been branded onto his chest by that flame thrower. From what seemed like another life completely, he remembered station gossip about similar crosses being branded onto the bodies of other unfortunate souls who'd also attracted the same sort of attention.

So far from covering his tracks, far from attempting to conceal the identity of Scott's persecutor, Yaroslav was going out of the way to advertise the fact. When his body was eventually found, there was going to be absolutely no doubt who'd done all this to him – meaning this was some sort of declaration of war.

See what I can do.

Look what I've done to one of your own.

Now, what are you going to do?

Which also made no sense. A murder committed for no reason along with a message that almost seemed like a suicide note, inviting the wrath of all the gods down on the perpetrator's head. Already that perpetrator should be running for the hills, only Yaroslav obviously wasn't. Yaroslav was sending out the most eloquent message possible that he wasn't going anywhere and that anyone sent against him would be similarly dispatched.

But as the light, thankfully, began to fade, as not even Yaroslav could now prevent the darkness creeping into Scott's vision, it was Bel, the beautiful Bel, the beautiful, pregnant Bel who was now before his failing eyes.

Of course he'd never now see the son or daughter she was carrying, but that wasn't the reason for the final piercing thought that twisted his guts. He wondered whether this would be the excuse he craved, whether DS Donovan Banks, soon to be DI Donovan Banks if once again that station rumour was accurate, would finally complete the job he'd started in that club, would now take his place in Scott's bed along with the place he'd already taken, in Scott's mind at least, everywhere else.

Then the door in front of him opened.

And everything changed again.

Ros let herself back into her one-bedroomed, second floor apartment, stood for a moment in the small hallway and thought of the Kincaids.

Or at least she felt an all-too familiar lead weight settle over her stomach and knew she was thinking about them.

Maybe she should have taken up the silent invitation proffered earlier by her Jacuzzi companion or the not-so-silent offer extended by one of the drinkers sitting at the bar. Or even the more conspiratorial offer from the teenage boy hanging around the rear of the club as she exited a few moments later. The local dealers were well aware what happened inside and well aware also that many of the participants occasionally needed some sort of stimulation to see them through the rigours ahead.

But she'd resisted. She'd declined each and every offer. She'd had – what was to Ros – an unusually uneventful night and this, it seemed, was her reward, standing in her hallway ambushed by memories, locked in a past she had no wish to revisit but which showed no sign of loosening its grip.

In her bag her mobile rang. For a moment she was tempted to ignore it and go to bed. Then Ros looked at the name on the display and changed her mind.

'Conor?'

Her new DC didn't waste any time.

'Uniform have been on from the hotel.'

Conor paused, as if he was taking some real satisfaction from this, as if some point had just been proved.

'Tyra's gone missing.'

MACKLYN, DI'S FATHER, could – as he'd been known to claim on more than one occasion – smell it a mile off.

Something in the way a driver would exit a cab, the way a telephone conversation would start with a special kind of pause. Sometimes it involved an employee, sometimes a customer, but it all added up to the same thing in the end.

Trouble.

And that's what Macklyn was looking at as he eyed the approaching twenty-one-year-old shambling across the yard towards him, the white Transit he'd been using, a van that had been purchased along with the rest of the new stock a few months earlier, parked a few metres behind.

He could almost see the thought processes going on in the semi-feral brain of his approaching visitor.

What could he get away with this time?

How much in the way of half-truths and evasions would his middle-aged employer be prepared to swallow?

The answer, if he had the wherewithal to see it, was evident enough in the pair of eyes that were now recording his every step across that yard; absolutely none at all. This was one driver who'd well and truly reached the end of his particular road.

His secretary looked from her boss towards his latest recruit. She'd been with Macklyn the best part of twenty years. She knew he took no prisoners. She knew he'd listen, even apparently take on board the litany of excuses as to why this delivery hadn't been made, those packages not collected. He might even shake his head in apparent sympathy as he was told about the roadworks that had played havoc with the schedule and had delayed his driver's return to the depot by at least two hours, a time lapse that enabled that same driver to indulge in a lucrative little bit of moonlighting, transporting a neighbour's possessions from one flat to another, cash in hand, no questions asked and no-one any the wiser or such, at least, was his fond and soon-to-be disillusioned hope.

Vaguely, her eyes on the approaching driver, she was aware of another vehicle pulling up alongside the Transit, of two men getting out, customers she assumed, or prospective customers at least, but she didn't take much notice of them, not with this sort of upcoming cabaret to savour. Their small freight company ran like clockwork, Macklyn made sure of it and his secretary liked to think she played her part too. It guaranteed job security, which was its plus point, but there was a downside. It made the working day more than a little dull. Interludes like this, a face-off of the type she was now confidently expecting to erupt, very definitely alleviated the tedium.

The young driver came into the office, his face already settling into a well-rehearsed grimace of weary defeat. She placed a mental bet with herself as to how far he'd get with his stumbling explanation for his extended absence.

Vaguely again, she was aware of the door opening behind and the same two men now coming in. She was just about to divert them into the small waiting area as quickly as she could, she really didn't want to miss any of this.

Then matters, at least so far as she was concerned, took an even more interesting turn.

Macklyn saw the flash of two warrant cards, then one of his new visitors moved beyond him into his own office and began to open and empty drawers.

Meanwhile the other officer swiftly and efficiently escorted the young driver into the waiting area along with his now open-mouthed secretary before taking Macklyn by the arm, escorting him back into his office where his companion now demanded a list of any personal documents or possessions he might have stored there.

At the same time as all that was happening he was also being told to get his coat and fetch his car keys while any attempt on his part to ask even the most basic of reasonable questions – like what the hell was going on here – was met with a total stone-wall.

Everything would be explained.

Just not yet.

Right now there was no time, for now he just had to do what he was told and he had to do it immediately.

Again the same warrant cards were flashed. The officers knew from past experience they'd need to be shown more than once in the course of a visit, sometimes several times and even then there were some who still wouldn't be able to take it in, who would refuse to accept the seriousness of the situation that was being spelt out to them and then, regrettably, force would have to be employed.

By now they'd been in Macklyn's office for less than two minutes. In that time his desk had been searched and cleared, a driving licence retrieved along with some family photographs, some car keys, a registration document, letters from the local tax office and some statements from the bank.

In the next office, the other officer was now emptying the secretary's desk in a similarly efficient fashion, the secretary herself watching from the other side of a glass door along with a driver who looked every bit as baffled as his employer.

One of the officers then tossed his car keys to the other while Macklyn was told to accompany him to the waiting, unmarked car. His own car would follow on, driven by the other officer.

All the time came the same stock responses to all his increasingly bewildered and increasingly agitated questions.

Everything would be explained.

Everything would be made clear.

Just not here and now, the only priority here and now was removing him from his place of work, his business, the business he'd started over twenty years ago, his own little kingdom in fact.

His kingdom, it seemed, no longer.

Options raced through his mind.

Tax.

VAT.

One of his drivers had been caught up in some sort of incident, smuggling perhaps, or fraud, but none of it made sense. And none of those possible explanations even began to make sense of the genuine fear he could see in the eyes of both officers, the constant checks they kept making on the yard as if they were expecting another visitor or visitors at any time.

In something of a daze, Macklyn allowed himself to be propelled towards the office door and the waiting unmarked police car, although in truth he had little option. He kept himself in fairly good shape but still he'd have been no match for the finely-honed officers who were now directing his every movement.

As he moved through the door he heard his scared secretary ask one of the officers when he'd be back, they had schedules to prepare, wages to pay and he just caught the short response.

He won't be back.

Then the door slammed behind them, slammed shut on more than just his former business as he moved in the space of just over three minutes from one life to a completely different life altogether.

F OR THE SECOND time in as many days, Ros took a right as she entered the main foyer, punched the button for the lift, then stared in something approaching blank incredulity as Conor, accompanying her this time, held back as he surveyed the lobby which was packed full of tracksuited footballers.

Ros kept staring at him as he enthusiastically began identifying the various local luminaries on show, moving on to detail that striker's latest goal, a save that had kept the Bluebirds in a recent cup game, the manager's recent run of results involving some tactic resembling something called, apparently, a diamond, before the lift doors opened and she could claim sanctuary inside.

Conor hadn't displayed a flicker of interest all the way over to the hotel in their missing witness or the case in which they were involved. Now he couldn't stop talking and, as he headed into the lift behind her, he launched into a new diatribe regarding the relative merits of the two midfielders currently vying, it seemed, for just the one position in the team. Conor, quite clearly, could demonstrate remarkable animation when the occasion and right set of circumstances arose. All of a sudden – and for the first time since Ros had made his clearly-unwilling acquaintance – the taciturn Conor had actually come to life.

The lift doors once again opened on the fifth floor and Ros stepped out, dismissing Conor and his encyclopaedic knowledge of the relative merits of the sweeper system. All that was on her mind now was Tyra.

Where was she? What had happened in the period between her attempt to single-handedly demolish a decaying snooker hall and the moment the uniformed guard detailed to check on her well-being every half hour or so reported her sudden absence?

Her bedroom door hadn't been forced and there was no sign of a struggle having taken place, strongly suggesting she'd simply opened that door herself and walked out. But something – instinct perhaps – or the evidence of her own eyes from their meeting the previous day – was already telling Ros that nothing involving the troublesome Tyra was ever likely to prove simple.

Masters was already inside the room as they approached. The look on his face as he saw her was an expression Ros recognised only too well. The world would be a simpler place if Murder Squad could simply keep their witnesses in one room preferably without windows or doors from the time of their arrest up to the time of the trial after which they could be released like wild animals back to whatever hellhole had raised and sustained them.

Look what happened when outside agencies got involved. Within twenty-four hours their chief witness had slipped through their fingers.

Ros had little truck with the first few sentiments. She had more difficulty when it came to the final, albeit unspoken, observation, because this was indeed beginning to resemble one gigantic fuck-up.

And it was about to get worse.

'Did you actually search this witness?'

Tyra had been searched on admission to the station, on her release into Ros's protective custody and the bags she'd brought with her would have been examined too. But obviously at some point those searches had been less than effective and as the final search took place in the care of Ros and her department it was pretty clear to Masters at least where the ultimate failure lay.

Because there was a failure, of that there could now be little doubt. The used syringe Masters was holding between two thin tissues was testament to that.

Ros stared at it.

'We found it behind one of the cushions. She hadn't even bothered to get rid of it properly. Other things on her mind maybe. Like where to get her next fucking hit.'

Ros kept staring at the syringe, her heart now sinking. It could have belonged to some other guest, could have been left behind in a room that had been inadequately cleaned, but she doubted it, making the only possible conclusion obvious and inescapable.

Tyra was not only the chief witness in a murder trial, she was also a junkie. And all of a sudden her decision to quit that room, to leave the protective care of her temporary custodians, to apparently exit the whole programme she'd agreed to join just hours earlier, became a whole lot more intelligible.

Yesterday, courtesy of the hit provided by that now-empty syringe, she'd functioned at least halfway normally, one attempted assault with a snooker ball aside.

But at some point in the night the effects of that hit had evaporated.

And Tyra had set out to secure another.

The train clattered over lock-up garages, mobile catering units and various car hire outlets housed in the old railway arches below. In front of Tyra loomed the new buildings of the old financial district.

Beyond that, unseen but still there, was home, the home of childhood memories, of friends and acquaintances, of playgrounds and teenage haunts. A place she could never forget. And a place, it seemed, she could not stay away from either.

As she passed Cable Street she looked down at the old mural on the side of the former Vestry commemorating the 1930s clash between the working men of the area and the Black Shirts; and found herself thinking about the copper.

Not Ros, the woman in charge.

The silent man at Ros's side. His mouth hadn't said too much but his eyes had said plenty.

It wasn't just the silent appraisal. She'd been used to that from men of all ages for years now. At first, in her early teens, it had frightened her. Sometimes the need in those looks was chilling. Later, when she became more confident, she began to turn all that to her advantage as she had, initially at least, with Yaroslav.

But with this one there was something else. She'd heard Ros use his name just the once and it seemed to suit him. Conor. He was Cardiff born and bred that much was obvious, a genuine Celt. That had given him his blue eyes and jet black hair, always a sexy combination. But it didn't explain the pent-up rage she could sense inside him.

It wasn't a rage directed at her. She'd seen enough of those sort of looks from the faces in Murder Squad, aware they had to deal with her, indulge her even, hating the necessity of having to so do. It wasn't a rage particularly directed at Ros either. He hardly seemed to even see her.

So what was it? What was it behind those eyes as they looked at and then beyond her? What demons danced before them? Something, Tyra didn't know what, but something told her it would be interesting finding out.

The driverless train slowed. Around her the last of the passengers collected bags, packed away mobile phones, made ready to alight. Tyra looked at the buildings now looming above her, the streets thronged with shoppers, the cafés packed with diners, city boys already spilling out from various wine bars and bistros onto nearby pavements.

Tyra licked her lips, fighting the overpowering sensation she always knew would claim her at this point, anticipating it, trying to absorb it in some way, but it didn't really help. Her throat, despite all her efforts to control her breathing, to will herself into some calmer place, grew ever drier.

All of a sudden Tyra felt afraid.

Ros, Conor, Masters and Banks had also travelled from the Welsh to the English capital, two hours earlier. Now they were in a small office high above the station concourse at Canary Wharf, the sounds of planes droning overhead, the four officers staring at a small army of faces as they flashed by on a seemingly never-ending loop.

They knew Tyra had taken the train to London. They also knew, courtesy of the same CCTV trail, that she'd then taken the tube here. But from this destination, Tyra could have gone anywhere and by any means. There was a river clipper embarkation point a short distance away that could have taken her east past Greenwich or west again, all the way up to Millbank, calling at any number of stops in between, accessing any number of onward connections to a million different destinations.

If she had taken the clipper then flight would most probably have been on her mind. Meaning that whatever Ros thought she might have achieved the previous day, whatever agreement she might have believed they'd concluded, Tyra had clearly decided it was no sort of achievement and no agreement at all in which case she'd be looking to put as many miles between herself and her former life as possible. In which case all Murder Squad's fond hopes for its new key witness would have evaporated, the celebratory champagne destined to remain uncorked.

The other alternative was that something else entirely was impelling the troublesome and clearly-troubled Tyra and she had a considerably simpler and shorter journey and purpose in mind.

Ros leant forward over the monitor, scanned the early morning commuters, most with briefcases in one hand, takeaway coffee in the other, streaming past the cameras, fumbling with travel cards, all with somewhere to be roughly five minutes ago.

Then a voice cut across.

'Guv.'

It was Banks who'd spotted her it seemed. On the edge of the frame, a hesitant figure approaching the station entrance, pausing before heading inside as if unsure of what she now had to do.

The same distinctively-willowy frame.

The same distinctive shock of blue hair.

But Ros kept her eyes fixed on the monitor as Banks grimaced in disappointment, that willowy figure now being joined by a young man, the pair combining to form a young couple, exchanging a last hug, a final kiss before the lovers finally parted.

Then Ros saw her. In among the rest of the commuters, no bag or briefcase in her hand, no takeaway coffee either, but moving with the same sense of purpose, a young woman with very definitely somewhere to go.

Tyra moved into the station and the CCTV operator changed cameras. Now she was seen heading down the escalator before taking a left, waiting by the glass doors for an east-bound train. By Ros's side, Masters barked at Banks.

'City airport?'

'Onto it, Guv.'

Banks was already making for the door but Ros didn't move. Neither to his credit did Masters. He might have wanted all options checked but that didn't mean he'd checked his brain out at that monitoring office door either. Sure enough, within five minutes – and after at least two if not more trains had sped down the line towards Stratford – she was seen moving back up that same escalator before heading out again on the station concourse where Tyra took the westbound DLR link instead.

Tyra was heading, presumably, for her old and familiar suppliers in one of her old and familiar places. And according to the time code on the CCTV tape she had at least five hours start on her watching pursuers.

Which meant it might already be too late.

Tyra took a left out of Kings Cross, turned down a side street. Ahead of her was a new development behind a gated fence. In time the intention was that all former residents would be driven out, leaving its recent and sordid past a distant memory. But in the meantime there were still plenty of rich pickings if you knew where to look.

And Tyra knew exactly where to look.

It was the blue hair he noticed first. The next thing he noticed was a certain truculence in the way she moved. Something told him this one would definitely be worth checking out.

He exited his car making sure to secure it behind him. Nothing was sacred any more, if it ever had been. Several of the more likely of the local lads wouldn't think twice about having it on their toes with a prize like that.

She'd already disappeared down one of the alleys that scarred and criss-crossed the whole patch by the time he'd taken all reasonable precautions, but he wasn't too worried about that. He knew the area well and he wasn't due to check back with the station for another hour or so at least. Plenty of time to bag himself a tasty little offering.

He turned into one of the alleys, ignoring the hostile stare of one of the working girls coming out of a nearby walk-up. Dimly, he remembered her. A particularly skanky piece of ass, but how could he be sure? There'd been so many lately. Faces tended to merge. Bodies tended to do so as well. That's why he'd noticed this other girl. Something was telling him she was going to be special and in his currently-jaded state that really was something to be savoured.

Ignoring the baleful stare of the passing whore – what did he do to her for Christ's sake, he really couldn't remember – he turned another corner, pausing as he caught another flash of blue at the far end of the next alleyway. She'd paused outside the entrance to a block of new-build flats.

Then, some sixth sense operating perhaps, she seemed to sense his stare.

And turned to face him.

Tyra really thought she'd underestimated them. She was sure she'd covered her tracks and even if she hadn't, even if the woman with the eyes that looked as if she'd lived a dozen different lifetimes had sussed what she was really up to, Tyra didn't in a million of those lifetimes think she'd be on her tail so soon.

But there he was. At the end of the street. Unmistakably a cop, something in the way he stood, the way he was looking at her. Proprietorial. As if he knew he could do whatever he wanted with whomsoever he chose. As usually, and as she knew only too well, they could.

She looked back at the door in front of her, still closed. Maybe it was best if it stayed that way for the next few moments. The cop approached and she didn't move. For a moment it looked like *High Noon*. The cop kept approaching. She stayed still.

When he was within touching distance he paused, just looked at her. Then his arm snaked out.

For a moment she just stared at the hand that had jammed itself, hard against her crotch, fingers already kneading at the tight material of her jeans. Then she looked back up at him, at his eyes darting now all over her body and all of a sudden she understood. And for a moment relief mixed in with amusement.

She knelt down on the pavement in front of him, uncaring of the grime now staining her jeans. Without saying a word, she unzipped his trousers, reached inside and took out his already thickening penis.

The cop looked round, checking, but couldn't see anyone. Then he looked back at the girl, delighted that his first instincts seemed correct. This one really did seem special. She held his penis up, stroking its length, opening up the head. He closed his eyes as she puckered her lips. Opening them again a moment later, he saw her reaching into her pocket and was just about to tell her not to bother with a condom, he'd take the risk. It was only a blowjob he had in mind after all.

Then pain of a kind he'd never experienced before blasted through him as she took out a razor from her bag, slotted it quickly, expertly almost, inside his now-gaping slit and yanked down, hard.

His penis opened like a burst sausage under a fierce grill. Blood spurted up onto his face as she kept tearing down with the razor, virtually splitting his penis in two, exposing a whole cat's cradle of veins all engorged with blood.

He thought he was going to die. He really did. He couldn't move, yet couldn't stay still. And he couldn't scream either, his voice seemed to have gone along with everything else. All there was, all he'd become, was pain. Everything else was blotted out.

Dimly he was aware of a nearby door opening, even more dimly he was aware of the girl turning away from him and for a moment he thought he saw fear on her face.

Then her face softened and a smile, almost beatific, blessed her features and she held out her hand and was led inside, leaving him writhing behind on the pavement outside, screaming soundlessly, his hands clasped over what remained of his penis, now unrecognisable as anything aside from offal.

From down the street another girl approached, the one he'd seen earlier, the girl with the baleful stare, the one he could hardly remember – and certainly couldn't remember what he'd done to her – but it must have been bad.

All that he'd realise later, for now he was in no state to even begin to form anything like a coherent thought which was perhaps just as well. His second female encounter of as many minutes wasn't going to be as barbarically savage as the first but damage – the inflicting of and making sure it was as painful as possible – was clearly the priority on this girl's mind too.

The cop was now curled into a foetal position desperately scrabbling with his fingers to stem the bleeding, an impossible task, even more blood now seemed to be spurting out from what felt like his very centre. He didn't present much in the way of a target but it was enough.

As he momentarily straightened, howled to whatever God might be listening to help, help him for fuck's sake, she brought her heel back, paused for a moment before cannoning the steel toe of her boot hard into the bridge of his nose as he lay on the road before her, splintering the bone, blinding his sight.

Inside the house, Tyra had already dismissed the encounter. That was a trick she'd used on several occasions in the past when wannabe boyfriends, usually of the mock-gangster variety, had tried to persuade her into bed or onto the bonnet of a car and had decided to dispense with social niceties like the gentle art of soft seduction.

Tyra had learnt early, courtesy of a middle-aged uncle, that it was never a good idea to resist at the start. Far better to flatter to deceive. To concede to the stronger force. Let them feel that surge of power, robbing them of their usual defences before administering what might be called the killer blow.

She stared straight ahead at the eyes now staring back at her. In a few moments time there'd probably be all types of emergency activity outside, but no-one would bother them in here. No neighbour, even if they'd witnessed the attack, would report the encounter. They simply knew better.

He was smiling back at her now, she could almost see him getting high just on her very presence and how long had they been apart, just a few days at most? It was love she read in his eyes, it had to be. Love springing from the most unexpected of sources perhaps, but love nonetheless. He'd give her anything, had indeed given her everything. And now he'd give her more.

Everything else could wait, would wait, all her plans and all her fears, all she wanted to do now was drink in this moment, let it intoxicate her as she knew it was now intoxicating him.

It was something she'd kept back from that tight-arsed female protection officer. A secret she'd guard, if necessary, with her life.

9

MASTERS DIDN'T WANT her there. It wasn't just his body language that made it crystal clear, Masters was never exactly shy when it came to expressing himself, usually in words of expletive-laden single syllables, particularly when something displeased him such as the presence of other departments on an operation that was supposed to be strictly his shout.

But Jukes was the same rank as Masters. And Jukes believed Ros might be of use. OK, she hadn't been able to prevent the flight of their chief witness but nothing would probably have prevented that given their new suspicions concerning her hitherto-unsuspected addiction.

No-one had any idea what they might find at the end of all this, a strung-out Tyra, a dead Tyra, a Tyra in serious need of some urgent and heavy-duty counselling or persuasion. In the case of the former, they'd need a doctor, in the case of the second, an undertaker, in the case of the third then Ros, as Masters was forced to grudgingly concede, could possibly come into her own.

For her part Ros just stared out of the car window at the London skyline. Conor had offered to drive the pool car they'd commandeered and she hadn't put up too much of a fight. Most of her thinking was revolving around Tyra, wondering how to play this, wondering if there was anything indeed left to play.

All that she could deal with. All that was purposeful, was moving all this forward.

The other part of her brain, the part she was trying at the same time to close down, was less purposeful, had nothing to do with moving on or moving forward.

It happened every time. Whenever there was any kind of setback, any kind of problem but lately – and even more worryingly – it was happening when there were no problems, no setbacks, when nothing had gone wrong, when the client had been successfully delivered to trial and then back to their former lives, unharmed and none the worse so it seemed for their experience. Unbidden, they'd creep into the edge of her vision.

The Kincaids.

Always, forever, the Kincaids.

Conor drove through the narrow streets of the city, avoiding buses and taxi drivers who clearly believed they owned each and every stretch of road. He'd lived here years earlier and knew the area fairly well but would still have appreciated a little help regarding a route that was changing every few metres as some fresh obstacle suddenly loomed before them. But he knew better than to ask his silent companion.

At first he thought it might be Ros's way of demonstrating the difference in rank. Social niceties were to be dispensed with, even common courtesy abandoned. Speak when you're spoken to, apart from that, just shut up.

Then he'd watched her with others – not just in their own department but in other departments too – and had witnessed them receive the same treatment. They were listened to for as long as any information they had to impart was relevant to whatever may be the matter of the moment, then dismissed.

So now he didn't think she was playing games. Now he reckoned she was a plain and simple ballbreaker.

Just like his wife.

In the second car, heading for their joint destination, Banks wasn't thinking about Ros. Banks was thinking about Conor instead.

Banks didn't like Conor and that was nothing to do with the different parts of the city they originally called home. Banks was Ely, Conor was Butetown. It was impossible to explain to an outsider, but Ely and Butetown boys just didn't mix. Then again, reflected Banks darkly, Butetown boys didn't mix with anyone.

But it was more than the simple claims of territory. Banks hadn't liked the new recruit from the moment he set eyes on him in that incident room some four years earlier. Banks had an instinct for them. Those who'd fit in and those who wouldn't. That instinct was usually spot-on too even if with some people the truth took a little longer to emerge than others. In the case of Conor it had definitely taken longer than most but his true colours came out eventually.

Banks parked and exited their unmarked car, Masters moving a short distance ahead. As he followed he could just see Conor himself driving onto the street, parking up a hundred or so metres away.

They didn't mind the occasional bit of violence. Justifiable force was how Masters described most of the petty – and some of the not-so-petty – assaults perpetrated by some of his officers on the sundry suspects that passed through the interview rooms and holding cells of their home nick.

It set down the ground rules from the start. A quick rabbit punch to the kidneys might mean a suspect pissing blood for the next few hours but it didn't leave much in the way of any other external evidence. And it worked wonders for concentrating the mind of that self-same suspect when their next interview came round. Conor might not have been quite as enthusiastic as some of the newer recruits in flexing his new-found official muscle, but he wasn't exactly to be found hiding behind the door when a ruck kicked off either.

A totally ordinary, fairly unremarkable member of the team in fact.

Until a certain piece of top totty walked in one night.

Actually, walking was putting it a bit strongly. It was more like stumbling, having to be held up every few steps by one of the grinning traffic rats who'd pulled her over. And she wasn't so much drunk as totally paralytic.

And she wasn't a merry drunk either. She was a vicious drunk. Booze very definitely didn't turn the world into a happy, smiley universe for this one. Once she'd taken on board more than enough liquid to float a medium-size minesweeper she looked out at that universe with eyes that saw one thing and one thing only.

Objects – usually human – to be attacked, mostly verbally, but sometimes physically too.

Relationships to be destroyed, people and situations to be abused.

They'd picked her up after she'd attacked a girl in a local restaurant. She'd been drinking alone after a man who was supposed to be her night-time companion had tired of her constant sniping and left her to imbibe the last of the wine he hoped they'd share, before being swiftly disabused of that fond notion by his drunken date immediately appropriating the first bottle they'd ordered at the same time as lining up its replacement.

She'd taken exception to some look her hapless fellow-diner may – or more probably may not – have flashed her way and had slammed her head down in her bowl of newly-delivered steaming hot mussels.

That little party trick over she'd left the restaurant and her now-screaming fellow diner – without paying naturally – and had managed to get into her nearby car. By now Uniform had been called and they tried to flag her down, only succeeding in diverting her towards and then into the side of a passing delivery van.

Dazed, she'd been brought in where it was quickly established that this was no ordinary paralytic drunk, this was a titled paralytic drunk with an address somewhere in old St Mellons and an ex who was something big in one of the local banks. It was all shaping up into the usual slap on the wrists and don't do it again routine when she came across Conor.

Conor shouldn't even have been there. He was visiting a low-life in the next holding cell who'd sliced a kid outside a kebab shop in Grangetown. But as their paths briefly crossed something in her obviously snapped because she suddenly flew at Conor although admittedly only with verbals. Jibes spewed out of her, mainly revolving around what she saw as his ill-fitting suit, his badly-cut hair, his generally grubby demeanour and his eyes which according to the top totty were too close together which was always a sign of something.

The problem being no-one found out exactly what that might be as the next second she was on the floor and Conor was on top of her, one hand round her throat which he was squeezing hard, so hard she was now gasping for what already sounded like her last breath. His other hand was bunched into a fist which was raining blows into her distended stomach.

For a moment no-one reacted. It all came completely out of nowhere – and it was all totally over the top too given the relatively mild provocation involved. But something she'd said – or maybe something in the way she'd said it – had obviously pressed all the wrong sort of buttons and the usually mild-mannered DC had suddenly turned into something just one step down from the Terminator.

Conor was pulled off his prone victim, she was cleaned up and the whole thing was pretty quickly hushed up too. She was never going to remember much about the evening anyway and a quick check-up by the station doctor confirmed no lasting damage had been done.

But later, reading the reports of the incident – and watching the video footage captured by the station CCTV – Masters grew more than a little uneasy. A show of force in the right place at the right time was totally acceptable. This was something else.

This was a sudden loss of control. Inexplicable in the circumstances and posing the question whether Conor was really fit for purpose in a high-pressure department like theirs? The incident may have been relatively trivial in itself but had it lifted a veil on something that may prove far from trivial in the future? A loss of control that may let them all down sometime?

It had all been done through the proper channels of course although Conor was no fool. He couldn't have bagged himself a wife like that if he didn't have something upstairs as well as probably below decks too. So he had to have understood all that happened at his next performance review and he had to have successfully decoded the suggestion that perhaps his career would benefit from a spell in some other department for a while.

There was no question of a demotion or alteration in rank. Nevertheless the fact remained that a DC in Murder Squad and a DC in any other squad were worlds apart and everyone knew that. So dress it up how you will, it was still always going to be a massive kick in the balls.

Banks grinned inwardly as he and Masters moved towards a plain door let into the large expanse of wall ahead of them. What happened next still gave him a delicious warm glow inside. Suppressed laughter leavened – sweetened indeed – with an invigorating, intoxicating, dose of bile.

No official record of the holding cell incident survived so no-one would ever know just what a loose canon Conor could become. Had he been busted back to traffic it might have caused a problem or two in the future. But to bust him back to that abode of bleeding-heart wankers – pardon my language,

Ma'am – to send, almost literally, a bull into that perennially fragile china shop was quite simply a stroke of genius.

Now there was only one thing better than looking back and marvelling at the neatness of this particular switch. That was looking forward and Banks had felt his mouth growing dry in anticipation on more than one occasion as he wondered just when – and how – and with what devastating effect – Conor was going to fuck up in the hopefully-near future.

And just how many of those low-life squealers masquerading as judicial witnesses he might drag down with him at the same time.

'Hello boys.'

The figure filled the doorway, a gun in his hand. Behind the unexpected visitor and visible through the open door, a waiting ambulance could be seen parked at the kerb. For a moment a weasel-faced medium-league dealer known locally as Jake didn't reply, just stared at the sudden apparition before him which was obviously a bad move because Masters suddenly raised the butt of his weapon and brought it crashing down on his skull.

As Jake fell, his companion also called Jake, stood up. In their world being known as the Two Jakes passed for class which was why they were never going to make the leap from medium league to anything even remotely bigger. The second of the Jakes had been rooted to his seat to that point but now some survival instinct kicked in and he just wanted to get the hell out of there. He threw the open bag of heroin they'd been cutting towards the gunman in a desperate attempt to distract him, temporarily blind him perhaps; but only succeeded in attracting the attention of a gun butt from a second gunman who'd appeared apparently from nowhere behind and he now joined his moaning companion on the floor.

The barrel of the first gun was then pressed into his neck and he was told to hold up his hands. As he did so he heard the other gunman shout the same instruction to the other Jake. He felt his arms being yanked behind his back and then his hands were bound together with thick rope. Then another rope secured the two Jakes together, back to back.

'Smell this.'

They did so and both gagged, nostrils recoiling at the sudden and acrid stench assailing them. Then they both felt paraffin being poured over their bodies from their chests all the way down to their legs.

Then both Jakes heard a click of a lighter and felt the heat of what seemed to be some sort of portable flamethrower.

The same voice spoke again.

'There's a young girl. Name of Tyra. Used to live round here, has now hooked up with a Ukrainian, name of Yaroslav. The word is you used to supply her, still do and some of Yaroslav's girls too, just a few substances, help them through their occasionally-stressful days.'

With a sickening jolt the second of the Jakes suddenly realised just who they were dealing with here. This wasn't some new outfit looking to muscle in. Faces, in other words, you could talk to, negotiate with.

This was the police.

And all of a sudden his bad day had become a whole lot worse.

There were rules even in tribal warfare, boundaries which, while pushed to the limit, were still observed. This lot didn't even begin to understand boundaries and as for rules they made them up, usually as they went along to fit any and every changing circumstance.

'Tell me where she is right now, taking absolutely no time out to think and don't even consider trying to send us off down any blind alleys and I'll turn this off.'

The second of the Jakes felt the flamethrower being waved closer to his paraffin-soaked shirt and jeans.

'If you don't I'll blow you out instead.'

'We haven't seen her for months.'

'Wrong answer.'

'It's the truth.'

'Still the wrong answer.'

The first of the Jakes began to whimper, then began to scream. A second or so later the second of the Jakes, face fixed on the copper in front of him, totally unable to turn his head to either side courtesy of the headlock currently being applied to it, caught the unmistakable whiff of flesh beginning to burn.

He started talking, quickly.

'She called, a few days ago, said she needed a bit extra, we thought she was going away on holiday or something.'

'And since then? She hasn't called, texted, contacted you via some social networking site, sent you a message by pigeon post?'

The second of the Jakes hesitated.

Who was he more frightened of?

The Ukrainian?

Or the police?

Masters registered his hesitation, sensed the unspoken question floating around inside his quarry's head and decided to answer it for him.

The second of the Jakes tried to curl himself into a ball in a desperate attempt to extinguish the flames ignited by the flamethrower but the rope fixing his arms and the tape securing his shins prevented him from doing so, not to mention the first of the Jakes currently strapped to his back.

Masters spoke again.

'In ten seconds we'll be talking third degree burns. Five seconds after that you'll be needing skin grafts. It's taken me three seconds to say all this so if you are going to tell me anything then I really do suggest you start talking right now.'

Four seconds after that the second of the Jakes was talking and wouldn't be requiring skin grafts.

The first of the Jakes wasn't so fortunate.

Masters listened impassively as the second of the Jakes finally proffered the information he needed.

Masters knew there were those in the department and outside who'd disapprove of what he called his information-gathering methods. There were those indeed who wouldn't have called them methods at all. Words like medieval and barbaric had been thrown around in the past. He'd thrown them around himself but not in the company of any of his fellow officers. Masters attended a local chess club each Tuesday evening and had been known to debate those very topics with a couple of the other members after the club closed its doors.

Those other members were a motley crew, retired college lecturers, a car mechanic, even a couple of old lags, but their brains were razor-sharp and they had no hesitation in chipping in with their own observations on the matter of the moment.

The greater good had been the topic of interest last week. Noble cause corruption. The manipulation of events by means that would certainly be called questionable to achieve ends that would very definitely be termed good.

How far would one go? How far should one go? If, to uphold the law for example, it became necessary to break that law too, then should one do so?

If a person or persons needed protecting from extreme violence and the only way to do that was to inflict that same violence on another then could that be justified?

Masters loved the cut and thrust of that sort of debate, hugely enjoyed exploring the contradictions involved therein.

A particularly intriguing philosophical conundrum that had most recently engaged him was Zeno's Paradox, a philosophical proof that an arrow shot towards its target could never actually reach it as in order to so do the arrow had to travel first half the distance, then half the distance again, then half again; meaning the arrow might cover ever smaller distances but could never ultimately reach journey's end.

The next day Masters, to the considerable bewilderment and quiet amusement of the rest of his team, had taken a longbow out on a raid on a particularly vicious gang of armed robbers working out of a warehouse bordering mudflats on the old dockside. As one of the villains attempted to evade the scales of justice by jumping from a second-floor window, Masters had let fly with an arrow. The arrow had struck the fleeing miscreant smack in the small of the back. He survived but the arrow destroyed a couple of his vertebrae and he was destined for life in a wheelchair from that point on.

None of that particularly bothered Masters. All he was thinking about was the contradiction between the philosophical proof he'd debated the previous evening and the practical demonstration of its failure he'd just enacted. It was an interesting lesson and one he'd pondered on many occasions since.

Across the room, Banks nodded at him. They now had the information they needed. They'd leave the second of the Jakes while the locations he'd supplied were checked out and if they didn't strike gold in any of them they'd just have to come back and pursue their enquiries some more. That meant the unfortunate second Jake's wounds wouldn't be dressed for a little while yet but the first of the Jakes was already being loaded into the waiting ambulance.

Masters moved to the door, the rest of the unit moving with him. He was caught in a classic conundrum right now too of course. Philosophically, he abhorred all he had to do. Ethically, it was indefensible. He accepted, admitted indeed and without reservation the necessity for standards, for rules, for certain codes of conduct.

The problem being that none of that was exactly much good when you came up against a Ukrainian who'd lacerate the face of a young girl with acid just to make a point.

Masters dealt day in, day out with the most venal forms of life and sadly they didn't understand the language of philosophy. There was really only one language they did understand in fact and that was nothing to do with an elegant argument or a carefully constructed thesis.

It all came back to the greater good. Which occasionally involved noble cause corruption of course; all of which dragged another question in its wake.

To protect the innocent, was it necessary to sometimes mimic the actions of the guilty? And even if one was acting for the forces of good, was it possible to adopt the procedures of the bad and remain unaffected? In other words did it corrupt those attempting to fight the corruptors? Was Masters making his very own deal with the devil daily, unaware he himself was turning into the very creature he was attempting to pursue?

All in all it was an interesting question but one that would have to wait for the next chess night. For now he had to hit the first of a small handful of clubs identified by the second of the now-disfigured Jakes and start inflicting some more of the punishment described by his detractors as medieval.

Tyra rose from the bed, her long back facing the man still lying underneath the sheet. A single tattoo in the very centre of that back, just down from her recent branding drew his eye, but it was only a lingering inspection.

She was perfection. In a few years' time she probably wouldn't be, although he'd thought that a while ago and her appeal had far from faded.

He wasn't exactly the poetic type. The face he presented to the world could never really be permitted to show any hint of sensitivity, any suggestion of what might be called finer feeling. So he kept the knowledge that nature had worked to create a vision of loveliness that still took his breath away, strictly to himself.

She knew it. That was all that mattered. She knew it in the way he traced the contours of her back with his finger, the way he'd stare into those eyes that held his stare as so few before had dared.

'I don't want to do this.'

He didn't reply, just kept looking at her. He felt the same but what was the point?

She had to.

She knew it and so did he.

'Just the thought of it.'

She turned those eyes onto him, large, almost beseeching in their appeal.

'Going back.'

He kept telling himself that he was the one who was supposed to be in control. He was the one who was supposed to be doing the thinking for the pair of them.

So why was he having trouble controlling his breathing right now? Why did his voice sound as if it was emanating from a stranger? Why, more than anything, did he want to tell her to forget everything, to close that door, shut out the rest of the world, let it just be the two of them, here, in this room, together, forever?

'It won't be long I know, but – .'

Another sentence unfinished. He knew she was waiting for him to fill in the blanks, to give her the strength she needed right now, but how could he when even the thought of her going back left him feeling as if he was lying on the floor, stomach ripped out, guts trailing behind him?

But he did.

'You go back. Then you come back for good. Then it's over. Everything that's hanging over us, then it's gone.'

And she smiled at the words she wanted to hear, the words she needed to hear to do what she had to do.

They'd always known this was going to be tricky. And she had underestimated just how keenly she'd have to maintain her guard, not let anything slip. Not a gesture, not a word, not one false note. She hadn't realised how closely they'd be watching her, how minutely they'd be observing her every movement. So every moment had to count.

Swiftly, she leant forward, kissed him lightly on the lips, then turned and, without looking back, closed the door behind her.

For a moment he just lay back on the bed. Then he rose, crossed to the phone.

Like Tyra, he now had work to do.

As it happened it wasn't the information Masters coaxed in his usual inimitable manner out of the two Jakes that finally located her.

Masters and Banks had visited the top two locations on the list supplied by the boys with the third and fourth degree burns and Tyra had indeed been to both. But by the time they'd arrived she'd left for pastures new and unknown and there was little point wasting time in trying to extract where that might be from any of their new informants.

Unlike the business-minded Jakes, most of them wouldn't have been able to say what day it was or even what century they were living in, let alone where a fellow worshipper at the altar of the Cocaine Christ might be at that specific moment in time.

Somewhat to Masters's chagrin it was Ros who provided the breakthrough on that score.

Ros was only supposed to have been there in a strictly observational capacity, on hand in case they needed to rely on the only relationship Tyra had managed to establish with any of them thus far. That relationship, as Ros herself had freely acknowledged, was tentative in the extreme but it was still all they had.

Ros wasn't meant to have taken any active part in the proceedings and certainly wasn't meant to come up with the only development that actually led anywhere. For his part Banks comforted himself with the opinion, voiced loudly and often over the course of the evening that followed, that the bitch had just struck lucky but Masters wasn't too sure. He had a sneaking suspicion it all went to prove the bitch might just have half a brain after all, but he kept that opinion very firmly to himself.

To Ros it was simple and it was summed up in one word. Desperation. She'd seen enough junkies taken into the programme to last her several lifetimes and they all exhibited the same personality trait when it came to whatever might be their substance of choice.

When deprived of it they became desperate. When reunited with it they wasted little time in fully renewing that acquaintance at all speed.

Which meant Tyra wasn't going to wait too long before shooting up. She wasn't going to be able to. She'd already demonstrated she was at the mercy of a compulsion that rendered all other considerations such as personal safety irrelevant, so having established that Tyra had indeed visited the first of the clubs sometime in the last hour or so, Ros let Masters and Banks charge away to check out the next likely locale on the list.

Instead she sat down with a detailed local street map, ignored the grumblings of Conor at her side who really didn't see the point of all this. She didn't actually see the point of Conor right now. And she tried to put herself in the mindset of a junkie.

Five minutes later and Conor was complaining even more volubly. He'd been trying to negotiate his way past two giant bins stuffed with food waste blocking a small alley at the rear of the club. One had overbalanced and had tipped its contents down his back as he'd tried to squeeze through the small space in between. And there was nothing in the alley as he ever more volubly pointed out, making this even more of a monumental waste of time.

Ros wasn't listening to him. She was listening to something else instead. Something that seemed to be coming from the other side of a far wall, from another of the local alleys. The sound of someone in pain.

Ros was over the wall and into the next alley in moments, Conor – brushing food waste from his jacket and shirt – following, habitually reluctantly, behind. Someone could now very definitely be heard whimpering, moaning even.

As it happened, the tramp who owned the whimpering if not moaning voice was feeling more than usually aggrieved. In truth, belligerence was something of a default position for him these days. Life, his life anyway, was a constant battle for food, drink and shelter as well as a battle against the attentions of almost every other fellow-unfortunate he came across in the course of his day.

Over the years he'd developed a persona that had become second nature. He looked angry all the time because he was. That anger might have been generalised, might have lacked any sort of focus, but it helped.

Because of it, people tended to leave him alone. The authorities tended to let him get on with his life without too much interference. There was always the possibility that some well-meaning social worker or volunteer might get hurt by some incautious intervention. There was also another much more over-riding feeling that there was little point in trying to help someone who didn't want to help himself.

His life hadn't always been like that. If his former family could have seen him now they'd never have recognised the figure he'd become. Four years ago he had a wife and two children, one about to go to university, the other beginning her teaching practice. His wife worked in the same port office as himself.

Then, one day, he rolled the small white van he'd checked out of the office a short time before into a deep part of a deserted nearby dock, watched as it disappeared beneath the surface, then turned and walked away from all he'd previously built up over the past twenty years, away from a wife he still adored and two children of whom he'd always been inordinately proud.

He supposed he'd had some kind of breakdown but it really didn't feel like it. All he knew was he just wanted out. Out of everything he'd previously known. In an instant he'd gone from a mild-mannered cargo assessor in a small office to a scowling, perennially angry, down-and-out with an existence where a life had previously been.

He didn't expect too much from his day. He certainly didn't expect too much from his fellow travellers on the road he'd now chosen for himself, one of the reasons why he refused to allow himself to relax. Even when he allowed sleep to claim him as even he occasionally must it was always fitful, a metaphorical eye and ear always open, honed to the first hint of any sort of trouble.

But every now and again he let his concentration drift as he had done a short time before and it was always in the most mundane of circumstances. It always happened when he stopped to take a piss.

Maybe it was something in the physical relief. He'd never

really bothered to analyse it. All he knew was that as he directed his piss over whatever he'd chosen as its receptacle, a wall, the side of a skip, the kerb of a pavement, he briefly allowed himself to close his eyes, to let his mind drift into a place populated by no ghosts from the past.

But now he'd never do that again. Because as he permitted himself his most recent moment of blessed relaxation, his world suddenly exploded in a fireburst of pain.

He couldn't work it out at first. He'd directed his piss onto an old bundle of clothes dumped by the side of a metal bin. He'd checked, a habitual reflex, whether there was anyone underneath the bundle of clothes but there wasn't.

But he was looking for a fellow-tramp, bulked out with all sorts of retrieved padding. He wasn't expecting a young girl dressed in next to nothing to suddenly rise up, yelling in protest at the stream of piss that was playing not only over her body but also on her protesting face and he also wasn't expecting the swift kick to his currently-exposed balls as a result.

As it happened that single kick was going to do what the intervening years since his disappearance had failed to achieve. The tramp was going to be taken into hospital for the removal of a badly-crushed testicle and during the course of his operation his real identity was going to be discovered and his former family informed of his reappearance.

Dimly he was aware of a man and a woman now coming into the edge of his agony-clouded view. Even more dimly he was aware of his attacker pausing at the sudden appearance of the couple who seemed anything but welcome to her.

And from what seemed to be a million miles away he heard one of the new arrivals, the woman, greet his assailant.

'Hello Tyra.'

Then he lapsed into unconsciousness and when he woke

from his upcoming operation the next faces he would see would be those of his bewildered and tearful wife and his equally bewildered and tearful children.

N O-ONE WAS TELLING Macklyn anything. The younger officer was sitting next to him in the rear of the unmarked car, the older one was now in the front, driving.

He'd kept trying to ask all the questions that had to be deemed as pretty well normal in the circumstances – what was all this about – where were they going – what was happening? But aside from one short, very short, explanation that all would be explained which was no sort of explanation at all as he'd somewhat redundantly pointed out, there'd just been silence.

Macklyn looked out at the familiar landmarks rushing past the window. This was the route he took to work. He knew many of the faces they passed, coming out of shops, buying coffee from a portable stall, he even saw the lady who ran a tiny sweet shop on the High Street, only ever enough room inside the cramped outlet for herself and her myriad collection of boiled treats.

There was a small stool in front of the open serving hatch that looked out onto the street and usually there was a child standing on the stool, peering inside, another waiting their turn on the pavement. Today there was nothing. No children waiting. Just the lady turning the pages of her paper. It all added to the impression of a world out of kilter. Out of step with the everyday. Not that the impression needed to be reinforced by anything outside that car window. Macklyn already felt as if he'd stepped straight into the middle of *Alice in Wonderland*.

They turned off the main street, travelled down a succession of smaller roads before they came to the outskirts of this small patch of suburbia. In the distance he glimpsed the main road heading east, the arterial thoroughfare for most of his drivers on their regular deliveries. Briefly, he recalled the driver he'd earmarked for the bollocking that day. That would have been the subject of his evening conversation when he returned home. Macklyn would have re-enacted it in its every detail to his wife, rehearsing all the evasions and stumbling half-sentences trotted out by his hapless quarry as he squirmed on the hook.

Macklyn looked out of the window again. That had all been more than a little usurped. All that was happening now was going to be much more interesting when it came to the re-telling stakes. When someone finally told him what the hell was going on of course.

They pulled off the road and headed down a small lane. At the far end was a five-barred gate that was raised as they approached by a uniformed PC. The driver kept the speed steady as they rolled over the potholes created, presumably, by successive generations of cattle but there was no sign of any livestock now. Macklyn saw a large, steel, barn-like building at the far end of the track, but nothing else.

The car pulled up outside. The officers who'd escorted him from his office exited, signalling to Macklyn to stay where he was. One of them briefly liaised with another officer who'd come to meet them, then both glanced back his way.

Something inside his stomach tensed as Macklyn registered the way they looked at him quickly, then equally quickly looked away.

All he could think was, what had he done?

What had he possibly done to merit all this?

But there was something else too, another voice telling him that they couldn't know, how could they and anyway, even if they did, wasn't all this just that little bit disproportionate for one, single, indiscretion?

How many other men did something like that for God's sake? Did they all get this kind of treatment?

For the first time Macklyn saw another unmarked car parked further down the track. And he could see that there were more people inside, so all this, whatever this was, obviously hadn't been staged simply for his benefit.

He looked round for more clues as to what was happening here. There were a couple of windows let into the steel walls of the barn but the glass was frosted, permitting light inside but barring access for any over-inquisitive eyes.

Then the car door opened again and the older of the officers slipped into the seat beside him. The younger officer stayed outside talking to his new companion.

Then, quickly, as if they had no time to lose which, as he was to later discover was exactly the case, the officer – prefacing all this with a stock apology for what was inevitably going to be a considerable shock – proceeded to inform him that his eldest daughter had been shot in the hallway of their family home just over an hour earlier.

Twenty minutes ago they'd received confirmation from the hospital that she'd died.

Now they were going to take him into the building ahead where he was to be reunited with his wife and youngest daughter who had witnessed, but were not directly caught up in the attack.

Then they were all going to be taken to a small military base nearby where they were to board a flight to a destination that was being kept a secret even from the officers themselves.

Then, finally, but only then, were they going to supply a few answers to what the officer knew must be a million questions.

It was only then that Macklyn realised something about his new companions. He hadn't noticed it before and had no idea why the sudden realisation should dawn at that moment. Maybe it was a way of blotting out everything he was being told right now.

These policemen differed from any others he'd previously encountered in one detail that he knew was significant even if at this stage he didn't understand exactly how. Because they were all, without exception, carrying guns.

As if whatever evil that had so clearly visited his home earlier that day was still an all-too potent threat.

As if whatever nightmare had just descended wasn't nearing any sort of end but was only just beginning.

Ros walked across the courtyard passing various cars, all parked in their allotted places. Each one was tucked neatly inside the painted white lines that marked off each bay from its neighbour.

Part of her – some defence mechanism perhaps, springing into life – sneered at the sheep-like mentality of those who so dutifully obeyed instructions and meekly observed boundaries. Another part of her wondered who on earth she thought she was fooling. One day she really was going to have to take that refresher course.

Ros slipped out past the barrier, didn't even look towards the concierge in his small hut, just made for the waiting taxi. The driver had already been told where she was going so she just settled back on the seat. Again – and as ever right now – Tyra dominated her thoughts.

The first issue had been substituting her opiate of choice. That old stand-by Methadone had been the initial thinking on the part of the duty doctor who was well versed in similar scenarios. It wasn't intoxicating or sedating meaning it wasn't likely to interfere with her ongoing duties as a witness. It could also be taken orally meaning there was no need for any medical assistance to be on hand, and it suppressed any withdrawal symptoms for twenty-four to thirty-six hours.

But in the end they went for LAAM or Levo Alpha Acetylmethadol to give it its full title. LAAM, like Methadone, was also a synthetic opiate but could block the effects of any other opiate of choice for up to seventy-two hours with only minimal side effects, one of the reasons Ros strongly preferred it. The fact that it lasted so long meant the patient, or witness in this case, only needed three or so doses a week.

Tyra had been given the first of the doses some six hours earlier. As the jaundiced, been-there, seen-it-all quack had predicted, she'd fallen pretty quickly into a deep sleep and would probably be out of it for the next ten hours at least. Meaning it was now time off for Ros.

Or at least time.

To do what exactly was a moot point.

The next hour or so would tell.

Masters was already waiting as she approached. His back was turned to her but some sixth sense seemed to be at work and he turned her way.

Then he smiled, which made for two highly unusual events as far as Ros was concerned in the same twenty-four hours.

First, there'd been the invitation to supper which had come so totally out of the blue she'd found herself answering in the affirmative before she'd even properly assimilated the fact of the request.

The second was the smile, the first time she'd ever seen his face without its seemingly-habitual frown or scowl.

Masters looked down at his watch.

Then he looked up at her and smiled again.

'Bang on time.'

Conor leant by the sink, listening to the voices from the next room, wishing he could just walk out of the back door, down the steps that led from the upmarket apartment onto the equally upmarket street and not stop till he'd found a pub, any pub – although in that area he knew he was going to have to walk a fair distance before he found the sort of pub he wanted.

He wanted a place where he could just sit and drink and let

the events of the day wash over him. Most of the local pubs had long ago turned into restaurants with every table booked for weeks, if not months, in advance.

From the next room he heard the latest not-so-hilarious anecdote, relayed by one of the not-so-hilarious colleagues invited to supper by his wife, Francesca, that night, a bow-tied dandy by the name of Frederick – call me Freddie – Lahr.

'So in he comes and I swear to God, this was the sixth time in as many days he'd been in my consulting room and like a complete tit I'd left his case notes lying on my desk.'

Conor stared out of the window at a small jet making for the airport a few miles to the south, its vapour trail evaporating as it passed overhead.

'So he sees it doesn't he, written in big black letters, right across the top of his file? TTFO.'

Gales of laughter greeted the acronym from most of the table leaving Lahr's puzzled girlfriend, the latest, they tended to change fairly rapidly, setting up the not-so-hilarious reteller of the not-so-hilarious tale only too beautifully.

'I don't understand.'

'TTFO. Told To Fuck Off.'

The teller of the tale was almost gasping now, partly in adoration of his own story, partly in admiration of what was to come next.

'So the total waste of space looks down at it – .'

Did that make him a TWOS as well, wondered Conor?

'And says, what does it mean? And I stare at him for a minute, don't actually know what to say and he's getting nervous now as if he's stumbled on some really bad news. His eyes just kept getting bigger and bigger as he looked at me. Doctor, he said?'

From the other side of the door he heard Francesca calling out to him.

'Conor? Any sign of that wine?'

Then the teller of the tale cut in again.

'TTFO, yes, I said, yes, it's what we call an acronym and for a moment I could see he hadn't a clue what I was talking about, I thought he was going to ask me if it was catching or something.'

Now he heard Francesca joining in with the rest of the laughter, the wine momentarily forgotten.

'So I gave him the old reassuring smile. Told To Take Fluids Orally, I said. He sat back in the chair nodding as if I'd just dispensed one of the Ten Commandments.'

Francesca cut across again.

'Conor!'

Conor took a bottle from the rack, went back into the sitting room.

'Two minutes later he was walking out when he suddenly stopped and looked at me. But I'm not prescribed any fluids, he said.'

Lahr nearly exploded.

'I had to put him on placebos for four months to stop the little shit sniffing a rat.'

Conor put the wine down on the table and the smiling ranconteur paused, looked at him.

'So how about you, Conor?'

His eyes twinkled across the table.

'Any police acronyms you can tell us about?'

Conor poured the wine and let the silence stretch.

And stretch.

And then stretch some more.

Masters was nothing if not surprising. When he'd suggested meeting by the large Ferris wheel that had recently been installed on the dockside of the new bay, Ros expected they'd dive into one of the myriad number of restaurants studding the nearby streets. She didn't expect to be steered into one of the pods or the well-stocked picnic he seemed to have brought along with him in a supermarket bag for life. The food was also supermarket-provided but all from the top of the range lines as Masters himself had pointed out.

It was odd and it was quirky and it instantly put her at her ease in a way that being shown to an intimate little table in the company of a man she'd always regarded as something of a professional, if not personal enemy would never have done. Which was no doubt the point. Masters might occasionally adopt the battle tactics of Attila the Hun but he also had his sensitive side. As all this was no doubt intended to demonstrate.

That was all clear enough. Why he should be going to such lengths to do so was still something of a mystery.

For the first ten minutes or so as the pod ascended it was all much as she might have expected even if she hadn't expected anything at all. Masters opened the wine, screw-top but a decent enough white Rioja, as he also pointed out. He sliced open the bags of salads, opened the dips, laid cold poached salmon out on some paper catering plates. He'd even brought small packets of salt and pepper sourced from the station canteen, she recognised them from the containers that were always laid out by the till.

And the strangest thing happened. Perched in their rising pod, gazing out over more and more of the old docks and the landmarks of the new bay – looking down on the Norwegian Church, the Millennium Centre, the new Senedd – she felt suddenly and unaccountably happy. Maybe because this was quite simply fun. An old-fashioned treat. And she felt herself start to relax more and more as Masters maintained a running commentary on some of the more esoteric sights increasingly exposed by their ascent. In a different world and time he'd have made a half-decent tour guide.

Then, just as she was at her most relaxed, just as she could almost physically feel the wine seeping through her bloodstream, massaging the tight spot in her stomach she could almost, but never quite, banish; everything changed.

All it took was one word. Or, more accurately, one name. A name she never wanted to hear again, a name she'd never forget and on the evidence of this now not-so-innocent seeming encounter, a name she was never going to be allowed to forget either.

Masters had been talking about a writer he'd been listening to on the car radio on his way into work that morning.

'He'd written his autobiography. It was why he was on the chat show, there's always some reason isn't there, a show to publicise, a book to plug.'

Ros reached for a salt sachet, battling feelings of guilt as she did so. Oskar had lectured her about her sodium intake in the past, showing her charts detailing the amount of salt already present in most foods, so why would she want to add any more? But then Oskar wasn't there.

'Only this writer had taken a really unusual approach. He hadn't written about the books he'd written, the films he'd scripted, the awards he'd won. He told the stories of all the books he hadn't written but wished he had, the films he'd scripted that had never been made, all the missed opportunities in his life, the lost chances.'

Masters had paused as he'd rolled the white Rioja around his mouth, savouring it.

'The ones that got away I suppose.'

Masters took another sip.

'He said it was like going to a restaurant. You look back and you never really remember the good meals, but the bad ones, they're always there, those are the ones you never forget.'

Ros indicated the picnic. They'd stopped now, right at the

top of the ascent, the whole of the city laid out on one side below them, the wide expanse of the Bristol Channel on the other.

'And that's why you go for supermarket take-outs these days? It's all down to one bad mussel?'

Masters didn't even seem to hear her.

'Maybe it's the same in all lines of work. Maybe in mine and yours too.'

Masters looked past her, reflective now.

'Which are the ones for me? The ones I've put away, the ones I've taken off the streets, the ones who won't be killing or raping anyone ever again?'

Masters took another small sip of wine. Ros hadn't realised it before but she must have drunk at least two glasses to his every one.

'Or the ones who walked away? The ones still out there, who probably always will be out there? The ones who burn inside you, right?'

And then he'd looked at her.

'So what do you look back on, Ros? Who creeps into your head in the dark? The ones you helped or the ones that slipped through your fingers? The ones you couldn't help, the ones you failed, the ones who fell by the wayside?'

Ros knew what he was going to say before his mouth had even begun to frame it, could see it in the way his eyes looked everywhere but at her right now.

'Like the Kincaids?'

The pod jerked forward, now beginning its descent and all of a sudden it was all-too clear – the phone call, the impromptu picnic, the ride above the city, the new Masters who was quite clearly still the old Masters albeit in a sweeter-smelling guise; still the same mendacious Masters underneath.

What this was all about was now crystal-clear. You may have scored a small victory with Tyra. You may have proved of some use in the apprehension of one troublesome young girl. But in the end you will fail. When it matters you will fuck up. And when you do so, you will cry out for the big boys to come and rescue you, to do what you cannot do yourself, clear up the mess.

Ros looked down at the ground. There was still at least twenty minutes before the end of the ride. In a restaurant she could have simply left. Masters had picked his location carefully hadn't he?

The supper guests had left about midnight. The conversation had swiftly moved on from the awkward silence Conor had deliberately initiated. Francesca had filled the gap, diverting attention onto some more hospital gossip. Another chance to dazzle in the acronym stakes.

Conor had caught Lahr glancing at him from behind his bow tie and matching breast pocket handkerchief as the evening ground towards its boozy conclusion. He'd like to have thought there was wariness in those barely-concealed, if not positively surreptitious, glances. He feared there was more amusement instead.

As the last of the guests had left Conor tensed, expecting some sort of onslaught but it didn't come. Francesca wasn't going to resort to anything as obvious as direct reproach, he should have realised that by now. The subtle art of the vicious put-down had probably been instilled into her at her expensive boarding school.

Where Conor had always been content to let his fists do the talking, his wife, several levels up the social scale, had rather more devastating tactics to employ. Francesca might have been attracted to her very own bit of rough, as he'd heard her friends refer to him on more than one occasion, but that really didn't mean she wanted to join him down in any gutter.

Instead, Francesca talked about a trip that had been discussed around the dinner table that evening. Some of the girls – they were always girls no matter their ages – had a big birthday coming up within a few weeks of each other. The possibility of a group trip abroad to a renowned gastro-hotel in southern Spain had been eagerly embraced by all – or almost all.

As another of the prospective celebrants had espoused the attractions of the hotel in question, even quoting seemingly word for word from the apparently-fabled tasting menu, Conor began to feel ever so slightly sick. But after the silence that had stretched and then stretched some more, he was already skating on thin ice that night and he knew it, so he'd pasted on an interested smile.

A decision had been made to book in for a long weekend in a couple of months' time. The issue of cost had been raised, but fairly swiftly dismissed. It would be expensive but what was the point of all their madly-busy lives if they couldn't enjoy themselves from time to time?

As they cleared away the dishes Francesca returned to the same topic. In a voice dripping with sweet acid she apologised for putting Conor in that position. They'd always led strictly separate lives in financial terms and she knew, particularly with his recent transfer, that times weren't as easy and money wasn't as plentiful for him as it had been in the past.

But Francesca didn't want him to worry about that. She'd advance him the cost of the trip if it was a problem. And any spending money he might need. It'd be her treat.

Conor seated himself on their balcony watching the lights outside extinguish as their neighbours in the gated community went to bed one by one. But Conor didn't go to bed. He remained where he was, his mind running on two matters.

The first was what to do about the problem of his ever more distant wife.

The second was even more pressing.

Money.
And how to get it.
And quickly.

The taxi dropped Ros back outside the apartment complex and Ros moved inside, past the concierge who'd once spent an entire afternoon showing her his family tree on the grounds of a superficial similarity in their surnames. He'd clearly done a lot of research into the whole field. Then again, what else did he have to do during the course of long and lonely days looking out over an empty courtyard as Ros, struggling to retain concentration all the while, kept reminding herself?

But sympathy only extended so far and she now kept her eyes averted as she headed for the blue door at the end of that courtyard, moving between two parked cars as she did so.

Ros felt it before she saw it. An alien presence as she approached the door, something that shouldn't be there. Then she saw it. A fox moving swiftly and silently past, heading for a small alleyway that led down to the river, something – a rabbit perhaps – still twitching in its jaws, the vixen trailing blood behind it.

The fox ignored the staring Ros, just kept moving. Ros watched it till it disappeared, then turned, fitted her key in the communal lock.

Only this time her sixth sense let her down. This time she didn't sense or see anything until it was too late. All she registered was a large dark shape to her left as an arm smashed down onto the side of her head, something – a brick perhaps – clasped inside the clenched fist that hit her. She felt a brief surge of sickness rise from her stomach before the whole world turned blindingly white, then as dark as anything she'd ever known.

And now she was back in it again. Back in that all-too familiar nightmare, looking down at the chasm, the sea raging at the bottom, the drainage pipes bucking in the storm-tossed waters.

And there they were again.

All those faces.

But this time there was one she'd not seen there before although she recognised her straightaway. It was the face of the girl she'd tracked to Jamaica, the girl who'd insisted on attending some family celebration, a party for an aged grandparent, the girl who would not be dissuaded, who'd already made two attempts to get out of the country and who'd made it clear there'd be a third and a fourth. The face of the girl who'd stood in the doorway of that small shack house in the small shanty town of Mandeville as Ros approached, smiling for the first time in all the weeks that Ros had known her, turning to introduce the family, all smiling shyly now too, grouped behind.

Which was when the first of the shots from the high-performance army-issue rifle rang out, literally removing her head from her shoulders, splattering those self-same family members with her blood, impossible to separate moments later from their own as the whole family was gunned down before a helpless Ros's eyes.

She was in that thrashing water now too. She was in the nightmare. Her head was still attached to her body by what looked like a single spliced sinew, but she was still alive. Looking up at her, eyes pleading with her as were all the others, begging her to do something, to reach down, to lift her from that abyss into which she'd been cast, into which they'd all been cast, to keep them safe.

Briefly, somewhere on the edge of consciousness, she became aware of a siren approaching. She registered feet which at first she thought were running towards her, perhaps as a team of paramedics arrived, but then she realised they were running away and it was just one pair of feet leaving the scene quickly.

Half-waking from one nightmare into another she watched the feet which she could now see were encased in trainers, white trainers, the kind you could buy in any sports shop the length and breadth of the city, disappearing round the corner of the building ahead, taking the same route as the fox, treading in the drying trail of blood as they did so.

Something about the way the feet were moving, the rhythm in the running, ushered in an association, a memory, some link or other, but it was unfocused, unreliable.

Was that part of her nightmare or something more real?

Then the ambulance, the ambulance that came from the real world, not a world that existed in her imagination, came to a halt by the gate, the sound of running feet were heard again, but this time it was the approaching paramedics.

Then, once again, as hands moved over her head, as other hands checked her vital signs she felt the sun on her face, felt the warmth of the Jamaican girl's smile as she turned to introduce members of a family she never thought she'd see again, then suddenly everything was darkness once more.

M ACKLYN NOW KNEW one thing. One of the wilder theories he'd silently rehearsed in the back of that police car had been well and truly blown out of the water.

This was nothing to do with any former indiscretions committed more or less willingly in the company of several other small businessmen at a transport conference in the lowlands of Scotland a couple of years previously. The entertainment provided by their host including a late-night visit to a local gentlemen's club wasn't about to be thrown back in his face. He wasn't going to walk into that anonymous steel building and see his fellow partners in formerly-drunken abandon.

Macklyn saw his terrified wife and his bewildered youngest daughter instead. And now he wished to a God he was having difficulty believing existed that his first uneasy suspicions had proved correct instead. It might have been more than a little embarrassing to have all the details of that night aired in front of Elsha, but it could have been explained away in time. Something was already telling him that nothing about this was ever going to be explained quite so easily.

Cara ran to him, an instinctive reaction. He and Elsha used to joke that it wouldn't last, placing bets when she, like Braith and Di before her, would change into the sulky teenager her two sisters had both become – temporarily at least – unable to even look at either of their parents during those troubled years, let alone bolt into the arms of a father at the first sound of his key in the lock.

Braith.

He'd heard what the police officer had said to him. He'd

understood the words, perhaps the reason why the officer in question hadn't pulled any punches. The officer knew they had a long road ahead of them both literal and metaphorical and didn't want there to be any confusion or doubt as to the horror of all that had happened or the present horror they now had to escape.

Macklyn held Cara in his arms, the young girl clinging onto him for what felt like grim death.

Braith.

Which had quite obviously been the grimmest of deaths if all he'd been told was true.

But how could it be true?

How could something like that happen to a family such as theirs? It made no sense.

Macklyn looked, helpless, beyond the clinging Cara to his equally helpless wife and all of a sudden something snapped. All of a sudden some instinct deep inside surfaced, an instinct born of habit. He'd spent so long taking charge, assuming control, that everything inside him raged at being simply moved around like some pawn on a chessboard, totally unaware of why, completely unable to see or even sense any larger picture.

Macklyn carefully prised the small arms from around his neck, ignored the protesting sobs as he placed Cara more roughly than he intended back on the floor.

Elsha moved over, an instinctive reaction again, to comfort her. Elsha was used to her busy husband having work to do, even at home, and escorting one or more of their clinging daughters away from his side as he sat at his desk in his small home study or worked on papers on the kitchen table had become second nature by now.

Macklyn crossed the few metres of concrete floor to the officer who'd earlier delivered the news about Braith, that officer currently liaising with a colleague, a mobile to his ear.

From outside he heard the sound of another car approaching, perhaps the one that was to take them if he'd heard right – he doubted everything he was being told right now – to some airfield somewhere.

A plane, an airfield, what were they all of a sudden, international spies? This was the stuff of a James Bond story, none of this took place in the life of a small-scale haulage contractor from a provincial town with a dozen or so lorries and vans, a long-suffering secretary and a more or less loyal workforce, the odd bad apple aside.

Macklyn had been stoking himself up all the way over to the officers. Ignoring the extended open palm of the officer on the mobile, a clear instruction that he really should not come any closer, Macklyn stood in front of the officer who'd delivered the little information he'd been offered so far and let rip, everything spilling out in one incoherent rant.

'You can't do this –

– can't just keep us here –

– what do you mean, Braith's been shot? –

– I want to see someone –

– someone in an actual uniform – .'

Why did he say that about the uniform? Even years later, replaying it all in his head over and over again, he still had no idea.

'Someone in charge –

– we've got rights –

– this isn't a police state –

– what hospital has Braith been taken to? –

– I want to go there, talk to a doctor –

– see for myself – .'

Macklyn barely knew what he was saying by now. Across the concrete floor, Elsha didn't seem to be taking it in either but she hadn't been taking anything in from the moment she heard what sounded like a clap of thunder inside their neat house and realised the sun was still shining and the sky still cloudless outside.

Only Cara, desperate for some sort of certainty in a world that had suddenly turned anything but, took in every word, registered and recorded every half-completed sentence; as if somewhere in the rantings of her father she might just find that sure foundation she'd come to take for granted up to then, already knowing perhaps it was a sure foundation she'd never know again.

What happened next, happened so quickly. One minute he was yelling at the officers who were standing in front of him, then there was a quick glance exchanged between them, some sort of unspoken agreement reached.

Then Macklyn was striding towards the door, intent on walking back to normality if need be, only the next moment he was on the floor.

Cara watched horrified, as her father – her father! – was smashed to his knees by one of the officers while the other applied an arm-lock to restrain him and his colleague, the one who'd hit him, secured both his arms behind his back with handcuffs.

Macklyn gasped and wheezed on the floor, trussed like a Christmas turkey. Across the room he could now hear his wife yelling at the two police officers over and over again, the same sentence repeated and repeated as if on some kind of loop.

'Who are you people? Who are you people? Who are you?!'

13

ALL ROS COULD see was what looked like a lace veil.

It was the strangest thing. It was covering her face, edged in tassels of some description. Through the lace she caught half-glimpses of what she believed to be her surroundings, although those surroundings seemed to change shape each time she focused on any part of them.

Walls moved, the ceiling seemed fluid. She made a mental note to tell Vorden, her regular supplier when it came to the occasional recreational substance, that she wanted a bulk delivery of whatever she'd ordered last time; then she woke up.

Ros didn't move for a moment. She just stared at the far wall of the small hospital cubicle some administrator had dignified by titling a room. From a corridor outside she heard the sound of a trolley passing, the voices of nurses on their rounds as well as the distant sound of an elderly patient just woken from an operation, disorientated by the after-effects of the anaesthetic still washing through his or her system.

The sex of the patient was difficult to determine. The words weren't all that easy to understand either. But the man or woman was clearly aggrieved about something judging by their incoherent yells. Ros knew how they felt.

Ros lay totally still. Flicking her eyes to the left she became aware she had company. Conor was sitting by her bed, absorbed in some paper or magazine. She couldn't at this stage work out exactly what it was but it was claiming his attention completely, for which small relief she gave much thanks. She needed a few moments to come round properly, to think.

Ros half-closed her eyes in case Conor suddenly lost interest in the object of intense attention on his lap, which, Ros now saw, was actually a loose-leaf collection of papers.

And she let her mind wander back, like a victim of toothache unable to stop themselves exploring the source of the constant pain with their tongue.

As if she was undergoing some sort of out-of-body experience, Ros saw herself once again walking across the paved courtyard towards the communal blue door of her apartment block. She once again saw the fox, blood dripping from its mouth, the small animal, a rabbit or maybe a rat clamped in its jaws. She remembered watching as it moved quickly past, intent on finding some safe haven to enjoy its recently-captured feast, then she felt the blow.

Ros must have instinctively tensed because Conor looked up from his papers. Ros stilled, but it wouldn't have made any difference if she'd remained immobile for hours to come. She wasn't going to remember anything else about her night-time attacker right now and she knew it. Ever more dimly she remembered the feet running away from her, registered again something in the rhythm of the running, something that seemed familiar but which she just couldn't place.

Besides, she now had something else to think about. Conor was obviously unsure if she'd come round or not. He was certainly unaware she'd been awake for the last few moments.

Conor must also have thought that if she was coming into consciousness she'd initially be all at sea, not connecting with anything or anyone around her. Otherwise he'd never have laid the papers he was studying down on the bed, on full view as he turned to press the button that would alert one of the passing nurses.

If Ros could lay bets as to his choice of hospital bedside

reading, she'd have been unable to decide between the sports pages of his tabloid of choice or maybe some lads' magazine.

Tits and soap stars.

Footballers and tips on achieving a stronger and longer lasting erection.

What she didn't expect were a whole pile of bank statements, heavily annotated in an untidy spiderish scrawl as Conor calculated and recalculated balances. Ros occasionally conducted a similar exercise but never in quite such a forensic manner. Either Conor was a frustrated accountant or the man had serious money worries. Ros doubted the former and was already beginning to grow concerned at the implications of the latter. Not that there was much time to probe this new insight into the private life of her new colleague.

The door suddenly opened onto the corridor. A man stood there clutching some flowers, his concerned face framed by blond hair.

Conor turned to him, his personal bank statements still on view on the bed, exasperation in his voice.

'The doctor told you, there's no visiting.'

'I just wanted to drop these off.'

Oskar indicated the flowers in his hand.

'Cheer the place up a bit.'

Oskar gestured round the functional, antiseptic little cubicle but Ros wasn't looking at him or at the flowers he'd sourced – so she'd later discover – from a small but obviously enterprising stallholder who'd set up shop just outside the hospital entrance and who was doing a roaring trade.

Ros was looking instead at his feet, encased in trainers, white trainers, the kind you could buy in any sports shop the length and breadth of the city.

Jukes studied the young girl sitting across the scratched and graffiti-daubed desk. In strict contravention of Health and Safety, Tyra was, once again, smoking. The smoke curled round a sign high up on the wall, prohibiting such an activity with the sanction of a hefty fine for the transgressor. Jukes reached across, extracted a cigarette from the packet he himself had provided and joined her.

Jukes had always been an occasional smoker at best. But he was also the consummate politician. You didn't rise to his exalted rank without being able to sup with princes and dance with devils. The young girl opposite might not be in the latter category but she'd been close enough to the real deal to warrant a bit of extra effort on his part to connect.

Especially now.

'Who did you see?'

'Lots of people.'

'People you knew?'

'No.'

'No-one at all?'

Jukes studied her as Tyra stared back, impassive.

'You're on your old home patch, you're in a part of the city you'd lived in for years. You're walking streets you'd walked every day and night for most of those years and you see absolutely no-one you know?'

'Chancer on the corner who hands out the free sheets, I saw him, don't think he saw me though, then again he never looks at anyone, just hands out the papers, some people take them, some don't.'

Jukes persisted.

'And no-one else?'

'I didn't exactly spend too much time walking round.'

'Because you were there to score?'

Tyra hesitated. Maybe it felt to her like an admission of weakness.

'Yeah.'

'So you went straight to the club, did what you wanted to do and then you got the hell out of there?'

Tyra hesitated again. They were bound to have looked at the local CCTV tapes, she knew that. That's how they'd traced her journey there in the first place. They'd have picked her out several times as she exited the station with the date and times stamped into each of the frames. There wasn't a lot of point trying to be too cute about this.

'I went somewhere else too.'

Jukes nodded. That much they knew, Tyra was right about that. What they didn't know was why. And a lot, one hell of a lot, the whole upcoming trial indeed might now just depend on her answer.

Tyra hesitated once more. They'd also have been checking the tapes covering the surrounding streets and she knew that too. And while she had mainly kept to the alleyways and walkways there were bound to be times she'd have been exposed.

And then there was that copper. He was unlikely to have made any sort of official complaint. The chances of his recovering anything like normal powers of speech by now militated against that for one thing, but even so some more than averagely clever plod might just have put two and two together.

Tyra eyed Jukes shrewdly. Even though his attempts to empathise via a shared cigarette might have been just that little bit too transparent, he wasn't exactly stupid.

'I went to see a friend.'

'Friend.'

Jukes repeated the single word flatly enough but inside his heart was racing.

What friend?

Why hadn't this been picked up earlier?

'Boyfriend.'

'I thought Yaroslav was your boyfriend.'

'One of them.'

Now the staring Jukes just waited for Tyra to continue, mainly because he was out of any other options. For now Tyra was in the driving seat and he had no idea where this was taking him, or indeed this case.

'I'm not giving you names. But, yeah, I met him a couple of months ago. Yaroslav was away on some trip somewhere, gone back home I think, can't remember. I'd seen him come into the club a couple of times. Him and Yaroslav had even done some business I think, I didn't know, didn't really care.'

Tyra shrugged.

'He was hot.'

'And brave. Seeing you behind Yaroslav's back.'

'It wasn't behind his back. Least not at the start. Anyway, what do you think this is, some sort of marriage? He sees people, I see people.'

'So he knew about it?'

'He didn't not know about it.'

'Meaning?'

'Meaning, yeah, he knew I'd seen him, like I'd seen some other people too.'

Tyra left the unspoken 'but' hanging in the air and Jukes supplied it.

'I don't know.'

Tyra ground out her cigarette and for a moment there was another young girl on show, someone more obviously and immediately recognisable as a twenty-something woman with a normal life to live, normal emotions on view.

'I just didn't want to, I suppose. See anyone else. Not after seeing him. Didn't even want to go back to Yaroslav.'

Tyra looked at Jukes, defiant still, but now shyly defiant in an odd and curiously appealing kind of way.

'So yeah, I want out 'cos of that too. Yaroslav's a crazy fuck who could do anything. And I don't want him fucking that up as well.'

Tyra paused.

'This bloke. My – .'

Tyra hesitated again.

'Friend.'

Tyra looked at Jukes.

'I don't want anything to happen to him.'

A visitor was unusual. An unaccompanied visitor – unaccompanied by Ros – was unique. Ever since Ros had delivered her to what she'd called a safe house, there'd been no other callers aside from her initial and original protector.

When she first arrived at the house, Kirino – the original witness in the case against Yaroslav – found it something of a disappointment. A safe house in her mind conjured up all sorts of images and associations. Something heavily guarded and fortified.

Armed guards at the entrance.

Maybe even a moat.

Ros had smiled at her initial unease. Apparently, real safety lay in anonymity, in this house being like any of the other houses all over the same town, small and unremarkable, its exterior and garden neither overly well maintained or neglected.

Just a totally ordinary small house on a totally ordinary street.

Since then the days had passed in a mind-numbing torpor. For the first week or so she'd welcomed that. It had given her time to think, to absorb the experiences that had driven her from her former life in the first place. But lately she'd begun to chafe against an imprisonment that might have been largely self-imposed and was most certainly voluntary but which was still deadly dull.

Every now and again she fantasised about going out to a bar, catching a movie. At one time – although not now for perhaps-obvious reasons – she'd have also quite liked to go out for a walk.

When she said as much to Ros, about the bar, the movie, she told her it was possible. They'd probably have to get someone to go with her, a single woman out on her own for a night especially in this small town in the wilds of mid-Wales, would probably excite comment and probably some unwanted attention too, but they could arrange most things if Kirino would just give them time.

The greatest enemy for most of her clients wasn't fear in the end, but plain and simple boredom. Cases could take months to come to trial and those months often proved a trial of their own for the impatiently-waiting witness.

But now there was a break in the routine. Now the tedium had been punctured by a car pulling up, a code exchanged on the mobile provided by Ros, an arrangement that told her she could open the door to whomsoever had come calling, that she was still safe.

So why – sitting in the small kitchen, across a tiny table from the man who'd conducted various interviews with her in the past – the man they called Masters – did she now feel anything but safe?

And why wasn't Ros there to mediate as she had been on all previous occasions?

'We need to get you moved.'

That had been the opening conversational bombshell from the second of the officers, an older man she hadn't seen before but who introduced himself as Ros's senior officer, DCI Jukes. Apparently he was taking over as Ros herself was on leave for a few days.

There'd also been none of the usual enquiries into how she'd been, no update, as had also become usual, on the progress of the case against Yaroslav. There was just this succession of short, almost staccato-like, sentences.

'You're in no immediate danger. This move doesn't need to take place for a day or so. We're still investigating a couple of possible options as to where to take you. But once we've found the right place we'll probably move you quite quickly.'

All the time Masters kept looking at her, cool, as if assessing her in some way, something else she hadn't experienced for the last few weeks.

That sense of being judged.

Of being judged and found wanting.

Kirino tried to ignore the unsettling presence to the side of DCI Jukes.

'Why am I being moved?'

'We've reason to believe this place might become compromised.'

'What?'

That was Masters, and Kirino stared at him as Jukes shot him a sideways glance that spoke volumes. Obviously that wasn't in the script.

'Compromised?'

'There's been developments.'

Now Juke was attempting to take charge again.

'What sort of developments?'

'And Detective Chief Inspector Masters didn't say this house had been compromised otherwise we'd have you out of here straightaway. There's just a concern that, at some time in the future, this place may not be quite as secure as we'd wish.'

Kirino was getting edgy now. What the hell else did they expect?

'Why can't you move me straightaway?'

'The next house will be unusual.'

'In what way?'

'It won't be just you living there. You'll be sharing the accommodation with someone else, another witness in the same trial.'

'Who?'

Jukes rolled on, ignoring that for now. Everything at present was on a need-to-know basis and Kirino very definitely did not need to know that information at this stage.

'It's not usual to put two witnesses together but in this case we think it's justified. It means the investigating officers can assemble the evidence they'll need more quickly and it means we concentrate all our available resources on just the one location as opposed to two.'

But Kirino wasn't listening. Her mind was running on other matters and a cold feeling – an all-too familiar cold feeling – was beginning to settle on her stomach.

'You don't know what he's like.'

'We know exactly what he's like which is why we want him behind bars.'

That was Masters again.

Kirino looked at him, more than a suspicion forming that all he'd said so far had been deliberate in its intent. She'd seen it before in their interviews back in the station. He never seemed to want anyone to relax around him, always wanted to keep everyone perpetually on their toes. Kirino might have understood it when it came to a potentially unreliable, even recalcitrant, witness. Why the same tactic should be employed against an officer of identical rank in the very same room was beyond her, but then so much lately had been beyond her that perhaps it made little difference.

'I don't know.'

'You don't know what?'

That was Masters again and Kirino met his stare full on.

'It feels like you're not telling me something.'

'We're telling you everything.'

Now it was back to Jukes.

This was fast becoming some sort of conversational tennis match. Kirino could feel her head jerking back and forth as her two visitors traded exchanges, ostensibly with her, in reality with each other.

'What if I don't want to move?'

Masters just looked at her, didn't reply as a concerned Jukes leant forward. And Kirino had the strangest feeling she was about to fall headlong into some sort of trap but was powerless to stop herself.

'What if I just want out?'

'Go.'

That was Masters again and, slowly, too slowly, she was beginning to understand. Jukes had probably sussed it from the start but he definitely wasn't in on it. His obvious irritation at his companion was too intense and too genuine for this to be any sort of act.

'Walk out now. You came in here of your own free will, you can leave the same way. Any time you like.'

Masters was probing now, testing, throwing a pebble in the pond. How far would the ripples spread? How unstable would the water become?

Unsettle her, panic her, how quickly would she crumble?

Masters clearly wanted to know the answer to a very simple question. Were they tying their fortunes in with the worst kind of weak reed, someone who'd run at the first sign of trouble? Because if they were, maybe they should get out now. Especially when, apparently, they had someone who could step into her place.

'Just like that?'

Masters stared at her, impassive again and Kirino could almost feel the rising panic in her throat.

'It's a free country. There is a belief in some quarters that we live in some sort of police state but that's simply not true. You're the living proof. Walk away.'

'And how long do you think I'd last if I did?'

Masters nodded at her. Point made. And she'd made it all by herself. It was always best in his opinion for a witness to work out the realities of a situation as opposed to having it explained to them. You could explain something a million times over to some people and still it wouldn't sink in.

'There's no difference really, is there?'

Masters kept looking at Kirino.

'You and him, I thought there was. Yaroslav's the bad guy, you're the good, but it's not like that, is it? You're both just the same.'

'That depends.'

'On what?'

Again he was surprising her. She'd expected an injured rebuttal, a self-righteous defence. Not for the crazy loon to lean forward, his brow creasing, his lips now pursed, his mind quite clearly working overtime.

'Is there such a thing? In the sense you mean, that is? Good, bad, what are they? Are they absolutes for example, eternal, immutable standards by which we judge and are judged or are they just categories of our own making, social conventions we've evolved over the years to make living with each other at least some kind of practical possibility?'

Masters hunched further forward over the table, more animated now than she'd ever seen him before.

'Take this.'

Masters nodded at a plate on the table, the remains of her morning toast.

'You seem to like your toast underdone, you put on a smear of what looks like some sort of spread and that's it. No jam, no honey, no marmalade.'

Kirino was just staring at him now.

'Now if that had been my piece of toast I'd have smothered it in whatever I had to hand. And I'd have toasted it for far longer and I've have used real butter too where you've used something else. Now that to me would be a good piece of toast. This – .'

Masters tapped the plate.

' – is quite obviously good to you.'

Masters shook his head, grimaced as if he was rolling around inside his mouth a particularly chewy piece of meat.

'So is that what good and bad really is, in the end? Not a statement of fact, just an expression of taste, of feeling, maybe even of vested interest? Is there actually no difference between, for example, the rules of football and the laws of the land? In an absolute sense, that is? Making the committing of a crime not actually sinful as such, but merely antisocial?'

Masters looked beyond Kirino and for a moment his eyes seemed to grow misty.

'But take the Good Samaritan. The opposite side of the coin I suppose. When we say he acted well, are we really just expressing some kind of circular prejudice about behaviour? We seem to approve of his kindness to a stranger but on what is that really based? Some sort of intuition that kindness is simply good in itself and that casual cruelty, for example, is not? Leading on to the next problem.'

Masters smiled at her and for the first time since he'd walked in that day his smile seemed genuine.

'Which I can see in your eyes and I'm sure it's something my well-respected colleague has pondered on more than one occasion too.'

Masters nodded across at Jukes.

'If we do accept the existence of absolutes, metaphysical, immutable absolutes of behaviour, then from where do they derive? It's easy to understand how social conventions come into existence as an agreement between more or less like-minded individuals. But absolutes that hold in all societies and in all cultures, for all time, where do they come from?'

Masters smiled again at the still-staring Kirino. By his side, Jukes was now keeping his eyes focused on the kitchen table. Maybe he'd heard all this before. Or maybe he was well versed in the dangers of interrupting Masters in full flow.

'And there's only one answer of course, one logical possibility. Absolutes of behaviour, of the type we employ to construct our laws and live our daily lives, really have to derive from some absolute elsewhere, something apart from the society in which they operate and the times and context in which they're applied.'

Masters sighed as if to acknowledge the impossibility of any other conclusion.

'Meaning, for want of a better word, some sort of God I suppose. If our behaviour really is open to absolute judgement then surely that means there must, logically, be somewhere an absolute Judge.'

Masters nodded at Kirino again and now a harder tone was creeping into his voice.

'The flip side being that if all the arguments about the existence of good have to lead to some kind of God, then what of men and women who follow different absolutes? They're then not merely acting against the society in which they live and the times into which they were born, they're offending against a greater force, they're following a much darker path, perhaps the reason why in less enlightened times they'd be burnt at the stake or hung, drawn and quartered and their bodies laid out for public view.'

That harder tone was creeping in more and more now.

'They then become disciples of what I suppose you'd have to call the Devil as they themselves become Devil-like in turn.'

Then Masters shrugged.

'In other words it's Good or Evil. God or the Devil. In the end and despite all the fine words, I suppose it all comes down to that painfully simple choice.'

Masters nodded at the young girl before him again.

'So? Which one is it going to be for you?'

Kirino stared back at him.

'Which path are you going to tread?'

Ros shouldn't have come back and she knew it. Her body was telling her that all-too obvious fact with each step she took down the corridor and it was still doing so as she seated herself, albeit constantly shifting position, in one of Jukes's high-backed office chairs with Jukes himself sitting opposite her on the other side of his desk, Conor to her side.

Now and again – and just to add to an already dangerously high level of discomfort – waves of nausea swept over her but wild horses wouldn't have dragged her out of that office.

Not until she'd got to the bottom of this.

Not until she found out exactly what had been going on in her absence.

'We can't take the risk it was an isolated attack.'

'Despite the fact there's absolutely no evidence it was anything else?'

'Nothing was taken. No attempt was even made to grab your bag.'

'Maybe whoever attacked me was disturbed.'

'How long does it take to pick up a bag from the ground, a second, less, even if someone had come through the gates or come out of one of the other apartments surely whoever attacked you would still have had time to do that.'

Jukes hunched forward.

'But they didn't, meaning that wasn't the point of the attack, meaning whoever did attack you had something else in mind.'

Ros cut to the chase.

'Tyra?'

'Possibly.'

'You think someone's made the connection?'

'We can't rule it out.'

'How? Someone's spotted me with her?'

'Or perhaps she hasn't been as discreet as she's claimed, we've only just found out about the other boyfriend for Christ's sake. Did she say anything to him, has he been picked off too or is he playing some kind of double-game, sleeping with Tyra, reporting to Yaroslav?'

'But if all that was to do with Tyra, why not wait till I was inside the apartment? If the whole point was to get information out of me why attack me outside in the yard, where anyone could see what was happening?'

Conor chipped in.

'Maybe the idea was to disable you outside, Ma'am.'

There it was again. The slight, deliberate, hesitation before the final address but if Jukes noticed he didn't let it show. Jukes nodded, rolling on instead.

'Then take you inside using your own key meaning there'd be no sign of a forced entry or any sort of struggle, nothing untoward to alert security, leaving all the time in the world to ask you questions and make sure they got exactly the right sort of answers.'

Ros paused and not just because her head was now throbbing. It was because they both had a point and she knew it. There were too many questions here and too few answers in a case where there were already too many loose ends.

Jukes leant forward again, building his own case all the while.

'In the circumstances the CPS have agreed to fast-track this. Putting the two witnesses together is crucial in that. And it helps us too. It means the prosecutors aren't then running backwards and forwards, constantly cross-checking one story against the other.'

'It also means Murder Squad are calling the shots, dictating the pace.'

'Which they wouldn't have been able to do if we hadn't temporarily lost one of their key witnesses.'

'We didn't lose Tyra.'

'Not my words.'

Ros fell silent again. There were no prizes for guessing just who'd coined that carefully-constructed phrase.

Jukes was looking at her, silent now. If he shared Ros's unfocused sense of unease about all this he wasn't showing it. If he understood it, he gave no sign. In truth, Ros didn't totally understand it herself.

But there was something behind all that had happened in the last few days – behind Tyra and her sudden flight – the attack outside her flat – the decision to accelerate the prosecution and bring forward the trial – something that gnawed away at her and wouldn't let her rest.

Ros stood, the exchange with Jukes over, the battle, if it had ever even been a battle, lost and she knew it.

Tyra would be moved. Kirino would be moved at the same time. She'd supervise first the one, then the other.

Business as usual.

Across the room, Conor stood too, folded the case notes that were open on his lap.

And for a moment, as Ros looked at him, she was back in that hospital bed, watching the unaware Conor as he bent over another set of papers, annotating bank statement after bank statement with a spidery scrawl, his almost frenzied calculations filling virtually every page.

Ros crossed the courtyard once again. This time nothing and no-one halted her progress towards the communal blue door. She took the stairs up to her apartment, stood on her small balcony looking down at the water, then looked across at a larger apartment opposite, a woman on the balcony reclining in a hammock.

Those apartments were bathed in sunshine most of the day, a natural pleasure denied to Ros by the other developments crowding her apartment complex on all sides, blocking out the sun.

Behind her the entry buzzer sounded and Ros moved back into the living room to activate the video link allowing her to see any visitor before allowing access. Not every apartment had the facility but in her line of work it had been deemed a sensible precaution.

Oskar was standing outside the communal front door, waiting more or less patiently for her reply. Ros looked at him for a moment, the Swede looking everywhere but at the camera set high into the wall, a spyhole she was fairly sure he didn't know existed. Ros's finger briefly hovered over the entry button but then she went back out onto the balcony.

Maybe she'd see him tomorrow. For today she'd had enough of loose ends that would probably, in the colder light of another rather more normal day, turn out to be anything but.

As she moved back outside her mobile rang. The name of the caller was flashing on the display.

Masters.

Ros answered immediately.

'We might have another one.'

Masters never did believe in wasting time with anything as superfluous as a simple greeting.

'Another witness?'

'The duty sergeant took a call about an hour ago. A woman. She didn't give her name or say anything about herself but she sounded young, he said. She asked for an email address for someone connected with the Tyra case. I told him to give her mine.'

There was a rustling of paper on the other end of the line.

'It came through about half an hour ago. It's a Hotmail account, can't be traced, probably set up just for this message. It's difficult to know if it's genuine but she definitely sounds scared.'

'What does she say?'

'She wants to know if we can protect her. Like we're protecting Tyra. And if we can, she wants to know what she'd have to do in return.'

Masters paused.

'If this is genuine, then the house that Yaroslav built really is sinking fast, wouldn't you say?'

'So what did you say to her?'

'I gave her my mobile and my office number. Told her to call anytime so we can talk it over. I also said we'd travel to meet her if she preferred, just tell us where and when and we'd be there.'

Then Masters paused.

'So how are you feeling?'

'Fine.'

'What happened sounded nasty.'

'I'll survive.'

'The other girl – Kirino.'

All of a sudden Masters had changed tack again.

'I think she'll come through. I was impressed.'

Masters paused again.

'Well done.'

Then the phone went dead.

Ros made to move back into the flat, then stopped. Down on the far bank, Oskar was now looking up at her.

Ros looked back down at him, holding his stare for a moment. Then Ros moved back inside, closed the sliding door.

14

MACKLYN AND ELSHA were sitting side by side, close but not touching. Elsha had held out her hand but her husband didn't even seem to see her. Instead he kept his eyes firmly fixed on the officer in front of him, his total concentration on the man who was about to make some sense, or so he hoped, of the last few hours.

Cara was in the next room in the company of a female officer. The officer had asked if she wanted the TV on, they had a film they could watch together, standard family fare, but the little girl had just shaken her head.

She didn't say it but it was obvious what she was thinking. Cara didn't want to do anything but sit and wait for the world to return to something like normal again.

Which would be a little like waiting for hell to freeze over thought the attending female officer, but she didn't say that of course. She just nodded and brought out a colouring book instead. Most of the drawings had been filled in already by other children who'd been brought there. But Cara didn't look at that either, just kept her eyes fixed on the closed door in front of her, her parents on the other side.

There'd been a change of heart since the initial briefing outside the steel, barn-like building. It had been decided they wouldn't wait until they'd escorted the family out of the immediate vicinity to tell them all that had been established so far.

Partly that was simple humanity. This was their daughter who'd been killed after all and in a particularly vicious manner, the mother and father really needed to know as much as it was possible at this stage to tell them.

Partly there was self-interest involved too. The father in particular was becoming dangerously volatile, there was always the risk he might do something stupid, try and get away, perhaps head for the hospital to see for himself the dead body of his daughter.

If he knew the truth, if he began to understand what they were all up against, what had provoked this seemingly-extraordinary response to a definitely-extraordinary situation, then it might help.

'They targeted the wrong person.'

The father stared at the officer, the mother staring too but she wasn't really seeing anything and wouldn't for months to come, possibly years. All she was seeing right now was the exposed skull of her dying daughter and her brains all over the wall.

'They identified the wrong sister. Braith wasn't the intended target.'

'It was a mistake?'

The father stared, incredulous.

'You're saying someone came to our house, to our front door, shot our daughter dead and it was some sort of accident?'

'The target was your other daughter, Divone.'

'Di?'

That was the mother. The officer looked across at her but in strict contrast to her husband she didn't look stunned at all. Maybe she'd had longer to get used to it all. Or maybe she'd already, partly at least, begun to work some of this out.

'What do you know of your son-in-law?'

'Emmanuel?'

The father paused a moment, glanced sideways at his wife, then shook his head.

'Next to nothing, he and Di met abroad while she was on

holiday, we'd seen pictures of him of course, talked to him a couple of times when Di had put him on the phone but she'd always told Braith more about him than us.'

The father paused again, a sudden memory of giggly, girly, phone calls sounding from the hall at home momentarily ambushing him, then he pressed on.

'That was the whole point of tonight, we were all to meet up, it had been planned for weeks, we had friends coming round, neighbours.'

He tailed off and the officer paused too.

So many people in the know.

So many ways this could have got out.

What possible chance did they really have of preventing any of this?

'We've known of your son-in-law for a while. He's been known to us for some months in fact. Or at least to our colleagues in Europol.'

'In what?'

'The European Union Criminal Intelligence Agency. It's like the old Interpol.'

Agreed to in the 1992 Maastricht Treaty, beginning limited operations a year or so later, not as well known in general folklore as the FBI or even MI5, but they preferred it that way. But all the father heard was one word and it wasn't anything to do with the European Union or any sort of Intelligence Agency.

Criminal.

That was the only word reverberating inside his head right now.

'Are you saying my son-in-law – ?'

He tailed off.

'Your daughter knows nothing of his activities, we're fairly certain of that. She probably doesn't even know his real name, Emmanuel's one of several he's used over the years. He presents himself to the world as a businessman. He's traded in various items over the years, at the moment his particular interest is antique rugs. To service that business he makes several trips a year to this country and to others in the European Union. It's the perfect cover for his more lucrative interests.'

Macklyn's eyes never left the officer's face.

'Which are?'

'For the last few years your son-in-law has been operating as what's known as a bounty hunter. He's part of a well-organised outfit that tracks down women and girls who've run away from homes, principally in the Asian community here and overseas, usually to escape a forced marriage of some description. His job was to recruit those who could provide key information on the ground – local taxi drivers and the like. He also targeted sympathetically-minded individuals in government organisations such as the Department of Work and Pensions in order to obtain National Insurance numbers, which has also proved a useful way to track down his various quarries. He's also been responsible for recruiting female bounty hunters who would pose as domestic violence victims to enter refuges to find their targets. It's a trade that's been growing a lot in recent years.'

The father just kept staring. He ran a small haulage company from a nondescript industrial estate in a small market town. He lived in a semi-detached house, played golf at the weekends and preferred lamb to beef or pork for Sunday lunch. He took pride in his very own mint sauce made from herbs grown in his rear garden. The officer before him was talking about bounty hunters. It was like listening to someone from another galaxy.

'As I said, the man you know as Emmanuel isn't a lone wolf, far from it. He's part of a well-organised group but lately Europol have reported divisions within the group. A couple of the women who've been tracked down in this way have ended up dead. No-one's too sure how or why. There also seems to have been disagreements on a couple of their operations, some dispute over monies received. We don't know yet whether that was behind what happened today or whether your son-in-law had decided he simply wanted to end his association with his former colleagues or whether – .'

The officer hesitated.

' – and there is some evidence to support this view – that he wanted to branch out on his own. What we do know is that a contract was authorised a week or so ago. We believed at the time that the contract was on his head alone. What we now know is that your daughter, his wife, was named as the first target. The likely idea behind her killing was that he may then be persuaded into a more reasonable frame of mind as regards any overtures made by his former associates. If he still proved to be something of a problem, then presumably he would then be eliminated too.'

Macklyn might not have been taking all of this in but it was, finally, having the desired effect. The officer could see it in his eyes.

Slowly he was beginning to understand what they were all actually up against.

'The gunman wouldn't be part of the same organisation. He'd have been a freelance, a gun for hire if you like. They're usually pretty professional and he would have been given photographs of your daughter so he could identify her. What complicated matters in this case was the strong physical similarity between your eldest and middle daughter. When Braith answered the door he quite clearly mistook her for Divone.'

'Di had gone shopping.'

That was the mother again.

'We needed some olive oil.'

The mother nodded at the father.

'For the salad.'

Elsha might have been saying the words but she wasn't even hearing them. All she was hearing was the momentary pause after she heard the door open in the hall, when the gunman looked at Braith, checked her face against the face he'd memorised and pulled the trigger.

'The most immediate problem we have now is that the contract was not completed. The target of the intended hit is still alive. Divone is a loose end and the people who authorised the hit will not be happy about that. They'll know the death of a sister-in-law isn't going to have anything like the impact on Emmanuel that the death of his wife would have. So now they'll be looking to complete the contract as quickly as possible, which is one reason you're not all together right now. You're all at risk courtesy of your association with Divone but she's at special risk, meaning we're having to put extra measures in place to guarantee her safety.'

The officer leant forward. The mother was still in some faraway land somewhere. But then she'd witnessed all this first hand. She'd held her dying daughter as she disintegrated before her eyes. The father could only imagine the horrors those eyes had seen.

'We can update you some more when we reach a proper place of safety. Despite all the precautions already put in place we have to treat all we're doing now as a holding exercise. We need to remove you to a place of total anonymity as a first priority and then assess what we do and what you do from thereon in.'

The father was quiet. He was looking through a window from a world he knew onto a world he never even knew existed. And now he had no way back to that world he previously knew. That world, as he was already fast beginning to suspect, was forever dead to him.

15

Ros didn't sleep. She knew she wouldn't. Partly that was the after-effects of all the drugs washing through the system.

Partly it was due to all the other bodies in her bed.

Masters's taunt had worked its desired effect. Once again, when she closed her eyes, all she saw were the Kincaids.

Petra Kincaid watched her young son as he darted among the aisles, identifying items, scooping them into the trolley. Usually, they managed the weekly shop in a matter of minutes. Cai had known where everything was in their old supermarket and even when the manager rotated the goods, he found the new locations speedily enough.

But this supermarket was a lot bigger. It looked more like an aircraft hangar from the outside. Flat screen televisions, all tuned to the same channel, blared out as they stood before them trying to get their bearings, thrown momentarily by the bilingual signs on every aisle. Their previous local store, a hundred or so miles to the north in the very heartland of Welsh-speaking Wales, sported only Welsh signage.

By her side stood a woman who up to a few hours ago had been a total stranger. It didn't help the acute sense of dislocation they were all experiencing right now that she was now going to be sharing their house, was going to be part of their lives indeed, for at least the next week or so.

Just while they settled, she'd told them.

While they moved from one life to another.

Petra looked at Cai as he moved from aisle to aisle, the young boy already identifying where his favourite brand of cereal might be found.

A few years ago, years that still seemed like days, she'd taken his brother, Rhys, on similar excursions. Then Rhys had discovered girls and had found something better to do with his Saturdays instead. Petra looked at Cai as he pounced on another of their regular purchases with a yelled exclamation of triumph, her eyes momentarily misting over as she did so.

Then Rhys had discovered guns and two nightmares began.

The first ended when Rhys was sent down for life with a recommendation he serve at least twenty years for the murder he'd carried out.

The second began the day Rhys commenced his sentence. And the family of his victim – exiles from the badlands of Walton and Bootle just across the border and definitely no angels themselves – decreed that Rhys's family should shoulder their share of blame for the crime.

The five bullets that had been fired through the window of their old family home two nights later had made it clear that this was no empty threat. One of the bullets had embedded itself in a wall just a metre or so away from where Cai had been watching TV. With just a fractional repositioning the gunman would have achieved his intended status of assassin.

Ros stirred in her bed, tried to focus on the far window, the rain now sounding outside, willing sleep to come, a blackness populated by nothing. But sleep wouldn't come, she knew that. And she also knew what she was now going to see.

Petra had called the local police earlier that evening. She'd seen someone outside, a figure lurking by the fence that separated their small garden from the Bluestone Hills beyond.

She'd called Seth, her husband, immediately but had made

sure not to alert Cai to anything amiss. The young boy had suffered nightmares since the attack on their old house and she didn't want this house to seem tainted too. She definitely didn't want him to even begin to suspect that it may be under anything like the same sort of threat.

Ros had given them a special number that was meant to trigger a code, alerting all available units in the area that this call was to be treated as an absolute priority. It was the first time she'd had to use it and it seemed to work well enough. A patrol car was at the property inside a couple of minutes and the two officers inside, one male, one female, had spent another ten minutes checking the fields leading across to the rolling hills beyond the house.

At the time it seemed reassuring. They were indeed in the safe hands Ros had promised. In fact, their death warrants had just been signed. The figure lurking by the fence, now parked up some distance away but still in clear sight of the property, noted the swift arrival of the officers and noted also the painstaking efforts they took to ensure the property was secured.

It was inconceivable such efforts would have been made for a normal householder reporting a sole suspicious figure. So he picked up his mobile, hit a speed dial button and told a voice on the other end of the line that their information was accurate.

They had located their quarry.

One hour later – and after the patrol officers were long gone – a neighbour had seen the car pull up. She'd also seen the four men exit, the driver open the boot and hand out the white boiler suit-type overalls to his silent companions.

Immediately visions of incinerated cattle flashed through her mind. They were on the edge of extensive farmland, it was a nightmare shared by every local farmer that some devastating epidemic would strike. The four men looked as if they were from some Government Ministry to her, which meant there had to be a problem.

Why else would they be clothing themselves head to foot in protective overalls?

The neighbour didn't waste any time. She called her brother immediately. He ran a small dairy farm four miles away. She told him to move his cattle and move them that very night. If those men were from some Government Ministry, if they did discover a new outbreak of some dreaded disease – foot and mouth perhaps – then no animal would move in and out of a steel-like cordon for weeks, possibly months, to come.

No animals moving meant no animals going to market. No animals going to market meant no income for the duration of the embargo. If her brother managed to get his animals away in time he'd be OK at least.

The more ethically-minded in the local community might have pointed out that if there was an epidemic and if those animals were infected then she'd have spread the disease by her actions. But in her view, ethics were something only the rich tended to observe and only when it suited them. The rest had to muddle along as best they could.

As she came off the phone she heard the sound of two shots in the distance and she closed her eyes.

She'd been pretty quick in alerting her brother to the potential danger that might be unfolding, but maybe she hadn't been quick enough. Maybe everything her brother and every other farmer in the area always dreaded had now started.

Maybe the slaughter had already begun.

Ros had never seen the assassins. All she'd had to go on was the odd eye-witness statement here and there. But it had been enough. From the moment she read the case notes the pictures were embedded in her mind.

All she could see from that point on was the front door being kicked down, the white-suited men, guns in hand, moving inside, one dashing upstairs to grab an already-whimpering Cai, the other smashing the butt of a rifle across the head of his father as he tried to make what he already knew would be a totally ineffectual protest.

From the position of her body it looked as if Petra might not have moved at all. It may have been fear that had frozen her to the spot. But – and more likely – she'd also have known there was no point.

No matter what they said, no matter what they did, from that moment on they were all already dead.

Later, the pathologist would chart the exact progress of the butchery that had taken place.

Cai had been dragged out of bed for a good reason as he'd been earmarked as the first target. Not that he was the first to die. He was paraded before his staring mother, his helpless, half-conscious father and then shot in both knees before being left to bleed to death before them on the living room carpet.

Next they turned their attention to Petra who'd been raped twice. On the second occasion she'd been anally penetrated by the barrel of one of the gunman's rifles before being finished off with a shot fired at point-blank range into her heart.

Only then did they turn to the father who would have been forced to watch as first they dealt with his son and then his wife. He was dispatched with a single shot to the head because by that time they'd have known it was time to go. The family would have had absolutely no opportunity to activate the code that would have alerted the local police. The men had cut the telephone line before they'd smashed their way into the house and they'd employed a makeshift but effective scrambling device that obliterated all mobile reception for a few hundred metres around the property as well.

But they hadn't been able to completely silence the screams – from the boy in particular – or the shots. At best, if someone local had called the police, they'd have around three to four minutes. And they'd probably planned each and every one of the seconds in each and every one of those minutes down its last detail. Three to four minutes of total hell for the family Ros had promised to keep safe.

A mile or so away, the farmer had already begun to move his cattle. He told his sister he owed her a drink and set off across an old track known only to a very few locals, towards the next village.

On the way a car had come up behind him. The driver obviously wanted to get past but the farmer was determined they should wait. They may have had the faster vehicle but he was towing the more valuable cargo. He looked into the mirror just as a bullet smashed through the rear window and exploded into his head. He yanked the steering wheel to the left, overturning the trailer he was towing, dragging his old Land Rover over a moment later. The car with the four men inside sped past, the temporary obstacle out of their way.

Ros had arrived twenty minutes after the local police. Murder Squad were already there. A roadblock had already been set up blocking off all local escape routes.

Ros moved into the sitting room of the rented house. She'd steeled herself for the blood. The room had to be drenched in it. Three bodies ripped apart by a combination of bullets and beatings, how could it not be?

She'd also steeled herself for the open, staring eyes that she knew would fix on her as she walked in, would follow her as she moved round the room, not really taking in all that Scenes of Crime would be telling her.

She also knew it would be one tiny detail that would ambush her, that would burrow inside her head, one image above all the others that day that would live on behind her eyes and she was right.

In this case it was a pair of knees. Or what had been a pair of knees. She could still see Cai as he darted down the supermarket aisles, changing direction in an instant, doubling back on himself, his limbs seemingly made of rubber.

Now there were just holes where those two limbs had been. The force of the blast had virtually severed his lower legs from the rest of his body. His dying moments would have been spent looking at slithers of bone, while listening to a mother who'd always protected him begging his attackers to finish him off.

Ros couldn't, of course, have known that. That particular refinement in the tale came on nights like these, alone in her bed when, not content with reliving the horrors she already knew, her mind for some reason added twists of its own.

And then there the eyes of the living too. Nothing was ever actually said but it was a natural reaction. Faced with something like that, everyone did it. They all looked for someone to blame. In time they'd catch two of the gunmen and put them away for what the judge promised would be life, although Ros doubted it. In the meantime there was one officer in that room who was supposed to have made sure this never happened and Ros felt her back burn as all those eyes bored into her as she knelt by the body of Cai and what remained of those rubber-like legs bent at an impossible angle underneath him.

But worse than their silent censure, of course, was her own. The system could have let the family down at any point. Perhaps this was all down to something as simple as a chance remark by one of the local officers to a colleague or to a partner or friend. Any system was only as secure as the weakest link in the chain and there were plenty of those. But it still didn't stop her feeling all those censuring eyes following her around that room.

Ros got up from her bed, picked up the duvet and went outside onto the small balcony. It was still too early for the dog-walkers or joggers. The hammock in the upmarket apartment opposite was also empty. For now she had the world to herself.

It wasn't just Masters's taunt that had ushered the Kincaids back into her head and she knew it. They always came back when there was another case to handle and something was wrong and she knew that too, something outside her control, something she may not be able to pin down, but which was there nonetheless.

A shadow in the corner. A shadow that might spread, like a stain, to infect the whole. And then they came. Then the faces of the Kincaids visited her again in her bed.

And she didn't know, looking again at their blasted bodies, whether she was simply reliving a past nightmare or whether she was looking forward to a nightmare to come.

16

D I WAS A model client. She'd made sure of it.

She hadn't asked any awkward questions, had told them, clearly and honestly, all she knew of the man she'd always called Emmanuel, where they met, how they met, how their relationship had progressed.

She'd told them of the business meetings he'd told her about, the trips he told her he'd taken, the few contacts and business acquaintances he'd either told her about or she'd seen for herself while she was out with him in some bar or some restaurant somewhere.

Di found the role easy to play. Partly that was down to her being naturally malleable. It was true what all the family said about her, she knew that. She'd always been forgetful, scatterbrained, call it what you will. A lifetime spent apologising for omissions, mistakes, lapses of concentration had made her more than pliable when she was in the presence of stronger characters.

Previously, the strong character in her life had been her father. Then Emmanuel had come along.

Now both had gone. Emmanuel had disappeared into some system somewhere and she knew there was no hope of seeing him again. If all they were saying about him was correct then she'd married a mirage, a fiction. A man who looked at her with one face while all the while there was another and quite different face beneath.

But her father was still out there. As was her mother. As was Cara. The sweet, innocent, little Cara. Who was perhaps no longer quite so sweet or quite so innocent. And, if she wasn't now quite so sweet or quite so innocent, if the events of the last few weeks had somehow bent her out of shape then that, like so much else, would be her fault too.

Di had decided very early on that she wanted to see her family at least once more. She didn't think of it as a final meeting but in her heart of hearts she knew it probably would be. The officers had talked to her of the day, sometime in the future, when all this might be over, when the organisation of which Emmanuel was, apparently, a key part might be crushed, its other members either dead or in custody.

At that point Di and the rest of her family could emerge from the shadows they now inhabited, could come back together in reasonable expectation of a threat extinguished, but she didn't believe it. She could see in the officers' eyes that they didn't believe it themselves.

One supposedly-carefree gap year, one chance meeting with a handsome stranger in a beach bar on what seemed like a paradise island, and her world was never going to be the same again and she could do nothing to put that right, could never give her dead sister back the life she should have had.

All she could do now, as a final gesture, was to lull them all into believing they had no reason to watch her, no cause for concern. Then she was going to escape from the house she'd already come to see as a prison, travel to meet the family she'd destroyed and say it to their faces.

Sorry.

Elsha had no problem playing the beaten victim either. But there was no subterfuge involved for her, no hidden agenda or ulterior motive. From the moment she'd watched her daughter die in the hallway of their former home, she'd been crushed. Now she looked out onto a world that had turned forever strange and cold and wished she didn't have to do so.

Deep down she didn't believe she would for much longer anyway. Something had gone out of her with the death of one daughter and the forced abandonment of another and the fact there was another child still with them, a daughter who still needed her, simply didn't seem to matter.

Later, years later, Cara would come across her mother's journal from that time, would read letters her mother had written to the deceased Braith in which she'd try and explain how she wanted to stay strong for her youngest daughter but simply couldn't. The plain truth was Cara just wasn't enough reason for her to keep going, to carry on. She wished it was otherwise, she knew there'd be those who'd blame her, who would see her as a coward in some way, but she couldn't do anything about it.

When she looked at Cara all she saw was the loss of her other two children. In fact she'd come to hate even looking at her. The one who'd been left behind was a too-cruel reminder that where there used to be three now there was one and in a sense she'd have preferred it if there'd been none at all. Nothing to remind her of the family they'd once been.

In those later years Cara would try telling herself these were the rantings of a woman still in deep shock. But the words still lacerated.

But in one regard Elsha was far from beaten. When it came to one matter she was flint-like in her resolve. Left to Macklyn, this might not have become an issue, he'd now become a pale imitation of his former self. But for Elsha the funeral of her eldest daughter was very much an issue. Braith was going to have a proper funeral and her family were going to be there too. And it didn't matter what anyone told her about security issues and clear and present dangers, on that she would not budge.

By whatever means were necessary she was going to say

goodbye – a proper goodbye – to her first-born, now first-dead.

And when they realised the strength of her resolve, realised that if they didn't accommodate this wish in some way then their most important adult witness to the shooting would simply close down, would refuse to cooperate with anyone from that point on, then they realised too that some sort of compromise had to be reached.

Late at night, when the individual handler who'd been deputed to look after her was sleeping – and making sure she kept well away from any windows – Di roamed the house. There was an unmarked car outside the property with two officers taking it in turns to maintain a watching brief in case security was breached in any way.

But they were looking for threats to the property. They were on the lookout for approaches from outside, not anyone moving around inside; but Di still took no undue risks. She knew she was likely to get one chance and one chance only.

Something of the resolve of her mother was clearly extant in her too, because in this regard Di would not be beaten. It took her three nights of silent wanderings, of holding her breath as lights swept the surrounding roads from cars that, thankfully, then passed by. Three nights when the different officers, asleep in the house, turned over, paused in their breathing, perhaps as they sensed some presence afoot before resuming their soft snores again.

But finally she found it. In among a pile of case notes there was a scribbled transcript of a telephone call made by one of the case officers some four or five days earlier. She'd caught snatches of his conversation while pretending not to hear a thing so she knew something was happening. Now and again she caught the end of a muttered and exasperated expletive yoked together with her mother's name.

Di stood in the semi-darkness looking down at the piece of paper, committed the location and the time to her memory, didn't even risk writing it down. Then she went back to bed, stayed awake as dawn broke and formed her plan.

KIRINO NOW KNEW the identity of the other witness who'd be joining her, the one whose testimony – along with hers – would hopefully dispatch the devil she knew as Yaroslav back to the underworld from which he surely must have sprung.

She'd known men who'd resembled Yaroslav before but none quite like him. She simply didn't believe he could have been borne from anything human. He'd come into the world by means that must have been totally non-natural or God help the rest of humankind was her fervent and heartfelt opinion.

Kirino preferred to think of Yaroslav as the product of some diabolical experiment that had gone horribly wrong. That was how you were supposed to think of monsters. The idea that at one time he'd played with other children, recited an alphabet, found infant succour at a breast, was unthinkable. Far better to think of him as some creature from another world completely. Even better to believe that this world might soon be rid of his unwanted and malignant presence.

It was ironic that it was Tyra who was to be her new friend and helpmate on a mission she'd embarked on perhaps rather more lightly than she should. When she'd first approached the police, offered them information in return for protection she hadn't quite expected it all to turn so serious.

In retrospect of course, she should have expected nothing else. Yaroslav was a heavyweight criminal. She was the first voice raised against him. It felt like every cop in the country was suddenly in her face. At least now there was another name in the frame, someone else to endure that heat as well. She just wished it wasn't Tyra.

She'd hated Tyra from the start. From the moment Yaroslav looked across the bar in that club, in what had been their club, had seen the ultra-slim figure in the artfully-torn jeans arguing her age with the barman – there was a strict over-twenty-one rule – she knew she'd lost him. She knew it had to happen one day. He always moved on. That was how she'd hooked him in the first place when she herself had replaced his previous favoured friend.

Tyra had opened her bag to show the barman the ID he'd demanded but had then sprayed him in the eyes with Mace before reaching past, picking up the bottle he was so resolutely refusing to hand over and pouring the contents over his now-bowed and agonised head.

Then she'd walked out.

'Who the fuck is that?'

That was all Yaroslav had said. But she knew. In that moment she knew for absolutely certain that he would make it his pressing business to find out just who she was and that she, from that moment too, was destined to be part of his past.

She should have just walked away.

There and then.

Just turned, walked out of that door and kept on walking.

Instinctively she looked down at her leg. If she'd followed her first and usually-correct instinct then she'd still be working the clubs, maybe even getting into the escort game, she'd had some good offers before she hooked up with Yaroslav. She could have had a good five or so years ahead of her at ten or so grand a week, plenty enough to keep her for the next twenty or thirty years if she'd been careful.

But she hadn't been careful. She'd been positively careless. And when she'd finally realised it was over, that she really had to get out and get out there and then she'd been even more careless.

She didn't think it was that much by way of a pay-off. Just a stash of something special tucked inside the hollowed-out heel of one of her Jimmy Choo ankle boots. OK, it would have been worth a cool quarter of a million once it had been cut but Yaroslav would probably never even have missed it.

But he didn't quite see it that way. He must have been watching her as she secreted her strictly unofficial pay-off – he had CCTV cameras in all sorts of hidden places – because when he stopped her on her way out it was the first thing he asked for.

He didn't want anything else he told her, just the shoes he'd bought for her all those months earlier.

By that time she was badly scared and would have just handed them over. So there was really no need for him to smash the door of that Jeep, time and again, on the exact same spot on her left leg, first breaking the bone, then fracturing that bone into smaller and smaller pieces as he held her in place, smashing the door onto it again and again until she lost consciousness before coming round in hospital to find he'd severed her leg just under the knee.

There was absolutely no need to do that just to retrieve an upmarket shoe, even with a more than usually-interesting package concealed in the hollowed-out heel.

That was very definitely out of order.

Ros pulled up outside the retail unit early the next morning. The sign outside, Mega-Bed Sale, had lost its B. Something told Ros the missing letter wouldn't be replaced. The whole place was coming to look more and more tired, more and more uncared-for.

Ros felt tired and uncared-for too and didn't hold out too much hope of any kind of quick fix for herself either. And she didn't feel much better when she walked in and saw Masters at the far end of the ground-floor reception area talking to Jukes.

'Should you be back in work so quickly?'

Ros didn't reply.

'It's not just the physical side of things. An attack like that.'

A musing Masters shook his head.

'It takes time.'

'What are you, a cop or a quack?'

Ros was rewarded with a dazzling smile. On another day and there'd been plenty of those in the past, she'd have been bawled out for her clear and obvious insubordination. Ros and Masters might have inhabited different departments but he still outranked her as he'd also pointed out on numerous other occasions in the past too.

Meaning Masters must be in an unusually good mood. And Ros was about to find out why.

'The other girl.'

That was Jukes. Some belated attempt to reassert authority.

'The third witness in the Yaroslav case. She's still not giving her name but she's been in touch again. We've offered her the same deal we've offered Tyra and Kirino. We'd need to meet, you'd need to talk to her, as would DCI Masters, but if she's genuine and it's difficult to work out why she's maintaining this contact if not, then we may have another face to feed before the week's out.'

Ros caught something, registered the half-glance exchanged between her immediate senior officer and Masters.

'We've given her a deadline. We don't want her to feel our patience is infinitely inexhaustible. Besides the CPS is already fast-tracking this case in the light of the earlier – .'

Masters inclined his head towards Ros.

' – difficulty. If she delays too long then anything she may have to say could prove academic anyway.'

Masters nodded at Jukes, dismissing Ros now.

'I've told her to get back in touch by the close of play tomorrow. After that, she's on her own.'

Tyra watched Masters and Ros together. It was better than having to listen to all they had to say. This session was routine, a straight rehash of all they'd said to her before, either together or individually – procedural stuff in other words and deeply boring.

So she entertained herself by trying to decode the body language of the two people sitting opposite her instead.

Ros was also trying to decode signals. This time she'd been given a Wrexham mug when she was offered the regulation station coffee. It was chipped and cracked. Masters had been given Arsenal. Not a crack or a chip in sight. Maybe there wasn't any signal involved here, maybe those were the first two mugs that came to hand. Somehow Ros doubted it.

Ros knew Tyra was looking at her. But she didn't look back. She just let Masters take the initiative although knowing Masters he'd have taken it anyway.

Across the table, Tyra kept studying them. Masters fancied Ros, there was no doubt about that. It was obvious in the way he refused to acknowledge she was even there. As if he was trying to make absolutely sure she knew he was ignoring her.

It was Ros she couldn't work out. Was she playing with him or genuinely not noticing the covert attention? Was she interested or genuinely couldn't give a shit?

Tyra prided herself on being something of a game player. With the circles she'd moved in lately and the people she'd mixed with, she'd had to be. She was used to people playing games, in fact she preferred it if they did. Everyone hid behind masks and once you realised that then most people were generally easier to deal with.

Tyra kept eyeing Ros as Masters reviewed her various

statements, still trying to work her out and still failing. Deep down she had the strangest sensation when she was in her presence, almost as if she'd stumbled on some sort of soulmate – which was ridiculous. She knew nothing about her, had never come across her until she'd been taken into custody that day, so why she should feel as if she knew Ros and that Ros knew her she had no idea.

They seemed, quite simply, to be the same type. And maybe that scared her too.

Then Tyra stopped eyeing Ros and started listening to Masters as, for the first time since this latest interview began, he actually began to move on to something half-interesting.

Masters had started talking about Kirino. He'd started to cross-check parts of her statement with that of her fellow-witness. A few minor discrepancies aside they checked out perfectly, each story neatly supporting the other as she knew they would, what did they think she was, some kind of amateur?

But now the interview began to turn infinitely more enticing as Masters moved on to more practical arrangements.

And told her that Kirino was coming to join her.

Soon.

Very soon.

He could easily have left work a good hour or so before the rush hour. One of the perks of what he supposed you'd call his flexi-time job. But he didn't. Today he wanted to be on that platform and catching a very specific train at a very specific time.

At one time in the not-so-dim and distant past, he'd visited prostitutes. The first few visits had all followed the usual time-honoured pattern but he soon wanted something different. A two-girl booking initially provided some extra spice but then he wanted something different again. That was when he'd investigated the S&M scene although most of the stuff he'd been offered was pretty tame. Little more than ordinary working girls with a whip in truth, so he'd abandoned that pretty quickly.

Deep down he'd always needed to refine the thrill, push whatever boundary he'd previously transgressed. And now he was doing it again.

He'd seen a girl in the station hall the previous week. She was young – maybe in her late teens – maybe even younger. He'd no idea what it was about her that had first caught his eye but once she had claimed his attention he hadn't been able to stop looking at her. He followed her up the stairs, across the platform and into the train carriage.

Then he alighted at a station a couple of stops down the line and caught the next train back. On a whim he'd gone back to the station at the same time the next day and there she was again. She was making, it seemed, a regular journey.

Now he settled himself just a seat or two across the aisle from the girl. If she recognised him as a regular fellow-traveller she gave no sign. Her head was buried in a book, perhaps some school text or other. At her feet was a small musical instrument protected by a hard case, perhaps a violin.

Maybe she was on her way to a private lesson. Maybe she was on her way home from that lesson instead. She looked up as he wondered and briefly, very briefly, their eyes connected and he felt a charge course through his body. It was the first time they'd actually exchanged glances, the first time he knew, without a shadow of a doubt, that she'd noticed him above everyone else.

He couldn't help it. He stole another glance in her direction only to see her looking straight at him.

The expression on her face was, she hoped, unmistakable. How many glances had she fielded on that very train from men like this? Perspiring, middle-aged men in grey suits, scuffed shoes, clutching cheap, laptop bags.

Looking at her and imagining the unimaginable.

They were scum, all of them and that included her pervy music teacher who hunched just that little too close as he demonstrated just where she should place her fingers, no doubt imagining all the while the very different places those fingers might touch.

Every now and again she stared back at them and they always ducked their eyes, caught out like the guilty schoolboys they all were, no matter their age, the job they did, the apparently respectable profession they practised.

But now and again she did something else too. She shouldn't do it, she knew she shouldn't, she'd told her best friend about it once and she'd been horrified. Didn't she understand the dangerous game she was playing, her friend had wanted to know?

And yes, she did, but she didn't care. These men were like small dogs chasing a bus. She'd heard her father say that once and liked the sound of it. They'd run after it for all they were worth, but wouldn't have a clue what to do if they actually caught up with it. It was exactly the same with him. The slightly-perspiring man a seat or so across the aisle.

She'd hold her stare just a fraction too long. She'd practised the look in the mirror so she knew its effect. There was just the hint of promise in that stare, the ghost of an invitation. She loved seeing the confusion on the faces of the middle-aged men in the grey suits when she did it. One of them had actually blushed.

But this one didn't. In fact he was a little disappointing in truth. He seemed to take it in his stride, almost accept it – extraordinary thought – as his due somehow. The girl dismissed him, concentrated on her book, her innocent little game forgotten.

Across the aisle, the slightly-perspiring middle-aged man in the grey suit didn't dismiss her quite so easily. So far as he was concerned there was unfinished business left to pursue. He checked his watch. But not now.

The middle-aged man in the grey suit stood and alighted at the next stop as usual before catching the return train back down the line. Then DCI Jukes took the stairs back down to the ticket hall, walked out of the station and made for a car park behind his nearby office where he collected his anonymous family saloon and travelled home.

Conor came back into the kitchen. Francesca – she insisted on her full name, she'd always had a horror of the dimunitive Frankie – was chatting away on her mobile to Lahr's impressionable girlfriend from the previous dinner party and making plans for the upcoming trip away.

Conor once asked her why she insisted on using her mobile in the house when the landline was just a few inches away and the call would be infinitely cheaper. The pitying look she'd shot his way ensured he'd only asked the question the once.

As Fransesca saw him, she paused, told her caller she'd find out. Then she'd asked Conor whether she'd be making the trip alone or whether he'd be able to get some time off and join them after all? He hadn't been too sure the last time they discussed this.

Conor told her that he wouldn't be flying out with the rest of the party but he would be joining them a day or so later – and then Conor put a Club Class ticket down on the table in front of her.

Francesca looked at the ticket, then up at Conor. He could

see the unspoken question in her eyes. She knew the state of his personal finances. With every single one of his personal credit cards cancelled, with the bank stopping each and every cheque he tried to write, with every penny of his salary going into a special fund set up by two specialist liquidation advisers where it was chipping away at his now-consolidated debt, how the hell had he just blown over two grand on a flight ticket?

Then Franscesca decided she didn't want her unspoken question answered and turned back to her call.

Conor moved on into the sitting room not wanting to think about it either.

And especially not wanting to think about what he'd just done for the sake of a slightly larger seat on an aircraft and some complimentary drinks.

18

I T WAS STILL like living in a nightmare. Actually, no, it was worse than that. At least with nightmares you woke up, the world reordered itself and something approaching a safe and familiar reality was usually restored.

For the past half-hour Macklyn had listened to some woman set out his life story, only it wasn't his story and it had very little to do with his actual life. In fact it was a million miles away from everything that had made him the person he was today.

Or at least the person he was a few days earlier.

Now she was telling him he could no longer be that person. She was even telling him he now couldn't go back to his normal means of employment. He'd been in the transport industry since he was eighteen which was, apparently, the problem. He was too well-known in the circles he'd previously inhabited. Even if he set up again a couple of hundred miles away or even in some different country like France or Italy, that old world of his was too close-knit. They couldn't run the risk that in some office somewhere, out on some yard, even in a remote café frequented by the most occasional of truckers, someone from his former life wouldn't stop as they looked at him and say the words that could sign his death warrant.

'Hello Macklyn.'

It was all right for Elsha. She didn't have a life, not in his view, although he'd never have phrased it in quite that way. Not a life outside the home anyway. It was going to be all-too easy for her to tell any future acquaintance about her past history. She'd married, raised a daughter, created a home.

All she had to do was remember how many daughters, as

he'd reminded her in a cutting aside he'd regretted the moment he cracked it.

Macklyn knew he was using his sporadic flashes of anger as some kind of defence mechanism. He realised he was stoking up the fires inside in a somewhat pathetic attempt to stave off the grief he knew was waiting to overwhelm him. He also knew that he was only postponing the inevitable.

It didn't help that there were other distracting factors right now too, like this total stranger telling him what his life was going to be like from this moment on, at the same time as destroying all that had been – and all he'd been – before.

He'd tried – once again – to reassert some measure of the control he'd always been able to exercise so effortlessly in the past over friends as well as family and his workforce. And as he'd done so he'd found his mind drifting back again to the confrontation that never was, to the employee heading into his office on the day he himself was almost forcibly removed from it.

What had they all been told? There were drivers there who'd been working for him since they left school. He wouldn't exactly claim them as close friends, he'd always believed in keeping employees at a distance but there was still a relationship involved. But whenever he tried to ask about them, about his former business and those employees, he was simply told that all necessary arrangements had been made and that as far as possible he was to forget that they or his business had ever existed. It would be better for him and them in the long run.

Which was when he'd blown. Not that it seemed to particularly faze the slight, youngish, female officer who'd been placed in charge of all this. She just listened, calm, as he ranted and raved, as he refused point-blank to continue with the charade she was initiating, told her – straight, much as he used to talk to the occasional truculent trucker – that he simply didn't care any more.

The slight young woman didn't say a word. She seemed to sense she wouldn't need to, that someone else was going to speak on her behalf; meaning she seemed to know his wife, currently seated at his side, rather better than he did. The last thing he expected was an intervention from that quarter but that's exactly what happened.

'Di's still out there.'

Macklyn looked at her.

'If we don't do what they say, what happens to her?'

Macklyn looked beyond his wife outside at the small garden. Cara was playing on a broken slide, another of the officers deputed to look after them maintaining a watching brief close by.

He'd watched each of his daughters playing in their garden at home a thousand times before. Cara looked as if she was just going through the motions. As if this was something that was somehow expected of her, a duty she had to perform.

'She got us into this mess. She can fend for herself.'

Even as he said the words he knew he didn't mean them. He was speaking for the simple sake of it, because he had nothing else to do. It was much like the crack about the number of daughters. All he could do now was inflict pain.

'Besides, look at us. All these people looking over us. There'll be even more people doing the same for Di, there's no way anyone will be able to get to her.'

'And if they can't get to her?'

'What?'

'If they can't get to Di?'

Macklyn just looked at her.

'They'll go for the next one down, won't they?'

Macklyn kept looking at her.

'They'll go for Cara.'

Macklyn looked outside at the small garden once more. Cara was now sitting on the bottom of the slide looking back in at them. For a moment Macklyn stared into a future where his youngest daughter grew up as someone else. And wondered if it wouldn't have been better if the gunman had simply finished what he'd started. If he hadn't taken them all when he had the chance.

Then he turned back to the slight young woman who'd just been watching the exchange unfold, hesitated a moment longer, then nodded, signalling her to carry on.

He'd only memorised his new life up to his early twenties. Now he had to absorb the rest.

19

THE EMAIL HAD come through ten minutes before the expiration of the deadline. It had arrived via the same, untraceable, Hotmail account as before.

The email comprised just one word.

OK.

Masters had replied immediately, wanting to know where they could meet, could she travel to see them or was that already not an option, was she already in too much danger, should they come and fetch her instead?

The reply took another half-hour and for most of that time Masters stared at his handset. Had he overplayed his hand at the last moment? Had he appeared a little too eager, pushed a clearly nervous witness just that little bit too hard?

Then came the reply and an address, or at least a district. Masters was to get to the intersection of two streets just off Atlantic Wharf. He was to call a mobile number which was again untraceable, the messenger obviously using a recently purchased SIM card. Then he'd receive his final directions.

Masters assumed the intersection would be overlooked by wherever this new witness was currently hiding, that she'd then be able to see who'd arrived to collect her. Which was a sensible precaution. All in all she sounded, as he remarked to Ros as they drove to make the meeting, as if she could be good news.

Ros and Masters pulled up outside the pre-arranged rendezvous a few moments later.

Across the road, high up in an apartment complex converted from an old bonded warehouse, Yaroslav's eyes bore down onto the roof of the unmarked police car.

Its progress had been tracked all the way along the Central Link Road before it had taken a left down onto the old wharf.

Its progress had been further monitored as it turned left again along the disused dock before turning right and parking by a former back-street drinking den that was trying to reincarnate itself as a gastro-pub and failing somewhat more than miserably.

It was time.

It was very definitely time.

Yaroslav's hand reached out, hovered over a speed dial button, the number that Masters had emailed over a few hours' earlier. But it wasn't that number that was pressed first.

First an attachment was selected and added to a message that had been prepared some time earlier. For a moment there was a pause as the anticipation was savoured. Then the speed dial key was pressed.

Down on the street, Masters looked at his mobile as a text alert sounded.

Masters paused. The agreement was that the witness would call. It was time for a bit of old-fashioned human contact, one voice speaking to another, closely followed by those same voices speaking face to face.

Masters grimaced. But what could he do? For all his bluster and game-playing, one additional face in the witness box, one additional and supplementary testimony could make or break the case they were now constructing. The truth was he wanted this witness no matter how she chose to make contact.

Masters flipped open the text to reveal an address. He repeated it to Ros who swiftly punched it into her phone, accessing the built-in sat-nav at the same time. They were, it seemed, only a few steps away.

Masters paused. There was nothing else in the message, just the address. Then he noticed the symbol to the side. The message came with an attachment. Maybe that would tell them more.

Masters hit the button that would download the attachment as he looked at a door set into a brick wall some few metres away.

The whole street had so far largely escaped the general gentrification that had blessed or blighted the area depending on your point of view, so everything pointed to the same thing. A young girl down on her luck and now scared, holed up in a run-down flat awaiting deliverance.

And for not the first time Masters congratulated himself on his foresight in bringing along Ros. Whatever her faults, witnesses very definitely responded to her. He'd still no idea why. There just seemed to be some sort of fellow-feeling established between them from the moment she came into a usually highly-charged room. Where that came from he didn't know and frankly didn't care. It was there, that was all that mattered.

Then Masters looked at the picture that had now downloaded itself onto his display.

High above, in the apartment, calculations were being made. The average download of this type took around five or so seconds. So it really should have completed by now. Give the officer down on the street a few more seconds to take it in. It wasn't exactly the kind of sight that could be absorbed immediately after all. The human eye always recoiled initially, even the odd surgeon might momentarily flinch at all he'd be looking at right now.

Then Yaroslav paused as the car door opened and Masters fairly bolted from inside. Then he turned, looked out across the neighbouring buildings towards the city's law courts just visible in the distance.

And the watcher smiled

A few days earlier Banks had looked at the email with some considerable irritation. OK, he'd never rated Scott but he'd never rated lots of his fellow officers either. Look at that other waste of space, Conor.

He had to acknowledge that it did still rankle that Scott had beaten him to the beautiful Bella in that club all those years ago. Partly that was because he didn't like to be beaten. But mainly it was because while some women come and go, pass before the eyes and are forgotten, Bella wasn't one of those.

It was one of the reasons he'd put heart and soul into bagging her that night. Maybe he'd tried too hard. He asked her, as casually as he could some time later, at one of their Christmas parties, why she'd blanked him? In strict contrast to most of the other cops, Scott always brought his wife along.

As if he was flaunting her in his face.

OK, you got the promotion but I got the girl.

Bel had looked straight at him, not fooled for a moment by the casual sounding tone he'd practised over the years and which usually stood him in good stead when extracting information from various witnesses.

But she didn't answer directly. She just told him he scared her. Momentarily nonplussed by that, he'd started to press her on what she meant. The last thing he thought he was being was scary. But then Scott was at her side – he never left her alone for more than a few moments on those occasions – and his question remained unanswered. But Banks didn't like loose ends and he knew he'd press her again.

But for once it wasn't Bel on his mind as he read the email she'd sent in, apologising for her husband's absence from work for the next few days, explaining that he'd come down with some bug or other and asking if the station needed a sick note because if so she'd arrange for one to be sent in.

Banks swore as he read it. Now they'd need to find someone

else to help maintain the surveillance on Yaroslav. Typical fucking Scott, couldn't even do a simple tail job without coming down with a runny nose.

Two days passed into three before Banks, with another officer now handling the surveillance, suddenly thought about Scott again. Bel hadn't been in touch with the sick note and Banks realised he actually now had a cast-iron reason to call her.

He earmarked a time the office would be quiet, later that same day. Maybe he could arrange to meet her away from the house, could hand over some files he'd pretend he wanted Scott to look at when he'd recovered sufficiently to do some office work at least.

And then he could press her a bit more on those still-unanswered questions, maybe tie up a few loose ends.

Banks looked out through the office window, already looking forward to it.

Ros stared at the image on the phone. All Masters had done was hand it to her before exiting the car. He was now moving at speed towards the door set in the old brick wall. Ros kept staring at the image, not really taking it in, aware of Masters, just a couple of metres away, now kicking at the door, that door first splintering, then giving way as he forced his way inside. By that time Ros had followed him, the phone with the image still on display left behind on the passenger seat.

High up in the apartment the watching eyes could see no more. Everything that was happening was now taking place inside thick brick walls, walls thick enough to drown out the sound of not just one, but two human beings as they screamed their last.

It was a location that had served its purpose well in the past but would be fit for nothing now which was a shame, but in the circumstances that was a small price to pay.

Ros stopped as she came into the room. In front of her, Masters had stopped too. In the first of the rooms – there were two as they'd discover soon enough – there wasn't the image they expected to see. It wasn't actually the image on the phone.

That had been shocking enough but this was something else. It seemed that the photo of Scott had been taken a short time before another – and quite separate – atrocity had taken place because Scott was holding something. Ros couldn't take it in at first but then she realised what it was, and at about the same time as Masters if the gagging retches she suddenly heard coming from his direction were anything to go by.

Scott's arms were wrapped around a human foetus. The foetus hadn't gone to anything like full term, but there were arms visible and legs and the head sported tiny eyes and ears. The back, though, was still not properly formed. Now it never would be.

Masters straightened up from his retching. Somewhere, on the edge of memory, he recalled station gossip about Scott and his beautiful wife, the beautiful Bella, the beautiful, pregnant, Bella.

Masters looked towards another door leading into what was obviously the second room, already knowing what they were going to find in there. Momentarily he hesitated but he knew the longer he did so the worse it would be. He thought of telling Ros to stay where she was but what was the point? Why leave her in one scene of primitive horror to spare her from what was quite obviously going to be another?

Masters walked through the door and stopped again. Bella was indeed in there, lying on the floor in front of him, arms and legs splayed out, ankles and wrists secured with tape.

Masters had no way of knowing whether she'd been killed before her stomach had been sliced from pelvis to chest and her unborn baby wrenched from inside, but his immediate suspicion, later confirmed, was that she'd remained alive, conscious and in agony, physical and mental, throughout the whole thing.

Masters stood before the eviscerated corpse, staring at her open stomach, her ruptured womb. From a place that seemed a million miles away he felt a hand, gentle, on his arm and he looked at Ros, who wasn't looking at Bella, the no-longer pregnant and no-longer beautiful Bella, but who was looking at him and him alone.

Ros nodded at him and he nodded back.

Then the two police officers turned, headed back outside.

Seeing them emerge into the daylight was something of a disappointment. Yaroslav didn't quite know what he'd expected, but he didn't expect the almost mechanical walk back to the car, the almost routine-looking call for back-up. Given the scene he'd staged he expected something rather more dramatic by way of a reaction.

But no matter. The game was long and it had hardly begun. There'd be plenty of time. At the moment everything was going absolutely to plan, the cards falling exactly where they should. He'd been a little dubious initially about this latest refinement, wondering if it was strictly necessary but then he'd become convinced.

He hoped she'd be pleased. He hoped she'd appreciate the savage beauty of it all.

If only he could see her. Describe what he'd done. Spell out every last little detail of how he'd done it.

But there'd be time for that.

Plenty of time.

Wouldn't there, Tyra?

CARA HAD ALWAYS done it. Actually, that wasn't quite true. She'd done it ever since she realised her sister did it, the sister who was still with them but who just wasn't around any more.

It was Di she'd seen keeping the diary. She'd even read extracts out to her and Cara had loved it. Di wrote about everything, about her friends and their neighbours and the teachers in school, even some of the people she'd met that day on the bus.

Cara tried to do the same but it was actually a lot harder than she thought. Looking back over some of her early entries it was as much as she could do to record the time she got up, what she had for breakfast and what time she got back from school. But over the weeks she grew better at it. She'd confide in the diary some of the more interesting details of her day, such as who said what about who, who fell out with who, who got in trouble with a teacher.

But the really big difference between her diary and the diary kept by her sister was that Cara kept hers secret. Mainly that was because she was embarrassed. She'd heard Di read extracts to Mum and Dad and heard them roar with laughter as she described some neighbour or other.

Then she'd looked at her own diary, read about what she'd watched on TV and decide Mum and Dad probably wouldn't find that quite so amusing. So she kept on with her diary, but kept quiet about it for the first few months, not even telling anyone of its existence, intending to bring it out when she thought there might actually be something interesting to share.

Then what happened to Braith happened. And all of a sudden

her diary became something she couldn't show anyone because it had become just too private. Because she then told the diary things she could never repeat to a living soul. Things she'd tried to say to her Mum but she just cut her off. Things she'd tried to talk to her about, like Braith, only to be told to finish her tea in a tone of voice that told her she'd just done something wrong although she couldn't for the life of her work out exactly what.

Late at night she'd read it over and over again, especially the early pages when she talked about what time she got up, what time she went to bed, what programmes she watched on the TV and what she had for supper.

Previously she'd found all that boring, but after Braith – everything in her life these days seemed to be before and after Braith – she found herself taking comfort in even the most mundane of entries.

Reading it, she could see herself getting up in their old house – the house she still called home despite the fact everyone now told her she shouldn't do so.

Reading it, she could imagine what it was like to open her eyes, to hear the sounds in the house with everyone already moving about, Dad shouting goodbye to Mum before she heard his car start in the driveway.

Reading it, she'd hear Braith going into and coming out of the bathroom, sometimes she'd hear exchanges between Braith and Di when one of them spent too long in there before Mum came upstairs and played peacemaker.

Reading it, she'd also remember the way her bedroom door would open and Mum would appear and she'd be told it was time to get up to go to school.

All that she'd actually see in a single entry on a single day. Got up, 7.45. It was amazing. Just three words; if putting the time down like that was a word, she wasn't quite sure, it was a collection of numbers, so did that count?

Normally she'd ask her Mum but now she didn't. She might have asked why she wanted to know and Cara didn't want to actively lie. Not saying something was just about OK. Saying something that wasn't true was different.

And then there were the entries that came a little later, before Braith, when things were still OK, where she talked about her schoolfriends and her teachers and the boys she hated and the ones who were OK and the lessons she liked and the ones she didn't. Reading all that, she could almost smell her old classroom, the games room, the playing fields.

Sometimes she put the diary away and didn't read it for a day or so because suddenly she'd feel tears stinging her sight. She'd been told not to think about the life they used to have, but that was easier said than done even for Mum and Dad. She'd hear them – again usually late at night – talking about things in low voices, almost whispering as if afraid they were doing something wrong and might be overheard, even though there was only Cara in the house and they thought she was asleep.

A few weeks earlier, she'd started in her new school. One of the teachers had taken her into her new class along with her Mum and she'd stood in front of the class as the teacher introduced her, calling her by a name she didn't know and explaining she'd moved to the school from another school miles away whose name she also didn't recognise. Then she'd sat down next to a girl who ignored her.

At playtime a couple of other girls had come up to her and she'd told them who she was, or who she'd been told she was, without them even asking and they obviously thought she was weird because they went away. That night Mum had asked her if she'd made any friends and before she could reply, Dad had asked her what she'd said to them and did she remember her new name? She found it really hard to do that, especially on the rare occasions when they were having fun, when they were out on the playing fields and there was a game of rounders or something and one of the girls shouted across at her, using the name she'd been given and she looked round wondering who they were calling to, before realising it was her.

Now and again when something like that happened she'd catch a quizzical look on the faces of some of the teachers as they looked over at her. The rest of the class just took it as yet more evidence that the new girl was more than a little bit strange.

But a week ago something changed. A new girl arrived and all of a sudden Cara wasn't the outsider any more. All of a sudden she was with the rest of the class looking at a new arrival. She'd talked to the new girl in the playground at break and they'd struck up a tentative friendship. They'd gravitated towards each other quite naturally and now she was wondering if she was to be the one.

She knew she had to tell someone the truth one day. She felt sometimes like her head would burst if she didn't. If she could just tell one person then she felt as if she could keep the secret OK after that.

And when the police officers and her Mum and Dad had said not to tell anyone, they had to mean another adult, didn't they? This girl was her age. And she'd come from a different place, miles away, just like her. What possible harm could there be in telling someone like that?

THERE'D BEEN A leak. Everyone knew that. It was impossible that all that had happened could have happened without someone passing on precisely the wrong sort of information so far as the police were concerned, precisely the right sort of information so far as the abductor or abductors were concerned.

At this stage there was still an official debate as to who that abductor or abductors might be, but no-one was in too much doubt. This had the hand of the Ukrainian stamped all over it.

It wasn't just the savagery of the attack. It was the sheer theatricality of it all. Yaroslav didn't seem to be content with a simple demonstration of force, it was as if it had to become something of a spectacle as well. Something that would pass into folklore. The slaughter of a policeman, his wife and child – that slaughter, in the latter case, taking place before the child in question had even been born – was always going to pass into the annals of station legend, handed down from one generation to the next.

That much was agreed. But why such an extravagant scenario had been enacted in the first place proved more of a stumbling block.

To Masters and the rest of the officers in Murder Squad it was a gauntlet thrown down. A more than usually devastating shot across the bows.

But to Ros that simply didn't ring true. To Ros it was almost as if Yaroslav was trying to impress someone. In her opinion there had to be something stronger at work here than a simple desire to demonstrate an almost invincible power. But, as Masters had pointed out, there was a rather more pressing matter to deal with than speculating on the twisted psychology of a madman. Because whatever the motive, whatever may have been driving him on, someone was helping him. And that someone was inside the force, perhaps inside that very station and once Ros had also reviewed the evidence she found it difficult to argue with that.

Initially it had been thought that Bella had been picked up following her husband's abduction. There'd been the clearest possible evidence of the torture that had been inflicted on Scott. Given that, it really wouldn't have taken too much effort on the part of his torturer, or torturers, to find out where he lived. They could have found some document in his wallet that would have led them to his home address even if he'd actually managed to keep his mouth shut. Officers on that type of duty weren't supposed to carry anything that could identify them but he could have been careless, left something in his jacket, even took along his home mobile rather than the untraceable handset he'd have been given.

Then they saw the tape.

It wasn't the first time Masters had lost it. Once, in the past, he'd been hastily transferred from a department he'd all but destroyed in an attempt to find the one bad apple who'd sabotaged an eight-month-long sting and all, as Masters later discovered, for the modern-day equivalent of thirty pieces of silver.

But the officer in question was a serious heroin addict. At the prices he could negotiate, that kind of money would have lasted him nearly a month. That might seem scant recompense for the four lives that were lost as a result of Masters not nailing a particularly vicious contingent of sex and drug traffickers but it was clearly a justified cost for the station junkie.

Masters had been put on indefinite leave while the police psychologist investigated what were called his anger issues. The psychologist failed to resolve any sort of issues at all but by that time Masters had discovered his own type of therapy in the form of chess and evening classes in philosophy. After committing most of his spare moments to the pursuit of one closely followed by the other there hadn't been a similar outburst since his transfer.

But his patience was now being sorely tested by all they were discovering about the murder of Scott, the beautiful Bella and their baby.

Bella was picked up before Scott was abducted. They knew that for a fact because a CCTV camera near to her home showed her being bundled into a van as she returned from the shops.

It was a classic sting, a van pulling up a few feet ahead, the passenger opening the side door, the driver getting out at the same time, momentarily blocking the path of the mark and that mark then bundled inside.

If it was a good team carrying out the sting it would be over in an instant – and this team was good. Bella hardly had time to cry out before the van door was slammed shut, trapping her inside.

The CCTV camera was time and date stamped. Meaning this wasn't some opportunist snatch, a refinement dreamt up as an afterthought. Someone had tipped off the Ukrainian in advance.

Masters was a coiled spring and everyone knew it. And Banks knew it better than most. Normally, in days gone by, he'd have relished being alongside his volatile boss when he was in one of these moods. Up to now those moods had always been directed outwards at some hapless villain with them all riding shotgun as that boss brought the offender to book.

But this was different. Now Masters wasn't looking outside. Now all his attention was focused on his own. Now he was looking at those he normally counted as allies and friends. He was hunting for someone – someone with something to hide, some secret they'd really rather remain a secret – and Banks was sweating, big-time.

It was only a relatively minor supplement to what some people would regard, he knew, as a fairly generous income. He had no idea if Masters knew about it. But if this kept on much longer he'd find out. And then some very serious questions were going to be asked, questions he really did not want to answer.

And then, all of a sudden, he had to.

Masters looked straight ahead into a pair of eyes that were only inches from his own. And then he began to speak, although what emerged from his mouth amounted more to a declamation than any attempt to initiate any sort of exchange.

'We maintain – .'

Masters paused, half-smiled.

'And here, I confess, I'm paraphrasing – .'

His smile wasn't returned.

'That all former moral theories are the product, in the last analysis, of the economic stage which society has reached.'

Masters paused.

'Marx and Engels. Or perhaps more accurately, Engels uncorrected by Marx. First advanced in *The German Ideology*, developed further in *Anti-Duhring*. It's all more than a little muddled in truth. For example Engels confuses absolute truth in the sense of unambiguous and self-evident statements with absolute truth in the sense of complete knowledge or the sum of all possible knowledge and there's a further confusion in that Engels, in claiming that all truth is relative, then claims for his truth an unambiguous and absolute certainty. But let's leave petty quibbles like that to one side, shall we?'

He wasn't taking any of this in. All he could see was the tip of the poker which had first been red-hot and was now white-hot, waving in front of his staring eyes. He had absolutely no idea if Masters was serious about using it or not but it had certainly claimed his attention.

'Marx didn't question it because, matters of intellectual rigour aside, it allowed him to formulate his own ethical ideology. It enabled him to disregard the notion of ethics as providing a set of rules or criteria by which man might resolve the dilemma of everyday moral choice. Marx didn't embrace the notion of duty, you see, in the sense we'd normally understand it. Duty was derived from good and if good was merely objective, deriving from the specific needs of society or a social organisation, then duty was similarly objective and derived from those same needs.'

The poker came closer.

'So what of our duty? What of our responsibilities in a society in which good may no longer be an absolute? Are we now into a free-for-all in which everyone can do as they wish? An initially appealing idea perhaps; perfect freedom to do as one chooses. The flip side being that if the concept of duty is fundamentally undermined then so is the concept of rights, the two being opposite sides of the same coin. Meaning if you've undermined the notion of duty then you've actually abrogated your claim to rights.'

All he could think was, he's going to do it, he's actually going to do it and then a terrifying thought ambushed him as Masters continued.

'Have you done that? Have you abrogated your claim to normal human rights?'

Was he competing in some way? Had this become some sort

of macabre tit for tat? All this shit about rights and duties and opposite sides of the same coin, was Masters trying to outdo that twisted Ukrainian?

'How much?'

At last, there it was, the first direct question he could understand.

'A few grand.'

'Normal villainy?'

'Normal – totally normal.'

He was gasping now. Sparks were coming from the end of the poker, as if they were looking to latch onto something, as if they could sense the skin just a few, tantalising, inches away.

'Turn a blind eye to a couple of drug runs, look the other way when a lorry-load of tarts show up at a couple of brothels?'

He gasped again.

'Nothing else, I swear.'

'How do you know?'

All of a sudden Masters was ranting.

'They could have got hold of your laptop. Hacked into it when some crackhead whore was sucking you off in the next room. Reprogrammed your mobile, how the fuck do you know?'

And now he knew Masters was mad. Totally and certifiably insane. He could see it in his eyes, in the way he hissed along with the sparks from the poker waving in front of his face and he knew that if something now happened it'd be buried, much as he'd be buried, he'd become one of the casualties of the Yaroslav case along with Scott and the beautiful Bella and their unborn child and Masters could do that because he'd done it in the past, maybe not with a copper but definitely with a few other faces.

Banks had been there with him and he'd actually helped cover some of that up too so he also knew that when you've an official sanction to ask questions it's all-too easy to strangle the wrong sort of answers.

And it was all so unfair, he was small fry, his misdemeanours totally insignficant in comparison to the crime Masters was now imagining.

So he did the only thing he could do. He closed his eyes, waited for the heat to bite, the agony to begin, knowing he couldn't tell Masters any more than he'd told him already, knowing also that he'd confess to the theft of the Crown Jewels if that poker came within just another inch of his sweat-raddled face.

Then, all of a sudden, there was silence.

Slowly, he focused on a pair of curtains at the far side of a bed.

His bed.

He looked to the left to the door that led to a bathroom.

His bathroom.

His breathing was every bit as panicked as a moment before and he was drenched in sweat. But there was no Masters. No white-hot poker scattering sparks in front of his face. His skin was no longer tensing in anticipation of a searing pain.

Banks lay back on the pillow and at least one part of his overheated mind began to calm at least. He hadn't been locked in some basement room with a psychotic senior officer. He'd simply been having a nightmare.

But another part of his brain wasn't calm at all. Whether that was the more paranoid or prescient part he couldn't as yet assess. That part of his brain was telling him to heed the warning, to listen to the message his night-time imaginings was forcing before his eyes.

He had to stop it – stop all he was doing – and he had to stop it now. He had to stop it for his own sake and also for the sake of his colleagues, past and present. If he didn't then all he'd just experienced in his head would become a pallid imitation of a reality he'd later – and inevitably – endure.

Banks closed his eyes.

Just stop it, stop it.

The problem being he really didn't know if he could.

Ros looked at Masters as he lay beside her. As she did so events from the previous evening swam before her eyes – the arrival of Scenes of Crime – the reaction to all they saw on the faces of professionals who'd seen everything, had experienced everything; shocked, as she and Masters had both been, beyond words.

She'd expected that they'd head back to the station but they hadn't. Masters had made for a small barge moored downriver instead, once a dredger working the nearby docks, now a bustling bar and restaurant.

Masters had ordered a bottle of red wine and two glasses. He'd poured Ros a glass, then poured one for himself. Both glasses were filled to the brim. He'd ignored the smiling waiter who'd approached with a menu and Ros had motioned to him to move away.

They'd remained in silence looking out over the water at the pleasure craft transporting charter parties, at the odd single canoeist bobbing around in the swell. When they'd finished the first bottle Masters had finally spoken but that was only to order another.

Then they'd moved onto another bar in the shadow of the old Coal Exchange. They found a table near the door and watched as a twenty-strong group of trainee financiers congregated, all carrying identical rucksacks with the name of their employer stencilled on the back. A waitress enquired if they were eating that evening. Again she'd been waved away.

The next stop had been a pub on the street near to Ros's apartment. There was a decking area at the back where customers could look out over the river. But Masters and Ros stayed inside under the almost impossibly steep stairs that led to a cramped restaurant that served, according to local folklore, the best Sunday roast in the city. That was all they served though. This time no waiter, smiling or otherwise, approached them brandishing a menu.

And Masters had finally talked but he didn't refer to the events of the day. He talked of a son, now aged ten, whom he hardly saw and a wife who'd remarried and had settled somewhere near Bath.

He tried asking Ros about her own emotional entanglements but gave up pretty quickly when he ran into the usual stone-wall.

But it would never have been the words that mattered that evening. Everything that was happening between them was happening at a level beneath any normal channel of communication. All he was doing and all she was helping him do because she wanted to do it too, was blotting everything out, the events of the day, everything they'd seen, the way they'd been suckered into that visit to the murder scene, the way they'd been played by persons or persons as yet – officially anyway – unknown; who'd visited an ordeal of unimaginable barbarity on three totally innocent lives.

Masters didn't try and make sense of it all. No-one could. There'd be investigations to come but for now all he could do and all Ros could do was look away from the clearest evidence they'd both encountered in a long time that there was indeed evil in the world and that a devil patrolled its walkways.

And there was something else going on here too. An experience like that either repelled or attracted, it either bonded those involved or blasted them apart. Ros didn't know which it would be for herself and Masters until they came out of the pub at closing time and he asked if he could stay the night.

Finally, hours later – hours spent just lying side by side – nothing more – Masters spoke about the day they'd just endured.

'We don't delay. We press on even faster than before. We put Tyra and Kirino together as soon as we can and then we bring him in.'

Ros just nodded, for once she and Masters in total agreement.

Then they both fell asleep.

High up in the apartment, Yaroslav studied the slowly-moving hands on an expensive Breitling Navitimer wristwatch. These calls were synchronised to the minute. They had to be. And the routine was always the same.

The calls were made and answered in the middle of the night. When everyone else in the house was asleep. If there wasn't an answer on the first silent ring he cut the call. Then he tried again the next night at the very same time. There'd only been the one night he'd not received a reply and that had been due to a mobile signal failing at the wrong moment rather than anything more sinister.

The rest of the time it had been like clockwork.

Just like everything else.

THE WOMAN WHO had once been Elsha, the woman who'd imagined she always would be Elsha, looked round the new-build school.

Already the paint was beginning to peel, the swings and slides in the playground beginning to show signs of wear and tear. The school had been built in the last two years and in ten it would be a maintenance nightmare. It had been put up quickly, shoddily, a hasty response to a large influx of local labour servicing a call centre that had closed in the last few months anyway.

Most of the children remained, but like the school that housed them they were also showing signs of wear as they rushed past in clothes that were cheap, largely supermarket-bought and looking it.

It was all a far cry from their old school, a local Victorian building that had been lovingly restored with help from a community that, in some cases, had sent several generations of its children to be educated there. These children were a far cry from those too. The woman who had once been Elsha struggled to maintain the fiction that she wasn't any sort of snob but the fact remained she really didn't like her daughter, her only remaining daughter, attending a class where at least sixty per cent of her fellow-pupils didn't count either of her two native tongues – English or Welsh – as their first language.

She told her husband, the man who had once been Macklyn, that she feared it would hold their daughter back, that she'd be marking time while the rest of the class played catch-up and he'd nodded in all the right places and made all the right sounding noises and even agreed when she said that perhaps they should investigate the question of additional tutoring, but he wasn't really listening.

He hardly listened at all these days. His eyes were on one thing and one thing only and she knew it, a past that could never now be recovered in a country where a wench was well and truly dead.

They sat opposite the class teacher on small chairs, their daughter's school work open on the desk in front of them. Across the room a young Asian girl with dyed yellow hair, a teaching assistant she was to later discover, cleared away some paintings and drawings.

Initially she thought the hair was some kind of fashion statement but then she realised most of the teachers had dyed their hair too, along with many of the children. It was all part of a fund-raising effort linked to a *Children In Need* TV appeal apparently, but it had rather passed the pair of them by. The teacher did sound a little surprised they'd not heard of it, the programme in question having seemingly dominated all television and radio stations for days.

The woman who'd once been Elsha didn't actually think they'd turned on a TV for weeks. She'd like to pretend it was because they had better things to do but of course it wasn't. Neither she nor the man who used to be Macklyn could bear the implicit reminder that the world was moving on in its usual way while theirs was not.

Her eyes strayed behind the teacher as she now started laying out different workbooks in front of them. A list of birthdays hung on the wall behind the teacher including the birthday of the girl who had once been Cara.

It was the wrong date of course. And for some reason, having a different name and a different life story hadn't seemed to worry the little girl as much as having to pretend she was born on a different day. The woman who'd been Elsha had tried to tell her it was a good thing because that way she'd have two birthdays – but then she'd been told to stop telling her that by the slightly-built specialist officer who advised them on such things.

She had to stop reminding the little girl of a life that was now gone. From now on they'd only be celebrating – if that was the word – just the one special day.

For the first few minutes it was the usual sort of encounter they'd experienced in most other parents' evenings. The teacher showed them work from their little girl's maths book, her spelling book, some work from her art folder. They all agreed she was doing well in relation to the rest of her year group and the two parents smiled in all the right places when the teacher assured them that the school was satisfied with her progress, especially given the fact she'd moved there midterm, which was never an easy thing for any pupil of any age to do.

The teacher had paused at that point, made the hesitant observation that she assumed the move was something to do with work – and she'd looked at the man who'd been Macklyn. The woman who'd been Elsha felt her husband immediately tense beside her. He always did when anyone, a postman, a delivery driver, a neighbour, made any similar reference to their past.

She knew what he was thinking. Why are they asking? What are they trying to find out? Is this just an innocent enquiry or something else entirely? And will I be the one to give the game away, to say the wrong thing to the wrong person, invoke the cataclysm they all feared?

She stepped in quickly, nodding back, made some veiled reference to her husband's unspecified business and the teacher moved on. They were a little concerned about what they called the little girl's social skills, she conceded. She didn't seem to have made many friends so far and she didn't take too much part in after-class activities but it was still early days in the settling-in period. Maybe they could review that in the next parents' evening in a few months' time.

But then the teacher had paused again. And now she seemed to be savouring what she had to say next, and indeed she was, because in a report that contained a few little negatives there was one massive positive and this teacher, like all the best teachers, always believed in saving the best to last, in sending not only the children in her class but also their parents home with words of encouragement rather than simply pointing out a litany of problems and faults.

The teacher spread another workbook out on the small desk in front of them. This was the part of the job she really loved, seeing the look of wonder on the faces of adults as well as children, watching as those adults looked at something on which their child had laboured, out of their sight, and produced something really quite remarkable along the way.

Because that's what this little girl had done. She'd conjured up a work of quite extraordinary imagination for a pupil her age. They'd even put extracts up on the wall for the rest of the class to read. A lot of children had imaginary friends or relayed imaginary conversations with their pets. But this child had constructed a whole different life.

She'd populated it with family and friends, adding in all sorts of small details that had really made it come alive. In fact it didn't read like a story at all, it was as if she was lifting a lid on something she'd actually experienced, it really was that good as she now observed to the two parents, their heads bent as they read the words before them.

Then the warm smile of the teacher wiped, the teaching assistant across the classroom stopped and stared as the mother looked up from the pages of the notebook she was reading and started to scream.

YAROSLAV TYPED THE coordinates he'd been given into the software programme that had been set up for him by one of his employees.

He didn't pretend to understand too much about this kind of thing. He didn't need to. All he had to do was enter some strange-looking digits and wait till the screen fired into life. Then he was staring at a street. Then he could drag the image across the screen until he was focusing on one house in particular. Then he could squeeze the image so he could focus on various aspects of that house, the front and rear doors, the windows, a skylight let into the roof.

In the old days Yaroslav would have had to mount some sort of covert operation, risking detection at any moment to acquire anything like this sort of data. Now he could sit in his penthouse and it was as if he was looking down on his neighbour a couple of storeys below.

The software wasn't commercially available of course. Critics had argued on its launch that the sort of forensic detail it provided could be used for all sorts of nefarious purposes. Yaroslav was delighted to see they'd been proved correct.

The house was well-chosen, like them all. Just another house on any other street a good couple of hundred miles away from anywhere its inhabitants might be recognised. The occasional neighbour who passed by wouldn't even give it a second glance and from the look of those neighbours, mainly immigrant types like himself, it seemed to be in a fairly run-down and transient area so the location was a doubly clever choice.

Yaroslav cross-checked the coordinates some more and was

further gratified to see his initial reading of the locale seemed to be correct. At one time the suburbs of Moss Side and Rusholme would have housed relatively well-heeled families in their larger than average dwellings but those days were long gone. Now – as well as a large immigrant population composed of many different and distinct nationalities – the area teemed with an equally transitory body of students. So taken together it was the perfect population – floating, the type of people who'd hardly be likely to put down roots; people unlikely in turn to concern themselves with any of their new neighbours or their backgrounds or interests.

Yaroslav adjusted the angle of the image, focused on the small front gardens of the surrounding terraced houses, most split into flats. They were all stacked with stray items of rubbish, old mattresses, bin bags, even an old fridge. Yaroslav smiled. More examples of general neglect, yet more evidence of a community in flux. Yaroslav looked away from the monitor and let his mind run on Tyra.

Two months earlier, in that same location, she'd been pacing the floor, even more furious than Yaroslav right now and he, were he to possess the vocabulary, would have described himself as incandescent.

In fact he did possess the vocabulary in his native tongue. In a previous incarnation and before he discovered rather easier ways of earning a living, he'd briefly considered teaching linguistics. But all he was concerned about at present was a young Japanese girl and a tip-off from a dependable and well-rewarded source that she'd entered into some kind of police protection programme with the sole aim of providing information to authorities who were already seeking to track him down before bringing him to trial.

'Were you fucking her?'

'She worked for me, I fucked her, I fuck them all when they first start, you know that.'

'And that was that, one fuck and you put her to work.'

Yaroslav paused.

He knew exactly what she was getting at.

'Not just the one, no.'

'How many?'

'I didn't count.'

'Where?'

Yaroslav struggled again, then conceded defeat.

'Here.'

'You moved her in?'

'She was a good fuck.'

'How long for?'

'A few weeks – maybe a couple of months – .'

'How much could she have found out living here with you for two whole months?'

Yaroslav didn't reply for a moment, didn't need to, his face the all-too clear answer.

'And now the cops have got her.'

It wasn't a question and didn't require an answer. Tyra was just thinking out loud, computing options, assessing the different possibilities now on offer.

'She's exactly what they've always wanted. Someone on the inside who now wants to be on the outside. And she's going to do that by putting herself where you can't reach her.'

Tyra exploded again.

'For Christ's sake Yaroslav, she might have been a good fuck but did you have to pick one that had a brain as well?'

'So what do we do?'

It was why Yaroslav had told her. She'd handled several problems for him in the past, leaving him free to concentrate on what might be called his core businesses. This was a somewhat larger problem than normal but he knew she'd come through and it looked as if his faith wasn't about to be misplaced.

Because after a few more turns of the room, an old and familiar light began to gleam in her eyes.

Something took over. He didn't know exactly what. It just always did.

Blood lust was a term they used back in his native Ukraine. The moment a mist descends before the eyes either through anger or jealousy. Or because at heart man is an animal.

He always thought it was like that old adage about war. They exist because, deep down, men like to fight. They like to inflict pain on others. And having inflicted pain on others they want to inflict more pain on even more people next time.

Yaroslav didn't know if the same applied to women. He'd known some hard bitches in his time but he'd never come across any who enjoyed the process of torture as much as he did. He didn't know if it was sexual at its heart but somehow he doubted it. It seemed to be something more than that somehow, more than the temporary rush of pleasure he'd experience during sex.

He'd inflicted the most appalling suffering on many people in his time, sometimes men, sometimes women, and had always experienced a different sort of rush. There was the sense of being transported to a different place. He could hardly call it a better place but it was definitely a world apart from the one he normally inhabited. Maybe there was something God-like at its heart. Perhaps because it involved the ultimate power, choosing life or death for another human being.

Tyra had said they needed some sort of sacrifice, the kind of atrocity that would panic a girlfriend into the kind of flight she was contemplating. She could hardly turn up at the local nick and tell them she'd simply got bored. She had to be terrified out of her mind by all she'd witnessed otherwise her story simply wouldn't hold water. Which made sense. As ever she left the details to him. Which made even more sense.

Which was when it took over once again. When the blood lust began to surge inside him. When he became entranced by the details of all he was planning like an animal examining the entrails of a recent kill.

He knew Tyra wouldn't like it but she'd be powerless to stop it, so that consideration was dismissed almost as soon as it was raised. But in any event he knew he'd be powerless to stop it too once it started. Once the process began, once he began to smell the flesh before him, witnessed the moments when something human turned into butchered meat, he knew what would happen.

Some men would stop, horrified by all they were seeing, but not many in his view. In his opinion most men would be like him. They'd want to push on, to prolong the process, to complete all they'd started for the plain and simple reason that they liked it. It was just the natural order. The way of the world.

Scratch a civilised man and you'd find a savage, Yaroslav had always been told; and in his opinion you really didn't need to scratch too deeply.

And there was one other plain and self-evident truth in all this too. Tyra had told him that she needed to appear terrified. She needed to be horrified and repulsed for the ploy to work properly.

And Yaroslav had always hated to disappoint a lady.

It all played out just one week later. Tyra had seen the patrol car a mile or so back. She'd seen the two heads inside turn as she flashed past. She was already doing a good thirty miles an hour over the limit and she was a young girl in an expensive Ferrari, what more did they want by way of an invitation?

Sure enough, a few moments later she saw a white flash in her rear-view mirror. Just to add a little extra special enticement to the unfolding scene she cut inside, carving up a small family saloon that was hogging the middle lane. Then she depressed the clutch, slid the gear stick through the change into fourth, hit the throttle hard. She didn't lift off till the rev counter was bouncing off the red line and the engine was screaming, the speedo now touching a hundred and fifty.

The cop car faded from view and she was momentarily worried she'd pushed this too far. Maybe they'd decided the battle was simply unequal and had opted for a nice quiet takeaway coffee in some layby instead. Then she saw a flash of sunlight reflect off a car in the distance behind her.

Tyra kept them in sight for the next two or three miles. During that time she undertook several lorries, even once detouring onto the hard shoulder. She didn't let her speed dip below ninety and the needle hovered more usually around the hundred and twenty mark. She committed, by her own conservative calculation, around fifty or so separate traffic offences in just a few miles. As chases went it had to be one of the most visible, which was exactly what she wanted.

The finale was something of an inspired improvisation. She'd imagined being surrounded on all sides by a posse of police cars and being forced to a gradual halt. Then she saw the service station. She'd been there with Yaroslav and now she remembered the large plate glass window looking out over the car park as they approached. Grinning widely now, she screamed left off the motorway exit, the police car swopping lanes to follow.

Tyra opposite-locked the Ferrari round the car park, looking for the best vantage point for her final manoeuvre, making sure also there were no stray children playing in front of the glass. She already had more than enough blood on her hands, albeit of the guilty variety. She really didn't want to spill any of the innocent type too.

With the coast relatively clear at least, she then gunned the accelerator, bulleted through the plate glass window, demolishing various chairs and tables before cannoning to a halt right next to a coffee outlet till.

Then she sat and waited as the screams from inside the service station died down. Then the police appeared at her window.

At which point – by rights she really should have been an actress – she turned her tear-stained face to the first of the arriving officers and told him she needed help.

Yaroslav caught it by chance. One of his drivers was channel-hopping on the radio in the front as Yaroslav worked his mobile in the back. They were separated by a screen that filtered out most sounds but Yaroslav just caught the start of the traffic report and told the driver to turn it up.

Then Yaroslav forgot all about the calls he still had to make and listened in a mixture of growing admiration and unease to the reports of a young girl who'd just crashed a red Ferrari – what did the colour matter for fuck's sake – straight into the front of a motorway service station on one of the main arterial routes heading across the border.

Yaroslav knew it was Tyra straightaway. Today was the day she'd planned on being picked up, so it had to be. The service station was a twist he hadn't expected but he could see instantly how it would play into their hands.

And, for not the first time, he wondered at the curious game of one-upmanship that always seemed to operate whenever the two of them planned anything.

Without ever making it explicit, she pushed him into ever more extreme acts, some of which fazed even him just a little. That, presumably, was what was behind her apparently suicidal headlong smash into that service station.

She'd never emulate him in the violence stakes, he knew she didn't experience the blood lust that swept through him as he embarked on another systematic bout of torture. But she still took his breath away sometimes by the twists she continually added to even pre-agreed plans and she'd obviously done it again and now he'd have to do something to similarly ambush her too. Sometimes he wondered where it would all end.

But he knew at least where this would end. Tyra would be taken at her own request into protective custody. She would volunteer information about his activities. The police would, with the right encouragement, put her together with the single other witness who'd come forward in the last few weeks to testify against him, believing that their joint testimony would make for an invincible case.

And at a certain point Tyra would tell him exactly where they were, exactly who was providing whatever security might be present.

And at that point he would move against them, freeing Tyra and killing Kirino and with the two witnesses removed by one means or the other the apparently invincible case would collapse.

It was all so simple.

Like all the very best plans.

Almost beautiful in its simplicity, just like Tyra herself in fact.

Yaroslav looked out of the window as the traffic bulletin ended and as his car began to move again along the clogged city streets and hoped he wasn't actually starting to fall for this one.

That really would make it a problem when, as had always happened and always would, he'd have to get rid of her.

Tyra was sitting opposite Ros. From the rear of the house – and across the small garden – came the ever present hum of traffic passing the highest concentration of takeaway outlets in any one street in any city in the country according to the driver who'd delivered her there a few days earlier. As a chat-up line, it wasn't the most inventive or impressive as her silence quite clearly attested and he soon shut up.

Now Tyra was silent again, but she was listening and she did nod in all the right places too as Ros ran through her new life story, her latest legend to use the department's own terminology.

She and Kirino, apparently, were distant cousins. They were both students waiting to begin courses at a local college in two months' time. Ros had liaised with the relevant education authority which was happy to enrol two late additions. Times were tough and numbers were down. They weren't going to turn away two new sources of fees.

At a certain stage, probably just before the college opened its doors for the new term, the girls would withdraw from the course. Ros, or more likely Jukes, would have to come to some arrangement with the college over a cancellation fee but as they'd been unlikely to fill these two places anyway, Ros doubted it would prove too onerous a burden for the hard-pressed taxpayer.

Both girls were to study business management, a catch-all, general sort of course. Anything more specific always posed a risk for the life story they had to memorise. Saddling them with the nuclear physics option really wouldn't have made much sense.

Tyra nodded again as Ros spelt out their histories including where they'd been brought up, separately of course given their clearly-different nationalities, how they'd come together in London a year or so before and had then shared a flat before both decided to take up their college course away from the capital to improve their joint employment prospects.

It wasn't recommended that either Tyra or Kirino go out of their way to make friends, but there was a fair chance they'd be doorstepped by postmen, delivery drivers, canvassers or the like. They were both attractive young women for one thing. In those circumstances it was always better to engage with any visitor rather than retreat and hide. Nothing was calculated to spike interest and attention more than an apparent recluse. Just ask Greta Garbo.

All the time Tyra kept waiting for the one piece of information she really wanted. She could barely disguise her impatience as Ros filled in the different parts of her imaginary life, refusing to commit to memory information she knew she'd never need. But Ros kept that one piece of information back to the very end, almost daring her to ask for it herself, knowing she must not because that really would make her sound too eager.

But, finally, there it was.

'Kirino arrives this Thursday. Probably sometime in the afternoon. We're arranging for a removal van to bring her stuff over even though she won't actually have any. We'll pack some boxes and books into the van so the driver doesn't become suspicious but in reality she'll be coming with just a few clothes.'

Ros paused.

'She left her last place in a hurry. Not in quite such a spectacular fashion as you maybe, but still pretty quickly.'

Ros paused again. Tyra hardly seemed to be listening to her. She'd noticed it before. It was as if she'd float off somewhere, was no longer connecting with anything. Then, suddenly, she'd be back with them.

'Did you get on? Before?'

'Couldn't stand the little bitch.'

Ros nodded. It was exactly the answer she'd have expected.

Tyra didn't even see the nod. She was away once more, far from this house, far from her keepers.

Thursday afternoon.

After that, all her careful plans would bear fruit.

2 4

THE GIRL WHO had been Cara was outside playing on the swings. Some of the other girls had been playing there earlier but now they'd gone, moved on somewhere more interesting. All around her there were high-pitched calls and yells as the usual wave of noise rolled round the playground, over the playing field and down towards the road where her mother dropped her off each morning and collected her each afternoon.

The girl who had been Cara swung higher and higher on the swing. Months earlier, on her own swing at the house that used to be their home but was their home no longer, she'd done this too. Higher and higher she'd gone, sailing up so she was almost level with the branches of the tree from which the swing was suspended.

Mum had shouted from the kitchen window telling her to be careful but she'd swung even higher, knowing she'd be safe. She didn't know why. She just knew nothing bad could happen to her while she was there, in the garden of her home. She tried sometimes now to remember what that felt like, that feeling of being cocooned and cosseted; but try as she might she couldn't recapture it. Maybe she would today. Maybe by swinging higher and higher she'd feel as she'd felt then.

Her friend, her new friend, actually her only friend, hadn't lasted long. She used to like to listen to her stories but once Cara had been told that she couldn't tell her any of her stories any more her friend had found someone else to play with. Now her new friend was part of a larger group and Cara was excluded again.

She'd once gone with Di – she mentally stopped, then

checked, corrected herself – she'd once gone with *someone* to transport her horse to a new paddock. There were other horses in there and they'd hoped the horse would settle with them, make friends. But the other horses stood in a tight circle and ignored the new arrival. When the newcomer tried to come too close, one of them bit her and she ran away.

The girl who had been Cara remembered being told this was totally natural, that the other horses would simply get used to the stranger in their midst in time and accept her and they did. When she went a week or so later the new arrival was part of the same circle. It had only taken a few days for the breakthrough to happen. Sometimes the little girl playing alone on a swing wished she was a horse. Somehow she felt that no matter how long she stayed here, in this new school, in this new class, she'd ever be accepted like that.

The sun came out from behind a cloud. Now it was in her eyes dazzling her as she swung ever higher. From somewhere to her left she sensed, rather than saw, someone approach. It wasn't a classmate, this was someone approaching alone and all the children in her class played together. If any one of them had come to reclaim the swing from her they'd have made sure to come in a pack.

And this was obviously an adult too, the way their body blocked out part of the sun made that obvious. Maybe it was a teacher coming to tell her to be careful just like her Mum had done all those months earlier.

Instinctively she slowed, decelerating all the while as the adult moved closer and then stopped. Now Cara knew she was being watched and she didn't like it. It had been drummed into her time and again these last few weeks that she must not do anything to draw attention to herself, that she must remain quiet, must only speak when spoken to. It was unsettling to be the object of this sort of attention.

The little girl was slowing now to a halt and she decided to get off the swing and go and do something else. There was a pond at the edge of the playing field and she enjoyed going down there sometimes, watching the bugs on the surface or the small frogs as they hopped from one stone to the other.

Then the adult, a woman, spoke. She addressed her directly. And all of a sudden one world crashed into another and the little girl just stared back at her open-mouthed.

'Hello Cara.'

And now she could see who was standing there.

Di didn't, of course, use the name Cara had been given. Maybe she didn't even know the name she'd been told to use from that point on, the name all her new classmates and teachers called her.

Di had used her actual name, her real name from her old life.

Then there was a sudden commotion as some teachers arrived and the girl who used to be Cara was ushered away. When she looked back across the small playground she could see Di being ushered away too.

That night she tried to tell her mother, who was even paler, even more tight-faced than normal, what had happened that day in school, only to be told it hadn't happened at all. It was all in her imagination. She hadn't been playing on that swing, she hadn't been approached by anyone and no-one had used that name while talking to her either.

It was like everything that had happened in their lives before they came to this place, to their new house, to her new school. It was like everything that had happened before she met her new friends who weren't friends at all.

It was all in her imagination.

But it wasn't and she knew it wasn't but she didn't say so. She just kept quiet.

25

KIRINO HUGGED HER small holdall as she passed the virtually identical rows of houses.

Inside the holdall were the only possessions she'd managed to retrieve from her former life, a few items of clothing, some family photographs. One was of her father, long-dead, another of a mother she wouldn't now be seeing again for a long time, if at all.

There was also an old christening gown, her very own christening gown in fact. Her mother had given it to her when she'd first started on what had been called her travels, had bequeathed it to her as a sort of lucky charm, something to pack into a case or even a handbag, something that came with love from those nearest and dearest to her and which would keep her safe.

Kirino was still alive, so in one sense it had worked. But she felt very far from any kind of safety right now.

Kirino glanced sideways at Ros. She was doing her best and Kirino couldn't say she'd actually felt threatened at any time since she'd come under her protection. Even that strange interview conducted by that even stranger officer from Murder Squad had been more unsettling than directly threatening.

But events were now gathering momentum. In a short time – how short she didn't exactly know, but soon – she'd enter a courtroom and look across at a man she knew possessed no human heart because no-one could do the things he'd done and still claim kinship with the rest of mankind.

She'd be protected, she'd be looked after, she'd been assured of that and she believed their assurances. But the power of her former boyfriend had only multiplied in her mind in the time she'd been away from him. If she'd been frightened before, now she was terrified. The people looking out for her, those now caring for her were well-meaning, but how do you protect against something you can't understand?

Ros spoke into her mobile, updating someone, her boss Kirino assumed, on their progress. Nothing to report, she was saying. No problems.

Kirino tried to focus on something else, something beyond the trial, beyond Yaroslav. She tried to imagine the new life ahead of her instead, the life she'd been promised once all this was out of the way.

But if she could have done, she'd have stopped that car there and then, opened the door and ran. But she knew she couldn't. Masters had made that crystal clear. She'd crossed a line without really thinking about it when she first picked up that phone and made that first call to the police, begging for help. Now that help was there but it came with the longest of strings attached.

Kirino looked up as the car began to slow, stared at the paint peeling on the fascia boards of the house that was to be her home for the next few weeks. Home for her and home for Tyra too, and from that she took some comfort at least.

At least she wasn't going to be alone.

At least there was going to be one other person with her who'd be sharing all her insecurities and fears.

Masters should have been thinking about all sorts. He should have been thinking about Kirino, about Tyra, about the upcoming trial, the endlessly twisting story in which he was enmeshed. But he wasn't.

Masters was looking at Kirino as Ros now fixed her some coffee and as Tyra explained the little she'd discovered about the local area, as both women began checking and cross-checking their respective life stories. But all he was thinking about was an old lady in a nursing home.

Masters had taken it upon himself to talk to Mrs Scott about the death of her son. It was the second tragedy that had befallen her recently. Scott had arranged for her to be admitted to a care home following a stroke some six months earlier.

When he first heard that, Masters felt his heart lift. He had a vision of a frail old woman dribbling spit. Then he walked into the home, past a semi-circle of other residents grouped around a constantly blaring TV and went into a smaller room at the rear, a so-called library although it housed only a pitifully small collection of books. That's where he came across a thin, well-dressed woman desperately trying to cling onto what was left of her faculties, a woman who was about to wish she'd lost them completely.

It was a good day of course. She had bad days too, according to the avuncular owner of the home who was supervising the installation of a small bar in one of the leisure rooms when Masters arrived. Masters wanted to know how much she'd be able to take in, whether he should have someone in with him to help, one of the care assistants perhaps, or even one of the trained nurses who'd call in most days to check on the various ailments and afflictions.

But even as he asked the question Masters knew he'd never take up any offer of help even if any were to be proferred. What Masters wanted to know was how much she could absorb, but as he couldn't ask the question without confiding the details of all he'd come to tell her he kept quiet. He'd just have to play it as he saw fit.

Mrs Scott understood everything. The news of the death of her son while on police duty had been relayed to her almost immediately following the gruesome discovery of his tortured body. But she hadn't been told anything other than he'd simply died during the course of some covert operation.

Then she'd been told about the death of her daughter-in-law and by implication that of her first grandchild too. She'd received even less detail on those deaths. That wasn't due to any sort of procedure having to be observed. The officer who broke the news simply didn't know where to start. Anyway, in his opinion the old lady was better off not knowing. The old lady disagreed and made a request for the officer overseeing the case that had cost her son his life to meet her.

It could have been buried, they could have hidden behind the cloak of an ongoing investigation, promised those details sometime in the future when the investigation was concluded, made vague references to that investigation becoming prejudiced if too much detail was divulged. The hope would have been that the old lady would die before she had chance to press the matter much further.

All Masters could think about was the classic philosophical conundrum of the tree falling in a deserted forest. If there was no-one to hear it then did it make a sound? If Mrs Scott didn't realise she was being lied to, then did it matter? What difference would it make?

A few years earlier, Masters might have simply ignored the inconvenient request from an old lady in an out-of-town nursing home. But that was before his regular stint at his local chess club. And so Masters called the home and arranged the meeting.

Within two minutes he was telling her everything. He didn't name names but he did describe the type of observation on which Scott was engaged and the nature of the madman he'd come up against.

He told Mrs Scott about the abduction and torture of her daughter-in-law.

He told her that both had been carried out for reasons they couldn't at this stage even begin to understand.

He'd no idea why he divulged all he did. Maybe there was something of the confessional about it. He'd talked to no-one about what he'd seen that day, not even Ros, who'd seen the same horrors. Both knew those sights would be imprinted on their memories for ever, just waiting to trip them up at unguarded moments, so what was the point of rehearsing it all again? It would only make it the more real and they both knew that. The more they chewed on the totally indigestible the longer it would linger. Yet here he was, telling every detail of that day to the one woman in the world who should have been protected from it all.

Mrs Scott didn't flinch. She stared at him, level, almost neutral, as he ran through his story. Finally he finished and thanked God he hadn't taken the owner of the care home up on his offer to have someone sit in with them. He'd broken just about every rule in the book in the last half-hour.

Mrs Scott didn't move for a while. She didn't even look at Masters now. She just stared out of the window beyond the few residents walking slowly by.

Then she looked back at him.

'One promise.'

Masters knew what that promise would be even before she asked. It was a promise he'd have no trouble keeping. It was a promise he'd made himself.

'Have you any children?'

'One.'

'Boy or girl?'

'Boy.'

'On his life.'

Masters didn't hesitate for a moment.

'On his life.'

The old lady didn't say another word. She didn't need to. The contract might have been unspoken but it was a contract nonetheless and one that had been signed and sealed in blood.

The blood of her son, the blood of her daughter-in-law, the blood of her unborn grandchild.

Deliver their killers.

And from that point on, Masters knew he would dedicate his professional life to that end and that end only until it was achieved.

Back in the safe house, Masters looked at Tyra.

Which was the only reason he'd accepted all he'd agreed to one hour earlier.

In that self-same house, Jukes was now present but he may as well have been miles away. Maybe he was losing his grip, Ros didn't know. All Ros did know was he'd let her take Kirino through the final check on her legend alone, hadn't stepped in once, hadn't added or embellished any detail and that wasn't down to some late demonstration of total faith in her abilities.

For some reason Jukes was simply on a different planet right now. Worse, Tyra had also absented herself for large parts of what was supposed to be a joint briefing on one spurious pretext after another and he'd done nothing to stop her. From time to time Ros had caught glimpses of her outside, dragging on a cigarette.

Jukes knew the score every bit as well as she did. He understood the absolute importance of maintaining discipline at all times. Lives, the witnesses lives, sometimes their lives depended on it. Yet Tyra was being allowed to sit out the briefing, to wander around outside as if this really was some sort of student house as opposed to a secure location for two women at the highest level of risk.

Ros looked across at Jukes for not the first time since the

briefing began, fell silent for a few moments, again not for the first time, expecting him to step in and pick up the reins. But Jukes just continued to stare out of the window, seemingly unaware of Ros's voice in the background, the occasional question from Kirino, unaware of anything it seemed.

And Ros snapped. She was trying to conduct a professional operation and Jukes was away in some neverland of his own imagining, Masters was keeping his own distance for reasons presumably best known to himself and Tyra was still doing exactly what she wanted it seemed and if it was all unsettling her it was very definitely unsettling Kirino.

It was also sending out an unfortunate message as to the pecking order in the house. Kirino was confined to the sitting room running through every minute detail of her story with Ros. Tyra was free to roam, popping in when she wished, absenting herself when she chose. Only there wasn't a pecking order here and Ros decided to enlighten her missing client as to that fact.

Before Jukes could do anything to stop her, Ros quit the room and made for the small garden at the rear. She'd caught sight of Tyra heading that way a moment or so earlier. Coming into the garden itself she was met by the sight of Tyra and Masters huddled together, conspiratorially, almost intimately; and just for a moment she wondered.

Surely not?

Masters and Tyra? It was inconceivable.

There'd been instances before of officers and witnesses crossing the line, of professional relationships becoming something rather more personal but Tyra really did not seem his type.

Then again, this was Masters.

But Ros dismissed it. It was still inconceivable. And indeed it was, but what was to follow was even more so.

'Five minutes.'

That wasn't Masters, that was Tyra. And it wasn't just the words, the fact of the curt dismissal as she approached, it was the tone, a tone that warned Ros that Tyra was going to brook no disagreement.

Ros stared at her, momentarily wrong-footed, and Masters stepped in, almost – and extraordinarily for Masters – hesitant; his tone bordering on the supplicatory.

'Please, Ros.'

Ros kept staring at them, the anger that had been building inside her on the point of exploding and Masters must have sensed it too because he hurried on.

Tyra didn't even seem to see her. Ros had been dismissed and Tyra clearly believed that was the end of the matter. To the young girl in her care, her protector had quite clearly ceased to be of any interest or concern.

'Technically, she does outrank you.'

Ros kept staring at Masters. She heard his words but didn't take them in, at least at first. Tyra just glanced at the staring Ros but still didn't speak. She just nodded at Masters as if giving him permission.

Masters hesitated again. He knew how he'd felt, so could understand only too clearly just what Ros would be going through now too. Then Masters reached into his pocket and extracted a warrant card he himself had been handed just one hour earlier.

Ros stared at a police issue photograph on the warrant card, stared up at the young girl still dragging on her cigarette, now looking back at her with eyes that seemed almost amused.

Ros looked back at the card, read the name.

Detective Inspector Teresa James.

The eyes that once belonged to a frightened young girl called Tyra who'd trashed a snooker hall, eyes that apparently actually belonged to a high-ranking officer in the Met kept looking at her, waiting for her, as she'd waited for Jukes and Masters, to catch up.

I T WASN'T THE first funeral she'd attended and it wouldn't be the last. But this funeral, like that of the Kincaids, would haunt her forever.

Ros watched as the coffins were taken out of the hearses, trying to avert her eyes from the final, tiny, coffin, completely unable to do so, then she followed the rest of the mourners on into the church.

There'd been some debate with Scott's mother and Bella's family as to whether there should have been two coffins rather than three, whether Bella, the beautiful Bella, should have been buried with the child who'd been so savagely ripped from her womb. But in the end the family had decided that the infant – a boy – should be accorded his own resting place alongside his parents. To do otherwise was almost to deny his existence.

That left, of course, the question of whether he had actually existed in any meaningful sense. Medical opinion was that he would have been killed before he was actually ripped from the womb, but if it was ever a question that was posed it was ignored.

The child had even been named – Keiran, after his father. Some of his former colleagues had told Masters that Scott and Bella had deliberately not named their child as they were worried it might herald bad luck, as if they were counting their chickens in some way. No-one commented on the implicit irony. No-one needed to do so.

Ros looked towards the church as the bearers steadied themselves and as the three coffins began to move through the massed ranks of attending officers. Then Ros tensed as she saw the watching Masters. He held her stare, steady, but she could see it in his eyes. That flicker of unease.

Yaroslav hadn't been the only one playing what turned out to be a deadly game, and while their Ukrainian adversary wouldn't lose any sleep over the consequences, Masters would. Ros would make sure of it.

They hadn't spoken since the revelation in the back garden of that terraced house but speak they would.

For now Ros just moved past him and joined the other officers as they filed, silently, into the church. A frail, but determined-looking old lady led the congregation inside. Despite needing the aid of a stick, she walked alone. She'd soon be joining the rest of her family in whatever after-life awaited her and the expression on her face said it all. That day and that reunion couldn't come quickly enough.

The pub was old school. The sprawling Adamsdown estate it served was the same. Strangers were a rarity. Old school and new school didn't mix, if they attempted to do so someone usually got hurt and there were no prizes for guessing, in any tussle between those two factions, which would generally come out on top.

And aside from the general sense of menace inside that old-style boozer, there was also the six-foot seven-inch gent dressed head to toe in a cream suit decorated with a blue handkerchief and sporting – as a final touch – immaculately buffed Chelsea boots. One look at him and most unwitting visitors usually turned tail and made a sharp exit.

Eddie Faulkner hadn't had the easiest time of it since hanging up his leotard. The wrestling game had always been the last refuge of conmen and bandits and any money he had managed to squirrel away over the years had quickly been spent. He'd gone initially into security like so many of his contemporaries, standing guard on the door at nightclubs, forming part of a ring of steel around various public events.

But Eddie had brain as well as brawn. He'd started talking to some of the faces behind the scenes, to the men and women who now dispensed his daily bread. He hooked up with one woman in particular who'd inherited a security business from her late father and together they'd managed to crack an attempted sting by a competitor, uncovering along the way some minor villains who were working from the inside to bring down what was perceived as an outfit dying on its feet.

Eddie and the woman had married and it was a genuine love match too, no union of convenience. From that point on he'd been used by various organisations including on occasions the local police to gather information, to delve into areas deemed too sensitive for the normal forces of law and order.

Or at least, areas that would require inconveniences such as search warrants and Home Office permissions. Eddie didn't bother with those sort of considerations which made him ultra-useful.

Eddie also always got results which made him even more so.

'So who is it this time?'

Ros slid a photo across the chipped and stained table towards him. Her companion picked it up, studied the young girl intently.

'She looks trouble.'

'She is.'

'So what's she done?'

'Been fast-tracked through our recruitment programme for one thing.'

Eddie looked up at her.

'She's one of yours?'

He went back to the photo.

'Doesn't look it.'

Which was probably one of the reasons she'd been fast-tracked as Ros had already realised. She could only imagine how useful a recruit like Tyra – she couldn't now call her by another name – could be.

Most coppers gave off something. Some criminals called it a smell but it wasn't. It went deeper than that; a distance inbuilt in the space between themselves and anyone outside the force.

Tyra looked as if the only time she'd been near a police officer was to answer a charge. She looked, smelt indeed, authentic street, the genuine article.

'So what do you want to know?'

'Everything I can.'

'You can get access to her records yourself.'

'I want the stuff that's not on record. The stuff she'd never have given away in any sort of interview, stuff that wouldn't have come up in any sort of background check.'

'Such as?'

'I don't know.'

'Because you can't imagine what it might be or because you don't know if it even exists?'

'Both.'

'Meaning this could be a wild goose chase.'

'Yes.'

Eddie liked Ros. He always had. For a woman more used to spending her life in shadows, constructing imaginary lives based on evasions and half-truths she was one of the most straightforward and honest coppers he'd ever met.

Maybe that was why. Maybe she simply had her fill of lies in her day job. When it came to anything outside those normal everyday duties she was as straight as a die.

'And the reason?'

Now Ros hesitated and not because she didn't want to answer. She hesitated because she genuinely didn't know. She didn't know why she wanted to find out all she could about a client who'd turned out to be anything but, about a frightened kid who'd turned out to be not only a fellow professional but one who outranked and who'd certainly out-maneouvred her.

In one sense this was now none of her business. She would, as Jukes had reminded her, simply have to adapt to a changed circumstance as would they all. End of story.

Only Ros didn't feel it was end of story. Not by a long way.

Then Ros turned her attention to the second item on her shopping list that day.

Conor stood outside Ros's apartment complex and pressed the entry buzzer. A moment later her voice wafted over the intercom. That voice, usually cool to his ears, became positively arctic when she realised just who was outside the gate. She told him to come into the yard, that she'd meet him at the door to the apartment block.

Conor hadn't expected a warm and effusive hug or enquiries as to his health or a welcoming smile. But a simple cup of tea would have been nice. The day was cold and it had just turned a whole lot colder.

He should have just handed her the file he'd been deputed to deliver and go. Under any normal circumstances, on any normal day he would have done so too. He'd no wish to spend any longer than was strictly necessary in the company of his unsettling and often downright unfriendly colleague. He didn't particularly enjoy the waves of distrust that positively washed his way every time she looked at him. He also didn't want to spend any longer than was absolutely necessary in a department he regarded as staffed by little more than imitation social workers. And even that was dignifying their job description in his admittedly-jaundiced book.

He was aware there was probably a connection between

Ros's attitude to him and his attitude to their work but he didn't care. Just one more thing to add to an ever-lengthening list.

So why did he do it?

Why did he try and build that one small bridge?

Conor nodded down at the file he'd just handed over, another of their cases.

'There may be nothing in it. Jukes has seen him and he's not sure. Apparently he's a bit of a fantasy merchant, has got quite a bit of form. But he reckoned we should have a word just in case.'

The fantasy merchant in question would turn out to be just that. Someone who wanted a fresh start somewhere new and was inventing all sorts of spurious ploys to secure police help and money to do so. It happened. For every genuine case that might lead to a conviction there were at least ten that led nowhere.

In one sense it was a relief to talk about a case other than Yaroslav. It was all that had dominated the department for the last couple of weeks. But even now, talking about a different case altogether, it still hung heavy over the exchange. Maybe that was why he did it, Conor mused later. Maybe that was why he'd overstepped the mark.

'I didn't know.'

Ros looked at him.

'Masters – all that with Tyra – whatever her name is – .'

Conor paused again.

'I didn't know.'

Ros just kept looking at him for another long, long moment.

'You were in his department.'

Conor nodded.

'I was.'

'Once Murder Squad, always Murder Squad, isn't that what

they say? It's not like any other department, more like a band of brothers, once in you're never really out?'

'Believe me, don't believe me, no skin off my nose. But just for the record I didn't get any late-night phone calls from any old oppos and no-one tipped me the wink in any pub.'

Conor paused.

'I just wanted you to know.'

And then, suddenly, incredibly almost, there it was. A slight softening of the features, an even slighter, but definite relaxation of the lines around the mouth, the hint, slight again but definite, of a smile.

Then Ros took the file from his hand, nodded at him by way of a dismissal, closed the door and was gone.

As an annoyed and frustrated Conor exited, he barely registered the young woman bent by the gate examining the entry buzzers for the flats.

He certainly didn't pay any attention to her as she moved past him as he headed through the now-unlocked security gate and the concierge in his cubicle didn't look up from his TV either.

Meaning she'd had one piece of good fortune and had penetrated the first line of defence.

Now it was time for the next.

Ros had just put the file down on the small table she'd managed to squeeze onto her tiny balcony when the buzzer sounded again.

For a moment she wondered if it was Conor returning. Had she given off the wrong signal by that slight smile? Had he come back on some pretext or other, hoping to build on it in some way? Ros really hoped not.

If any sort of relationship – any sort of strictly professional relationship – was going to build between herself and Conor it was going to be at her pace and on her terms and very definitely not his.

Ros put a mug down on the file – stray gusts of wind had blown case notes all over the water on more than one embarrassing occasion in the past – then moved towards the buzzer.

As she walked the small distance across the open-plan living room to the door, the strangest sensation crept over her. In some way she'd felt as if she'd done this before, not here, but somewhere some association was stirring, something she couldn't pin down.

Ros shook herself. What the hell was she imagining now? She'd done this a hundred times, walked across the living room to answer the buzzer. Oskar had been an almost nightly visitor these last few months and, as she'd never let him have a key of his own, it had become an all-too familiar ritual.

Which ushered in another unwelcome possibility as to the identity of her new visitor. But how could it be? Even if Oskar had made it past the security gate – all-too possible as she knew – he knew in turn that he'd never get access to her actual apartment this way. He'd be much more likely to hang around and wait for her outside.

Ros activated the video link but her visitor had stepped out of range.

Ros hesitated a moment, then depressed the speaker button, spoke a simple greeting and waited for a response. But all she could hear was the sound of someone breathing.

Nothing else. Just the sound of someone outside, a flight or so down, on the other side of a locked door.

Not answering.

Just breathing.

And there it was again. And this time she couldn't dismiss it quite so easily either. There was that definite and highly curious sense of déjà vu, of having been enmeshed in something similar before.

That sense of waiting.

Of a world outside that had suddenly stilled, that was almost holding its breath.

The woman outside the door couldn't speak. She simply couldn't form the words.

She opened her mouth, goldfish-style, but nothing came out. Her breathing had deepened, had become shallower as her heart pounded inside her chest but she made no other sound.

And the reason was simple and she knew it.

What could she say?

How do you begin this sort of exchange?

Ros felt a sudden surge of anger. She'd no idea who was downstairs, who'd rung her entry buzzer, it could have been kids, they'd had them before, slipping into the courtyard when some resident drove away, their entertainment for the evening handed to them on a plate as they moved from apartment to apartment summoning resident after resident downstairs.

Or it could have been some drunk, a finger pressed on the wrong button, an incoherent figure leaning against the closed front door which may not even be their front door, it was just the same sort of colour.

Whoever it was they'd caught Ros on a bad day. And she flung open the door, didn't bother with the lift, just headed down the stairs to the front door, blood pounding in her ears as she did so.

Ros was a woman used to taking control, to being in charge. She organised the lives of those around her. Maybe that was why she'd taken the Tyra deception so personally. It undermined everything she'd put in place over the last few years, both in her personal and professional life. She'd become the puppet master in that time, had worked so hard to make sure she was no longer the hapless puppet.

Ros opened the door and looked out at a woman, older than herself by a good few years. The courtyard lights were behind her and her face was partly in shadow. Ros just stood on the step waiting for some sort of explanation and then one came.

It may only have been two words long but it was still all-too clear as an explanation and all-too devastating as well. The woman moved slightly, so more of her features were revealed, although even then Ros still didn't recognise her.

Then the woman said those two simple words, words she'd last heard years earlier, words that were to change everything.

'Hello Cara.'

S TANDING OUTSIDE THAT flat, in those few moments before the door in front of her opened, Di also had a sudden flashback.

It was a matter weeks after the murder of Braith. She was still in the first of the safe houses that had been provided for her. She'd been quite the model client up to then – as she seemed to be that night too.

She'd gone to bed at the usual time after watching the programmes she always watched. She'd eaten all that had been put in front of her. There was absolutely nothing remarkable about that evening, she'd made sure of it. Then, around two in the morning when her live-in escort/companion/guard was asleep, she'd slipped downstairs, opened the door and walked out into the night. She hadn't taken any change of clothes and only enough money to last her a few hours. It was all she was going to need.

Whether they realised that or thought she'd simply had enough, had maybe wandered down to the nearest river, jumped from the nearest bridge, she didn't know. She'd heard them talking, late at night, when they thought she wasn't listening. She knew she was officially at risk. They were concerned for her mental state, not only now in the immediate aftermath of what must seem like the most massive of betrayals, but later too. To find out that a new husband was not all he said, to discover that new husband was a different person altogether, would be enough to send even the most balanced of individuals over the edge.

Let alone Ditzy Di.

But add to that the realisation that all those she'd previously believed would be at her side for the rest of her life – her mother, her father, her siblings – would now be absent from that life perhaps forever, and it was easy to see why they were so concerned.

And then there was the guilt of course. She'd introduced death and destruction into a formerly happy family home. She'd initiated the sequence of events that had unleashed a horror that had then engulfed them all. Moreover, there was nothing she could do now that could put it right, as she'd also heard them say. But they were wrong about that.

Di now knew she could do one thing – aside from saying sorry. She could tell her mother, her father and her only surviving sister the truth. She could tell them what else she'd discovered on her nocturnal wanderings. It wouldn't make things right, it wouldn't turn back the clock and it wouldn't restore Braith to the family. But at least they'd understand she didn't get everything wrong.

She'd seen them as they'd walked into the church where Braith's funeral was being held. As good luck would have it the building was sited on a busy shopping street. If it had been out in the country she really would have had a problem. But it was easy enough to keep watch from the surrounding shops and cafés.

Cara was as she remembered of course and Mum looked much the same as well. She was pale, which was understandable, and seemed to have lost weight, which was even more understandable. But it was Dad who provided the real shock. At first she didn't even know it was him, she imagined that in his grief he'd decided he was unable to attend.

Then she recognised the stooped figure by the side of her mother. Before, he'd walked tall, his back ramrod straight. It was his proud boast that he looked the world in the eye. She knew he dealt with some pretty tough individuals in his line of work so he made it a point of principle always to look as if he wasn't to be trifled with. Now he looked like some aged incarnation of the figure she remembered from just a few weeks or so earlier. As if he'd lived thirty years in the last three months and maybe he had.

She waited until they came back out of the church. Briefly, they had to pause on the pavement as a car was brought from a parking space round the corner. There were double yellow lines outside the church and it would have attracted too much attention to park a car there for the duration of the service and, more importantly, to have to explain why to some zealous traffic warden. Far better to keep a low profile, not do anything to draw any undue attention.

Cara saw her first. And an instant smile lit up her face as she saw her approach, a smile that almost broke Di's heart.

Instinctively Di smiled back. Then her mother saw her, then her father looked up, his back, still stooped, but stiffening as he did so. Then the plain-clothes officers made to move towards her but by then she was already at their side and had scooped Cara up into her arms, holding her almost as if she was a shield, the little girl clinging onto her in turn.

The plain-clothes officers looked at each other, momentarily thrown. What the hell were they supposed to do, rip the young girl out of her arms? What would that do to all their efforts to keep a low profile, to not draw any undue attention to themselves?

'I've found something out. Something about Emmanuel.'

One of the officers, the one whose smile never quite reached her eyes, touched Di on the arm, but she didn't even look at her, just kept her eyes fixed firmly on her parents.

'Just let her go, yes?'

Di rolled on, refusing to be deflected.

'He wasn't what they said, he wasn't part of any kind of gang.'

'There's a café round the corner, let's go there, talk properly.'

But Di wasn't listening. She knew she'd have no more than moments, just enough time to say what she had to say. Cara, still clinging onto her for dear life, may buy her a little longer, but not much.

'He was involved with them, yes, like they said, but he wasn't one of them.'

Passing shoppers were beginning to give the huddled group of adults and the child with her face buried in one of the adult's shoulders, curious glances. The female officer looked across as the unmarked car came to a halt beside them. Pretty soon they'd be into damage limitation. She really didn't want to drag the young girl, probably crying and screaming, away from her elder sister, but the time was fast approaching when she'd have little choice.

'I knew it right from the start, right from when they first told me, I knew it couldn't be true. OK I didn't know everything about him but I knew I hadn't married a bad man.'

The female officer had now received and decoded an urgent silent signal from her companion in the unmarked car.

Get her away.

Get them out of there.

Whatever it may take, just do it.

And the female officer, whose smile wasn't now within a million miles of her eyes, put her hand much more firmly this time on Di's shoulder.

But Di still only had eyes for her parents.

'He's one of them. He's a policeman. He's not a criminal. He was working undercover, but no-one knew that, they weren't lying to us, they just didn't know themselves, not at first anyway, but it's true.'

And then, all of a sudden, all the fight seemed to go out of her. For the first time she looked at the female officer at her side and nodded.

It was over. What she'd come to do, she'd done.

Di looked back at her mother, her stooped father.

'I didn't fall in love with a bad man.'

Then Di, gently, took her sister's hand in her own, softly peeling back her fingers, caressing them all the while she did so. Then she watched as the female officer escorted her mother, father and sister into the waiting car while the male officer stood with her, waiting for back-up transport to take her away too.

Inside the car Cara looked back as they pulled away but no-one else did. Her sister looked after them but didn't wave. Then they turned a corner and she was lost from view.

Cara turned back which was when her father spoke for the first and only time that day. Without looking at anyone, without seeming to address anyone indeed, he just stared straight ahead through the windscreen and said:

'Well. Now we really are fucked, aren't we?'

By his side, the woman who'd been Elsha – and who'd already come to much the same conclusion – nodded in mute agreement.

Two days later and with the genie well and truly out of the bottle, the female officer who now didn't even attempt to smile, had provided a fuller explanation.

'It seems your son-in-law had been working undercover for a couple of years. In the nature of the way these things work that was only known to a handful of officers and those officers were all stationed back in Europol headquarters in The Hague. That means the story you were initially told was believed by the officers back here in the UK to be true.'

The female officer paused, ordering the sequence of events she'd only just been told herself in her mind.

'At the time your son-in-law was recruited he'd already been working for European intelligence for some two or three years but his new colleagues didn't, of course, know that. He joined those new colleagues on several missions in the UK and France all aimed, as you know, at returning errant wives, sisters or daughters back to their families in different countries, mainly in the Middle and Far East. Some of these were high-profile defections but all the evidence was that just as much care was taken over runaways lower down the social scale. This wasn't just about money, which was one of the reasons Europol has become increasingly interested in the activities of these outfits. Much of this was motivated by notions of honour.'

And infinitely more dangerous as a result, although the young female officer didn't say that, at least not yet.

'Emmanuel was able to forestall several of the planned snatches without attracting suspicion. Attempts often went wrong anyway. He was also able to feed back to Europol hugely useful information regarding the group for whom he worked, their methods and the main characters involved.'

The female officer paused.

Was any of this going in? She had absolutely no idea.

'As you know, Emmanuel and your daughter met in the Seychelles. Emmanuel had returned to his home island on a break and your daughter was visiting on holiday. It seems that meeting her marked something of a turning point. Apparently it happens quite often. An undercover officer falls for someone and all of a sudden living a life that's, effectively, a lie becomes insupportable. He staged a disagreement over some detail of one of the operations, a dispute about pay we believe, and hoped thereby to extricate himself as a disgruntled and disillusioned ex-member. People had left in that way before, it wouldn't have been that unusual.'

The female officer paused.

'Unfortunately in this case there was a complication. The girlfriend of one of his colleagues took his defection badly.

Apparently she'd always harboured hopes of something developing between the pair of them. She tracked him down to an apartment he was using in Paris. She was hoping to persuade him to return to the fold and presumably begin the liaison she desired. There seemed no reason, once he'd left the organisation, for any of the other members to follow him there so perhaps Emmanuel, as he himself has conceded, had become a little careless. The young woman broke in, clearly not meaning to leave until she'd achieved all she'd intended.'

The female officer paused again.

'Emmanuel managed to get rid of her easily enough. But he couldn't be sure she hadn't come across something incriminating. On his arrival in the UK to meet yourselves and the other members of his new family, he reported this encounter to the Europol representative but the general feeling was that his original cover had not been compromised.'

All the woman who had been Elsha could think was, what world is this?

What twisted version of reality had they all unwittingly entered?

'We now know that was incorrect. We know that, not only because of the shooting of your daughter but also because a message was received a day or so later making it clear that your son-in-law's real identity had been established and that the organisation of which he was previously a member would not rest until he and his immediate family had been eliminated as a warning to others who might be tempted to follow in his footsteps.'

The female officer had experienced the same difficulty in taking all this in on first being briefed. This was a world so far away from the one she knew, the world of normal policing, she also might well have been listening to a tale from some other universe entirely.

There had been some debate as to whether they should be told anything at all. The police back in the UK had only discovered all this themselves a day or so before Di, on one of her nocturnal trawls, happened on the true story. Had she not, it was possible it would all have been simply hushed up.

But the female officer believed they deserved as full a version of the story as was possible. In the months and years to come it would be the only thing they'd be able to look back on by way of a partial explanation at least of all that had happened.

Oddly enough it was the young girl – Cara, there at the insistence of her mother for some reason – who seemed to be the most successful at absorbing all this. The mother and father still just seemed out of it.

'Practically, this means we can't contemplate any sort of return to your previous life for any of you for some considerable time to come. It's possible that life is now closed to you forever.'

The female officer hesitated.

'This isn't just another criminal outfit. As I said, many people in this organisation aren't motivated by money at all making them even more dangerous than many of the outfits tracked by our colleagues in Europe. They believe in and hold to a deep personal code. Your son-in-law has broken that code and they believe that must be avenged. So for now we need to move you again and in the light of your daughter managing to track you down we need to invent new identities for you along with new names of course and new life stories.'

The female officer nodded at Cara.

'We'll need to find a new school in a new neighbourhood for you too.'

All Cara could think was, a new name. She was going to get yet another new name. She didn't like the name she'd been given in her new school. She'd never felt like a Pamela or even a Pam when they tried shortening it to make it more palatable. She just didn't feel like a Pam.

She liked her new name a lot more. When you said it out loud, in its full version, it was a bit of a mouthful.

Rosalind.

But when you abbreviated it then it sounded fine.

Ros.

Much like her visitor some few moments earlier, Ros also didn't speak. For the first time in her life she knew what it meant to be literally robbed of the power of speech. She'd read about it in the pages of novels but imagined it to be a storytelling construct. Now, looking out from her apartment door at a woman from another life completely, she knew she'd been mistaken. It was possible for words to shrivel, unspoken, on the vocal chords. All it needed was to espy a ghost where you believed none existed.

'He's found me.'

Di plunged straight in, no preamble, and for the first time since it had happened Ros was back to the aftermath of Braith's bleak funeral, her sister wasting no time then either, knowing that any moments she had were rationed, maybe feeling the same now.

'I don't know how. I've asked, but he won't say. He says it's not important, not now.'

Di took a step forward and instinctively Ros stepped back.

I don't know her name. It was all Ros could think. Of all the million and one questions roaring inside her head right now, all she wanted to know was the name her sister had now been given.

'He's found you too. I'd never be here otherwise. He wants us all to meet. You, me, him, Mum and Dad.'

Di faltered.

'He wants to make everything right.'
Di nodded at her.
'For all of us.'

28

ROS TOOK A seat opposite Jukes, the first time she'd been in his office and the first time she'd walked past the Mega-Bed Sale sign – still missing its B – since the revelation of Tyra's undercover sting. Jukes had suggested, politely but with steel, that Ros might like to take some time out. She was due some leave anyway.

Ros had accepted the implied instruction. It was either that or inflict some serious grievous harm on something or someone. And as she'd walked away from that terraced house and Tyra, feeling her eyes watching her all the way, she really didn't know if she'd be back.

Then she'd had that late-night visit from that most unexpected of faces from a past she'd been told to forget. And then she really did need some time out.

Ros spent a few days travelling, hopping on one train after another, moving from one destination to the next. There was no grand plan at work, the only aim being to keep moving. Ros had always made every major decision in her life on the move. She had no idea why she needed the sensation of motion to accompany any choice. When she was moving it was as if her mind began to move too. Then she could pore over options, debate possibilities. And the upshot was she'd returned.

Jukes had started talking almost before she'd sat down. He'd obviously decided not to waste time in attempting to explicate all that was now past and incapable of being changed. Jukes always was the quickest to respond to any changed circumstance, the least likely to waste time and effort in contemplation of times past.

'We still have Kirino. She knows nothing about her companion other than the story she's been told up to now. As far as she's concerned, everything is as it always has been. And being with Tyra has been a positive experience. She now quite clearly feels that she's no longer alone, that the entire weight of the edifice that's being constructed isn't just on her shoulders any more.'

'Even if it is.'

Jukes acknowledged the qualification with a slight incline of the head.

'Kirino will still testify. She'll remain unaware of her companion's real identity and the reason for this subterfuge until after the trial. She may even remain unenlightened after that. It depends how things work out. So she's going to need us before the trial, during it and after. She's going to require all the usual support we offer anyone in her position in fact.'

'So how's it going to work?'

Jukes hesitated. He knew at some stage – and probably at some early stage in her return to the fold – that Ros would cut through what he and she both knew was his habitual bullshit and latch straight onto the real matter of the moment.

'This charade. How's it going to play out?'

Jukes hesitated again, expelled a silent, relieved breath, then started to explain.

Earlier that same day, standing on the small waiting area watching the water taxi that connected Penarth to Cardiff power towards her, she'd sensed him, behind.

She'd expected some sort of approach. She thought he might have left it another day or so but since when could you second-guess anything Masters might do? These last few weeks had shown her, if she hadn't realised it before, that the man revelled in the unpredictable.

Partly that was habit. It was a time-honoured tactic to unsettle anyone of a criminal leaning.

Mainly it was the man himself.

The water taxi came in, the pilot reversing expertly until the craft was alongside the dock. Portable stairs were hooked from the craft to the landing station and a couple of passengers disembarked. Ros moved along the steel steps and headed for an open deck at the rear. No-one else was venturing outside today, most were grouped inside, around the bar.

Masters moved after Ros, settled next to her as she looked out over the wash as the pilot gunned the engine heading for the midpoint of the river before continuing on.

'I didn't know.'

Ros didn't reply.

That was what Conor had said too. Maybe it was a default reflex drummed into everyone in Murder Squad.

'Not at the start anyway, the whole thing was sanctioned at a much higher level at the same time as it was decided to keep even the operational officers in the dark. The reasoning was that if she fooled even us then the whole thing really did have a chance of working.'

Ros looked out at the converted warehouses that lined that stretch of the river, at a spot where the currents converged called Dead Man's Pool, a cauldron of churning water where bodies that had gone in the water for whatever reason, crime or suicide, were traditionally washed up close to the shore.

All she could think about now was a name.

Scott.

Yet another name to be added to the list.

The Kincaids.

Now Scott.

Those two were the most memorable, but there were others of course. As well as those living lives of sometimes not-so-quiet desperation.

'You can walk away from all this and maybe you will. To be honest I was tempted myself. But talk to Jukes, don't hear it from me, let him explain and then decide.'

Masters paused.

'And yes, before you ask, he does seem to have been in on it for longer than us. He was probably under strict instructions to keep it all on a need-to-know basis but he's a slimy little fucker, always has been. I knew him when we both started out, there's always been something about him, something hidden, deep down, that you really wouldn't want to dig up.'

He was building bridges. Or at least, trying to. She knew it and he knew she knew it. That wasn't really the point and they both knew that as well. The point was that he was trying.

Because this mattered. Maybe because they mattered too in some way, but that was nothing to do with the evening when they'd all-too briefly connected. It was all to do with Scott. Everything would be from now until the day the Ukrainian stood in the dock. Then another face and another name would take his place.

Then, suddenly, her mind focused on something else. On a nearby bridge, looking out over the water, not looking at anything, just staring sightlessly upstream, was Conor.

By Ros's side, the same honeyed tone dribbled into her ear.

'Don't do anything hasty. Kirino is still your charge. With her, with all we've planned, we can still nail this one. If you remain on the case it stands an even better chance of success because she trusts you. She likes you. To change the handler at this late stage would cause all the wrong kind of complications.'

Ros kept looking at the sole figure standing alone on the bridge. As she did so, Conor pushed himself away from the guard rail and moved on.

Now her companion's tone altered, ever so slightly, a new and harder note beginning to creep in.

'But if you are getting out, do it now. Don't waste any more time. If we need a new handler we need to know and we need to know quickly.'

Masters nodded at her as he stood, another stop reached, more passengers now disembarking, Masters joining them.

'Your call.'

Ros remained seated at the rear of the craft as new passengers embarked, as the steel steps clattered and clanked back and forth and as the taxi churned away again and continued on upstream.

Ros stayed in her seat, calmer now. Her head, previously spinning almost beyond control, was spinning no longer.

Because she now knew exactly what she had to do.

Conor walked away from the bridge and cut across the highway. He'd intended to head over to Rumney and a badlands estate sinking into the estuary mud on which it had been unwisely constructed some couple of decades earlier. He had a client there, encamped on the top floor of a council-run flat complex due to give evidence in a drugs case in Newcastle in a few weeks time.

It was all relatively low-level stuff but threats had been made and the client was of a nervous disposition. He'd been moved the few hundred miles south purely as a precaution. He'd also been told to stay inside and only open the door to officers from the protection unit and pizza delivery drivers, an instruction he had no trouble in observing to the letter. From his top-floor eyrie he looked out on pavements stained with vomit and excrement as well as the blood of victims of various late-night muggings. This was one client who was never going to break the terms of his mutually-agreed contract with the protection department.

On an impulse, Conor paused by a fast-food café opposite a row of businesses encamped in some old railway arches. In that momentary hesitation, he was lost and he knew it. And instead of turning left he cut right, through a rat-run of alleys and on into a square he once called home.

It was the strangest thing. At one time he couldn't wait to get away from the place. Now he found himself returning to it more and more. And for what? It was hardly the view. Mattresses still littered the communal walkways, debris from overturned dustbins was still strewn all over the playground, towels still hung up in windows in place of curtains, dogs still roamed, unchecked and unfettered, among the concrete alleyways in the sky.

All he'd done while he was growing up here was dream of getting away. And he'd done it. He'd graduated from a local college, had secured not just a job but a career, had traded on his looks and youthful wide boy charm to ensnare a posh girl with genuine class. Certainly enough class not to turn her nose up when he took her along to meet his aged old Mum that first time even if she'd, gently but firmly, steered all future meetings in the direction of an expensive local hotel where they served an equally expensive afternoon tea.

If you'd told him then how spectacularly it would all go wrong, he wouldn't have believed it. Everything he touched in those days turned to sold in the words of another old friend of his who now made a fairly spectacular living as a bond trader.

And he had the law on his side too and not just the Black Rat version of the law either, this was the copper-bottomed, gold-plated variety, Murder Squad, the elite of the elite, something of a law indeed unto itself.

Now he was trying to find the pattern underneath the happenstance. He was trying to trace the link from those days to these. If he could, then maybe he could pinpoint the moment when everything that was good turned to everything that was not and if he could pinpoint that moment then maybe he could work out how to reverse the momentum and make everything right again.

Conor wasn't going on the overseas trip with his wife and her companions after all. His gesture with the airline ticket had pretty quickly been revealed as the cheap stunt it was in truth. A few late changes of itinerary and a couple of additions to the schedule had pushed the price of that particular trip way beyond anything he could remotely afford.

Unless – and now he exercised a belated act of will, refused to contemplate even going where previously he'd been unafraid to tread. He'd made his excuses to Francesca and she'd pleaded pressure of work on his behalf to her friends. They made all the right sort of sympathetic noises but he could see the quiet gloating in their eyes.

What hurt even more was her willingness to accept his absence. He hoped he was wrong, but he feared that might have been due to her now being a free agent on the upcoming trip. There were to be other free agents too, including Lahr, the storyteller from the dinner party who'd just ditched the latest of the girlfriends apparently. Maybe that explained the small smile that played across Francesca's face as she told him not to worry, that they'd have a trip later in the year, just the two of them, to make up for his missing this one.

It was the second small smile he'd seen recently and he was unable to decisively decode either. He didn't know whether he'd witnessed a momentary weakness inside Ros when he'd called in on her, unexpectedly, that evening or whether she was also looking out at him with amused and contemptuous eyes too.

And, once again, there it was.

That word.

Unless…

Conor paused, looking at the two tower blocks looming above him, both pointing towards the sky in what he'd always thought resembled a giant fuck-you gesture to the rest of the city.

And now Conor did allow himself to think about it. To think the unthinkable in fact, everything he'd done his level best not to do for the last couple of weeks.

And all the time an old proverb he'd first learnt here on this very square reverberated inside his head.

You may as well, an old lag had once remarked to him, be hung for a sheep as a lamb.

The complex was in one of most fashionable postcodes of the capital, the throw of a stone – if one threw stones in such an area – from the Ritz. On the ground floor was one of the most famous restaurants in London although being a resident didn't apparently guarantee preferential seating. That much Ros had gleaned from the friendly face on reception as he waited for Masters to answer the phone. Then he'd broken off to relay Ros's name to the owner and occupant of Apartment 685.

The receptionist had paused as the owner and occupant of Apartment 685 hadn't responded immediately. For a moment the receptionist wondered whether he'd been heard, whether he should repeat the message, but then Masters had cut across, telling him to send his visitor up, that he'd be waiting for her by the lift.

Whatever else Masters might have expected that Sunday morning, he clearly hadn't been expecting company.

Masters led Ros into an apartment with a direct view of Green Park. Down in the communal gardens a lone gardener tended manicured bushes and shrubs. Ros didn't even begin to wonder how an officer in the force, even one of his rank, could afford an apartment in a complex like this, let alone use it, as he quite obviously did, as just a weekend retreat. The question would have been naïve in the extreme and she knew it. Besides she wasn't here to enquire into his personal circumstances but to advance a private matter of her own.

'I'll work with you. I'll make sure Kirino isn't spooked. I'll do whatever's necessary to maintain the charade you and Jukes have planned.'

His eyes never left hers.

'And in return?'

Ros slipped a piece of paper across an outsize table towards him. Either Masters did a lot of entertaining or he moonlighted as a surgeon. Or practised some other dark art.

Masters studied the name on the paper, then looked up at Ros.

'So who is he?'

'That's what I want to find out.'

Ros nodded at the name of the man who'd changed so much in her life and about whom she still knew next to nothing.

Previously that hadn't really mattered. Now it was absolutely vital she find out all she could. She had no way of penetrating the veil of secrecy that would inevitably cloak this character but she had no doubt Masters could.

A man who maintained an apartment in one of the most prestigious blocks on one of the most prestigious streets in one of the most prestigious areas of one of the most expensive cities on the planet, and who did all that on a Detective Chief Inspector's salary had to have done the odd deal with the devil in his time.

D I WASN'T SURPRISED to discover that Ros wasn't married. In fact she wasn't surprised to find absolutely no evidence of any sort of permanent relationship at all.

Just the one toothbrush in the bathroom. No photographs showing her with any significant other. Ros's apartment was much like her own in fact. Functional, barely-lived in, as if the occupant was passing through on their way to somewhere else. Their homes closely resembled both their lives in that and in every other respect.

It would have been the same stumbling block for them both, she imagined. Always the same obstacle to be surmounted, the same test they'd both inevitably fail. How could they not do so? She'd gone out with men, quite a few men and for the first night or so it would be fine. Then, when things began to deepen a little, when the pace began to relax, when they began quite naturally to luxuriate in each other's company, the questions, always those same fateful questions, would start.

Where do you come from?

What do you do?

Where were you born?

What do your parents do?

Where did you go to school?

What was your first job?

Tell me everything.

Which was natural. Totally normal. Di would have wanted to know all about the lives of those who might become significant others too, so why shouldn't they wish to know the same about her?

At first she thought it would be simple. After all she'd become well-practised over the years in repeating the details of the life story she'd memorised. And so she trotted it out. The problem being that while that was fine for every other sort of acquaintance, even for a few fairly close friends, it was different, totally different when it came to a lover.

Maybe she was old-fashioned. But she just couldn't help it, to her a lover meant love. In the time-honoured version of the word.

Someone to love, someone to cherish, if not necessarily obey.

But very definitely someone to trust.

But how could you do that? How could you enter into a loving, trusting relationship when it was based on a lie? When, right from the start, you yourself were telling a lie? When you were in the arms of a man you wanted to love and every word you were telling him was a giant fabrication?

And they knew too. They always did, they always picked up on the slight hesitation in the voice which gave her away. It would start with an amused enquiry – what's she holding back, what isn't she saying?

The more she insisted she wasn't holding anything back and was hiding nothing, the more they pressed, still amused – in the early days anyway – convinced it could be nothing awful, some embarrassing former lover perhaps, some indiscretion of which she was illogically ashamed.

It couldn't be anything else. She was too normal, too nice. And she was. That had been her downfall. She'd seen the best in a man who'd seen the worst in others. And she'd paid the price.

Then, as she continued to hesitate and evade, the mood

would change, amusement would give way to irritation and then irritation would give way inevitably to mistrust.

And she couldn't blame them. Who would want to be with someone who was always holding back? And then she would change too as the strain became too acute.

And then it would end as it always ended, sometimes in a screaming match, sometimes – and this was worse somehow – in an awkward parting at a train station or a bus stop with a mumbled agreement that one or other would call or text, an arrangement both knew neither would keep.

She'd wanted it lifted from her shoulders for so long. That cloud to disappear. But how could that happen? Who could she ever talk to openly, freely, without fear of entrapping someone else in the nightmare?

In her mind there was only one person and that was the man in the same nightmare, the man she'd fallen in love with and had married even if she didn't know absolutely everything about him, the man she'd never been able to forget, the man she still couldn't forget after all this time and despite everything that had happened.

Emmanuel was the only one who'd ever properly understand what she'd been through, was still going through indeed, but he was lost to her forever – or at least so she thought.

Then, all of a sudden, there he was.

The ritual was always the same even if the setting, a mile or so from their latest house, still felt alien and probably always would.

Friday afternoon, three o'clock, the last of the small children collected, everyone looking forward to the weekend which was just about to kick off with an after-work drink in the local pub. It was a much-cherished routine.

No-one got overly drunk, misbehaved or attempted to go

home with anyone else. It wasn't like that. It was just a way of winding down after the week, chewing over some of its key moments, looking forward to the next, swopping plans for the couple of days ahead.

The man who had once been Macklyn never went. They always tried to get him to go along, to join in and he always made sure he declined with humour and grace. It had taken a long time but he liked his new career, liked his colleagues and didn't want to do anything to upset them.

When they pressed a little too firmly, he mumbled some half-excuse about having to get home, hinting at some situation or other and they, nice people that they were, would immediately back off.

But he watched them head away with real envy in his eyes. At heart he'd always been a social animal. He'd have loved to sit in that pub with them, drink with them, laugh and joke with them but how could he risk it? That way he'd have relaxed and how could he ever do that?

Aisha brought him the last of the books. She was always the last to leave, her mother waiting patiently for her at the door. The little girl had been the quietest in the class when she'd first arrived and he'd taken special pains with her and it had paid off.

The breakthrough had come on a trip to the local airport. He'd stayed up half the previous night when his wife was asleep and fashioned thirty pieces of red card into makeshift passports. One of the check-in staff at the airport had gone along with the role-play and had stamped all the new passports with immigration and destination stamps.

Aisha had been given a stamp from Nigeria, a country she'd only left a few months earlier in the company of just her mother, her father having stayed behind for reasons no-one seemed to know. Aisha had clung onto her makeshift passport and stamp all the way through the rest of the trip and, on the way back home, had told him a little of her old home far away across the sea and of her old school too.

From that day on he'd had a shadow. Everywhere he went she was there, helping put out the books, even helping tend to some of the very young children when they fell over in the playground. Her reading and writing was coming on well and her social skills, just as important at her tender age and given her difficult background, were improving all the time too. He'd made a connection with her, and Aisha was turning into a real success story as his headteacher, a woman some ten years younger than himself, had pointed out.

Which made it all the more important that he never – ever – let down his guard.

He knew the stakes that were involved here. He knew the way the minds of those who'd already wrecked his life worked. They could have gone after his son-in-law alone all those years ago, could just have been content with him, but they weren't.

That was too clean, too quick. It's what made them so terrifying. They'd first take those nearest and dearest to his new family – as they'd taken Braith – and as they would probably still be trying to take Di – before turning their attention to the main quarry.

That main quarry, so far as he could glean, was still alive. It was possible, again from the little he could glean, that this situation would still endure even after his death. The people Emmanuel had wronged had long memories and he'd broken what they seemed to regard as some sort of sacred code.

So the man who had once been Macklyn thanked little Aisha for all her help, watched as she skipped across the classroom to her waiting mother, then he turned off the lights, exited the school gates, said goodbye to the caretaker who was waiting to lock up before turning right along the street and heading for home instead of turning left with the rest of his colleagues and heading for the pub.

The woman who had once been Elsha knew what had changed. At one time she didn't think anything would or could. She believed that as well as living in a place that was always going to feel like some sort of temporary billet, as well as watching her remaining daughter turning in on herself more and more, becoming ever more isolated in her new schools and their new communities, she was also going to have to watch her husband spiral down into an inevitable decline.

It was depression of course. Not the sort of depression you get when you've had a bad day, when it's rained for weeks, when a planned holiday falls through or when you've bumped the car.

This was depression of the clinical variety. This was depression occasioned not only by the violent loss of a child, enough reason in itself. This was what happened when you're wrenched from a life you'd laboured long and hard to bring into being and forced to live another and totally different life instead.

And there was no counselling that could heal that wound. This wasn't a case of simply adapting to a changed circumstance in the way you'd have to if you'd suddenly lost your sight or the use of a limb. This involved the complete destruction of a previous personality as well as the assumption of another that was never, in a million lifetimes, going to replace it.

But then she'd become the unwitting key to what was his partial recovery at least.

The woman who'd once been Elsha had struggled so hard to keep the family together, to provide some sort of focus and reason to keep going. She'd taken over many of the roles he used to perform, the roles he used to take pride indeed in performing.

She negotiated with tradesmen over work that needed to be done in their various new homes. She met with teachers and discussed with them the girl who'd once been Cara. She decided what they'd do at weekends, where they'd take the growing girl, what family treats and small breaks they could still permit themselves to enjoy in the light of their suddenly and inevitably-straitened circumstances.

The days when people such as themselves were guaranteed a lifestyle and income commensurate with the one that had been taken from them were long gone. They were now on little more than subsistence, designed to keep them ticking over until the day one or other or both of them found a job. As she was trained to do absolutely nothing save look after a home and bring up her children, and as he was now debarred from even tangential contact with the industry he'd worked in all his life, that day seemed a long way off.

And she'd cracked. She'd tried holding it all together, she really had, but the strain was simply too great. She couldn't even look at her youngest daughter, she was so far removed from the cheeky, happy, little girl she always saw in her mind's eye when she thought of her; the girl she was just a second or so before that clap of thunder that wasn't a clap of thunder at all.

Conversation with the man who'd once been Macklyn was even more of a trial, not because of what was said but because of what was not. Neither dared even approach all that had happened to them, so they talked of other things instead.

The weather.

An item in some magazine.

A book she'd started but hadn't yet finished, there were countless such abandoned books all over the house.

And all the time she watched his back as it bent ever more out of shape, watched as he became ever more hunched, ever more stooped.

One evening she'd remained sitting in her chair when he went up to bed. She didn't join him. She couldn't. She didn't actually put it to the test by trying to stand up but she seemed to have lost the use of her legs. Or maybe she simply couldn't be bothered trying to use them any more.

She remained in the chair as the central heating clicked off on the timer, growing colder and colder as the night wore on but she didn't seem to care about that either. She didn't do anything, just stared at the far wall which was where the girl who'd once been Cara found her the next morning when she came down to fix her own breakfast as she always did in those days before going off to school.

The little girl ran upstairs, shook her father awake. He came down and tried talking to her, but as well as apparently losing the use of her legs she seemed to have lost the power of speech as well, or maybe she just couldn't be bothered speaking any more either.

She'd been visited by a doctor summoned by the police contact they'd been told to call in the event of any sort of emergency and had been immediately hospitalised. Which was when things began to change.

In retrospect it was all so blindingly obvious. All of a sudden he was needed again. It wasn't just that the little girl needed looking after, it was the fact she herself had stopped trying to fill the void.

It was the smallest of steps he took by way of a response, little more than opening a drawer and taking out a saucepan and heating up a tin of beans for their tea, choosing a book to take into the hospital with them on their next visit. But that small step led to more steps until he announced some months later that he'd seen an advert in the local library and was thinking of retraining as a primary school teacher. Apparently there was a shortage of male teachers in that field and he wanted to give it a try.

The upside was he now had something to do and while he was still a long way away from the man he used to be at least he'd moved on from the creature he'd become.

The downside was it all seemed dependent on her remaining locked in her very own downward spiral. He seemed to need that to feel as if he had a purpose once again.

She didn't know what would happen if she managed one day to lift herself from the bed she now occupied almost permanently, if she re-engaged with the people around her again, whether that would wreck the fragile recovery he'd enjoyed. But as she didn't want to lift herself from that bed and had no wish to re-engage back with anything then it didn't really matter because they'd never find out.

Ros had grown up hating them. How could they have expected anything else? Part of her knew it was unfair, all that had happened was hardly her parents' fault. But the rights and wrongs of any given situation hardly matter when you're a teenager. All that matters is the impact on your life, never mind the reason for things being as they are in the lives of others.

Walking out at the age of fifteen and disappearing for a full six months, living where she could, with whoever she could find, was perhaps a bit extreme but she didn't care. Not then. Not about anything.

Every now and again she wondered what they were doing, what steps were being taken to track her down, whether she was going to walk down a street the next day only to be stopped by some police officer, her photo in his hand.

But no-one did anything of course. She was a girl from a fractured background who'd walked out on an old life to begin a new life somewhere else.

Same old, same old.

There was a complication in her case in that she was

still officially living inside a protection programme but that programme was always, at its heart, optional. Again, how could it be anything else? The protectors could do nothing if the protected person chose, as she seemed to have done, to remove herself from their care.

Years later she herself would trot out the various reasons why a protection programme may be terminated reciting the different causes by rote.

Security could be compromised by the behaviour of the witness.

The witness may violate the rules laid down in the original memorandum.

The witness may refuse to give evidence at trial.

The seriousness of a threat against the life of the witness may have lessened or be no longer relevant.

In reality what could anyone do when faced with a teenager bent, so it seemed, on self-destruction anyway?

How can you protect someone who doesn't want to be protected?

Then Ros had been found. She'd been picked up in a raid on a basement club in Kilburn, just one of a number of wayward and underage kids. Once her identity had been established – both her real and assumed identities in her case – she'd been transferred from the police station to a local hotel. She'd been kept there for a night or two before a protection officer from the local force came to talk to her. He was old-school, firm but kind. He didn't act the heavy-handed authority figure as some of them had in the past and didn't insist she return home to her parents either.

He had teenage children of his own. He knew better than most that at a certain point in the life of a teenager, parental control was little more than a fond illusion.

He'd come with practical matters in mind instead. They

hadn't been able to do this before given Ros's sudden and unannounced flight from home, from the care of her parents and from the programme inside which she'd lived for the last ten or so years. But now they'd found her they could observe at least one piece of outstanding protocol.

Ros was handed a letter giving her the statutory twenty-one days advance notice to terminate her participation in the programme.

Ros signed the form straightaway. It should have felt like some cloud lifting but it didn't. Something else happened instead. Sitting in the foyer of the anonymous hotel that hosted their meeting, with business-type guests checking in all around them, Ros suddenly asked the old-school protection officer a question she didn't even know was in her mind.

Was there ever a case she wanted to know, could it ever happen, that someone growing up inside a protection programme could, later in life, become a protection officer themselves?

If the old-school gentleman was surprised by the question he didn't show it. He just looked at her for a moment, a smile playing on his lips, a smile that very definitely reached his eyes.

Then he leant forward and told Ros that not only could it happen but perhaps it already had.

Years later Ros would wonder if that was more prophecy or prediction than anything else, but by then the old-school gentleman had retired from the service and emigrated abroad and she never had the opportunity to press him further.

Ros had never thought too much about the obvious subtext to it all, that far from embracing a future, she was actually going on a journey into the past; trying to understand in the lives of others something about her own life and her own experience of a situation thrust upon her at an age when she could do little but simply accept it.

But even if she'd never actively considered it, she knew that others would certainly do so. Which was when she'd reinvented herself again, taken up her first posting in a city where no-one knew her, erasing all trace of her past life aside from the name she'd been assigned and other details held on only the most secret of records.

That was all made possible by the extreme nature of the threat that had dogged her and her family most of her life, a threat that even now could not be said to have gone away. It was always going to be safer for her and for those around her if her real identity, her actual history and back story remained hidden from view. And so for the last few years she'd worked with colleagues who knew nothing about her save the few facts about herself she chose to present to them.

And they were few and very far between. She was in her twenties, she was single, she was dedicated to her job and a good and effective handler. If anyone wanted to find out any more they were going to have to dig deep and so far no-one had cared enough to make the effort.

Which had its upside and its downside. She preserved her cherished privacy. She was untroubled by questions from the concerned or the curious. She lived a life apart. But living that life apart meant she had no-one to consult at times like these and no-one with whom to discuss developments such as the one that had now landed in her lap along with the sudden appearance of a sibling she could barely remember.

Who was this figure who'd suddenly reappeared out of a dim and distant past? Could Ros trust her? She was certainly who she said she was, matters of identity were simple enough to check. But what had really impelled her to get in touch after all this time?

Was she acting of her own volition or at the behest of someone else? Who was this ex-husband who'd made contact after all these years and what game might he be playing? The one thing Ros had learnt, even in her relatively short time in her new calling, was that there was rarely anything in this field as heart-warmingly simple as a happy ending. And she doubted this would end happily now.

30

A FEW DAYS later, Ros once again made the two-hour train journey from one capital to another. She took a tube to Monument, then crossed London Bridge looking down on a river clipper as it passed underneath. Another clipper approached from the opposite direction, its klaxon horn blaring as it did do.

One had obviously beaten the other to the only navigable section under this particular landmark and was luxuriating in a victory that might have been small but had quite obviously enlivened a day no end.

Maybe it was the same in all lines of work. No matter who you were, prince or pauper, river captain or rent collector, there was nothing like putting one over on someone else. And if that someone else was someone you worked with day-in, day-out, then victory was all the sweeter.

Ros moved off the bridge, looked down the street. Borough Market was just around the corner. Now it was time to see whether that was true for protection officers as well as princes, paupers, river captains or rent collectors.

When she'd first lived in this city as a runaway teenager, Ros used to spend each and every morning in that market, a place renowned for its food stalls. She'd never return to her succession of squats with much more than an out-of-date sandwich. Any attempts to even begin to follow any of the recipes thrust at her by enterprising stallholders always ended in disaster. She'd always been as adept at cooking as reverse parking. Why she loved the place so much she had no idea.

Maybe it was just street theatre at its purest with the

stallholders continually proclaiming their wares, their audience assessing and judging each offering in turn.

Or maybe she was just a plain and simple voyeur. Maybe it was like most things in her life. She liked to be in a situation where she could look but had no need to touch; to be involved without necessarily having to participate.

Ros crossed the road, joined an already large throng of people heading in the same direction. Now she had the market in sight but she wasn't on this occasion following the crowd streaming inside the various entrances towards the already-bustling stalls. Ros was looking at a small café serving Spanish breakfast fare to a discerning clientele instead.

Sitting by the window on a high seat, his food in front of him on a bar that ran the whole length of that self-same window, was Masters.

As she seated herself next to him Ros caught the unmistakable whiff of truffles. Masters was eating a simple breakfast of boiled egg mixed with the supposed delicacy. Ros told him it stank to high heaven and so did he. Masters told her it was considered a treat in Seville. Ros pointed out they weren't in Seville and to her truffles were an abomination. Social niceties and the pleasantries of the day dispensed with, the real business began.

'I want to be there.'

Ros paused as Masters looked at her.

'Correction, I want myself and Conor to be there.'

Masters kept looking at her.

'There's no way this is going to work if we're not.'

Masters still didn't respond.

'From everything I've heard about this character he's bright. Twisted, but sharp. Look at the lengths Tyra's had to go to. One false move, one wrong step and the whole thing would have gone belly-up and it's the same with the next step too. If I'm not there and if Conor's not with me, if we're not doing exactly what we should be doing, then he's going to wonder why and the minute he starts doing that is the moment you can kiss goodbye to any chance of bringing any of this off.'

Masters bent his head to his eggshell, finished – mercifully so far as Ros was concerned – the last of his evil-smelling concoction. When he lifted his head, Ros caught a pungent blast as he replied softly, even insidiously. Something told Ros it wasn't accidental. Nothing Masters did or said ever really was, the odd lapse, courtesy of a tortured officer and his wife and unborn child, aside.

'There's something cold right at the heart of you isn't there, Ros?'

Ros just stared back at him, her turn to remain silent as Masters dabbed his mouth with his handkerchief.

'Something controlling. Controlled. Something that never allows you to give way. I saw it the very first moment I met you. It's almost like there's some sort of self-censorship at work deep inside, something that goes beyond nature or instinct, a gap between everything you think and all you say.'

Masters paused, examined his handkerchief which was immaculate, no trace of the egg. Ros remained in supreme control, perhaps making his point for him. As Masters probably intended.

'I've only ever come across it before in senior politicians – or maybe high-ranking diplomats. That same sense that they have to be careful of each and every action, have to watch every single word. It's curious and, I have to concede, quite fascinating at the same time.'

Masters didn't expand on his sudden diatribe. Both he and Ros just let the silence stretch instead.

Then Masters stood and for a moment Ros wondered if he was just going to walk out without saying another word.

But then he looked back at her and nodded.

'I think you're right. If you weren't around it would look suspicious. I'll brief Jukes on the exact sequence of events as we expect them to unfold and he can brief you in turn. Till then we should keep out of each other's way. For purely operational reasons of course.'

Then Masters turned, headed for the door and was gone.

A day or so earlier, Tyra had been out in the small garden of the Manchester safe house. She'd adopted a smoking habit and didn't, considerate soul that she was, want to inflict it on anyone else in the non-smoking house. In truth, it was the only place she could make and receive phone calls. Tyra had a pathological aversion to all-matters nicotine but she'd adopted a sixty-a-day habit as naturally as she might have put on a new top.

Detail, Tyra had learnt years earlier, was everything. Kirino rarely ventured outside so she should be safe from the kind of interruptions that might give rise to awkward questions, but that wasn't really the point.

As the day of reckoning approached it was more and more important for her to remain in close touch with all that was happening. This was an operation that had been at least three years in the planning. Like all such operations, the last couple of days were always going to be the most critical.

Tyra eyed Ros as she came out into the garden behind her, offered her a cigarette. Ros took one and for a moment the two women simply stood in silence, smoke curling beyond the bushes to their side.

Then Tyra looked at her.

'No hard feelings?'

Ros just looked back.

'There would be if it was me. I'd have gone ballistic. All that time and effort. All that bridge-building.'

Tyra smiled thinly again.

'That contract stuff was great by the way, I told Jukes what a professional you were, actually managed to put together a fifty-break and still spout all that protection shit at the same time.'

Ros mottled. What Tyra was hoping to achieve she had no idea. But maybe there was no object, no end in view. Maybe, as with Masters, it had just become second nature. Attack before you're attacked.

Ros waited a moment, metaphorically counting inside all the while.

'I should have realised, shouldn't I? If you weren't going to understand, who would?'

Don't respond, Ros kept telling herself. Don't rise to the bait.

'A woman who lies for a living. A woman who teaches others to lie as if their lives depended on it, which in most cases they probably do. After a while it must become habit, right? To deceive, dissemble. Why should I have to justify an act of fiction to a professional fiction-teller?'

Ros kept looking at a pair of cool eyes looking back at her, assessing and appraising her. There had to be a reason she was being singled out for what she knew was special treatment but for now she didn't care. All she could think, as she stared back into those ice-white pools, was an old proverb about dishes being best served cold.

She'd learnt that a long time ago and the old proverb was right.

Revenge always tasted the very sweetest then.

Four hours later on that same day and Ros, now back in Cardiff, had known where to find him. Those few moments in that hospital room, moments when she watched him pore over bank statement after bank statement unaware that she'd come round, hadn't only told her that Conor was in deep financial trouble.

It had also, courtesy of some of the debits clearly visible as he'd turned over page after page, told her exactly what kind of financial trouble he was in as well.

Tracking more closely the activity behind those numerous debits had been the second of the tasks she'd deputed to the peddler of dodgy ringside stories, ex-wrestler Eddie Faulkner, now digger of dirt and exposer of even dodgier stories outside that ring.

Cracking that second story had been the work of moments.

Getting even close to what might be called the heart of the first story had taken a lot longer.

Ros let herself in via a side door. There was some token hired muscle in attendance but a quick flash of her warrant card sent him back into the chair he'd half-vacated speedily enough.

Further down the corridor Ros spotted a couple of bored girls, waiting, smoking, their duties not really kicking in till the evening got under way. The only game in town at the moment was for the pros and they didn't need inducements of the type these girls had to offer. Those players had no hesitation in extracting and laying down the contents of their wallets on that all-too seductive green baize.

Ros pushed on past a small kitchen, moving into the presence of some more hired muscle, only this one didn't even half-rise to his feet as she approached on account of his being asleep.

Ros occasionally fantasised about moving out of her current line of employment, taking up Eddie on his perennial offer of going in with him in private security instead. She knew she never would but she'd still got into the habit of tipping him off about places that might benefit from his professional help. Now she added another location to the list.

Moving through a door ahead she came into a small room.

The air was thick with swirling smoke but that was the least of the threats to the health of the small cluster of men currently inside. A small sea of desperate faces swam into Ros's vision.

A rather more energised example of hired muscle detached himself from a wall at the far side of the room and began to move across to her but Ros hardly saw him. Ros had spotted her quarry and Conor had now seen her too.

And as he did so Conor felt his world, not exactly at its most secure right now, come crashing down around his ears.

After seeing Masters in the Spanish café, Ros had taken the river clipper to Embankment. She'd cut across the Strand to Trafalgar Square making for her favourite gallery in London. Once inside she'd waited, staring out at a thousand eyes staring back at her.

Large, wide eyes, narrowed, almost vulpine eyes, smiling eyes, tired eyes that had seen all the world had to offer and now didn't want to see any more, eyes that danced in private ecstasy, eyes that had died decades earlier.

Then Ros stood up from the seat she'd been occupying in the very middle of the floor, gave a half-wave across the room as another émigré walked in. As always, people parted as he approached, an instinctive reaction. Eddie just had that sort of presence, not to mention that six-foot-plus frame, encased today in a mustard suit. That definitely helped when it came to the parting of the ways as well.

Eddie joined her, nodded round at the images lining the walls, rock stars, novelists, politicians, poets, the odd major league criminal, even a collection of Great Train Robbers. The choices on offer in the National Portrait Gallery had always been more than a touch esoteric, one of the reasons Ros had always loved the place, but to her admittedly untrained eye they'd become positively wacky of late.

'I'm in here somewhere.'

Ros stared at him feeling as if a recent private opinion had just made the leap into accepted fact.

Eddie nodded without even looking at her, anticipating the quizzical reaction.

'Serious. Some chancer calls up, wants a photo from the old days, me with some of the other faces. McManus, Johnny Saint, that maniac Kellett, Bert and Vic. They're going to be doing some display about the golden age of wrestling. I told him to keep looking and when he'd found it let me know, I'd hate to think I'd missed it.'

Ros felt just the same about her not-so-hallowed sphere of human activity. Somewhere, sometime, there'd been a time when everything was in place and everyone worked together for some kind of common end but somehow she'd missed that too.

Eddie looked round the walls, lost for a moment in a dreamy disbelief that he might soon be part of a genuine rogues gallery. Then he looked at Ros and got down to business.

'Anyway. First of all, Tyra.'

Eddie brought a sheaf of papers out from under his jacket and from the expression on his face Ros knew he'd struck gold of some description and now rather wished he hadn't.

That few days earlier, the conversation had been the last thing Conor had expected. The drive from the gambling club down to the old docks was unexpected too. His senior officer had just come across clear evidence of activities in his private life that could be definitely and positively prejudicial to his professional conduct.

So by rights they should have headed straight for his new nick. By now he should have been clearing his desk – not that there was too much to clear – as well as preparing for an extended period of leave while a disciplinary machine swung into action.

It wouldn't have taken long. Once his debts had been revealed he'd probably have been tramping the private security road like so many before him, trying to call in favours only in his case, as he hadn't actually done too many for anyone over the years, he wouldn't have counted on too many being returned.

His marriage, needless to say, would have gone the same way as his career before much more time had elapsed. It was already hanging by a thread as it was. The news that he'd turned into a house-husband overnight would have been unlikely to go down well with the high-flying Francesca.

Within a few short days he should have lost the lot, his job, his income, any pension rights he might have – he really had no idea any more – closely followed by his wife and the last few friends he'd just about managed to hold onto.

But none of that had happened. He was standing on a river walkway instead looking out across the barrage and Ros had started talking. And for the first time since they'd met she actually talked about herself. She talked about an old case from years earlier and how she felt about it, both then and now. And she lifted a lid on some of the most extreme emotions he'd ever heard or could ever expect to hear from the mouth of anyone, let alone a woman who was supposed to never lay herself bare in this way.

Maybe that was the point. Maybe she wanted to see if anything in what she was saying struck a chord.

And it did. In fact it was like listening to some kindred spirit where he thought none existed.

And so he'd reciprocated, not because he thought it might help him rescue a career he'd come to care little about, he'd reciprocated because he too wanted to drag it all out, to say the unsayable, to give voice to that which up to now had remained unsaid, would probably always have remained unsaid if it hadn't been for this encounter.

But there was a point to all this, aside from an unexpected

discovery of common ground. Ros had initiated all this for a reason. A reason connected to the disciplinary incident that had triggered his transfer to Ros's department. An incident he'd been assured had been buried and would never resurface, so long as he played ball of course.

And he had played ball but the incident had resurfaced. Whether that was down to the efforts of the department he'd left or his new senior officer in the one he'd just joined he didn't know, but he was already beginning to have a shrewd suspicion.

Conor stared as Ros handed him some papers. She told him not to read them just yet. She just wanted him to answer one question instead.

He was never going to get rid of what was inside him. She knew that. Maybe because it was inside her too. Maybe it was inside most people, she didn't know, didn't care in truth. All she did know was it destroyed most of the people she'd met, twisted them out of shape, turned them into something unrecognisable even to themselves. They couldn't understand it and so they couldn't control it which was what she was asking him to now do.

Ros wanted him to channel it. She didn't want him to do what so many others she'd met had done – pretend it didn't exist – try and bury it so deep it couldn't come out because it would always come out. It would always burst to the surface at some time and it would usually be at the worst possible time as well, the time that would spell almost certain destruction not just for the specific object of their wrath but for themselves.

Ros tapped the small sheaf of papers, now in his hand.

Unleash it on that, she told him.

And let the pair of them do it together.

That same night, Ros had watched Jukes as he charged around the court. For a man who had to be pushing his mid-forties he was in undeniably decent shape. Presumably that was down to regular squash sessions such as this.

Ros turned her attention to Jukes's companion, the taller, slimmer, younger Masters. Not that his extra height, trimmer frame or relative youth was gaining him much of an advantage in this encounter. Honours were fairly even. For every point Masters managed to add to the scoreboard, Jukes would reciprocate.

Ros had no idea how the match would end and she wasn't going to stay to find out. Ros wasn't there as a simple spectator.

She'd slipped into the observation gallery that ran the length of the courts a few moments earlier. There were some other people sitting on the hard-backed chairs, a few bored children waiting for their fathers or mothers to finish their games as well as the odd girlfriend trying to look interested in the floorshow. Ros looked like just another appendage as she peered down into the central court.

It was the impression she wanted to cultivate. She didn't want to do anything that might attract attention to herself. That way she'd have a chance to study both men while they were unaware she was watching, while they were concentrating on something else, when they might, just might, let down their guard, let the masks behind which they habitually hid slip a little.

Ros had become used to it over the years. People-watching, her father used to call it in the days he used to notice such things. She remembered it being said with a sense of amusement when she was small. Before all that happened had happened. In later years it had become like so many things, a stick to beat her with, a barbed missile.

Ros bent low over the rail, watched Jukes grimace a congratulatory smile as Masters prevailed at the end of an extraordinarily long rally. Masters just about mustered the same when Jukes won the next point after an exchange of just two shots.

Because she needed to read these two right now. She needed some lid to be lifted on them both. She needed some moment, however fleeting, when they might stand exposed in some way. All she'd seen of them up to then was what they'd chosen to let her see. Even Masters, that night after the Scott discovery, had held plenty back. There was still so much he would not permit to be revealed and Ros had allowed him his efforts at concealment because she didn't think it mattered.

But now it did matter. Charging round the squash court below her, oblivious of her unblinking examination, was something treacherous. A man who was a traitor, not only to himself but to them all. A man who was about to put them all in the severest possible jeopardy.

Ros had begun with a list of possible suspects and now she'd narrowed it down to just the two, but she couldn't get any further. She couldn't decide which of these two it was. And watching them as they continued with their game, she still couldn't.

A short time later Ros stood to leave, still unseen by the two men below, but on her way out of the observation gallery she paused, looked back.

She hadn't noticed it before. She'd been too busy watching their faces, trying to read some sort of hidden language.

So it was only as she was leaving she registered the two pairs of feet running around the court below, both of which were encased in trainers, white trainers, the kind you could buy in any sports shop the length and breadth of the city.

YAROSLAV WOULDN'T BE able to resist it. The police knew that. He knew that. And both parties were to be proved right.

It was never going to be simply left to Tyra. Aside from everything else she'd then have no exit strategy and while she was a loyal and willing lieutenant she wasn't about to literally fall on her sword. Yaroslav wouldn't have expected that, indeed would have been instantly suspicious had her devotion to their cause extended that far.

Tyra was the Trojan horse. The diversion thrown into the mix to form the bridgehead for the main attack. Once she was in place and once she'd fed back to the Ukrainian all the fine details he needed to know, the security arrangements, the geography of the house, then he'd take over and not only because there was still some element inside him that regarded all this as work for a man, not a woman.

It wasn't even down to the blood lust that would inflame him at such times, still impossible for him to resist.

It was all down to the message this would send out, the shockwaves that would ripple far and wide.

He'd seen it with the acid attack in that butcher's shop all those weeks earlier and he'd seen it with the brutal slaughter of the police officer, his wife and unborn child.

The whispers had quickly started, not only among those he still needed to influence in some way, but among those pitted against him too. There was a reluctant awe in the reporting of those excesses and he could smell the fear behind that reporting too.

There was a growing realisation that they weren't dealing with an ordinary mortal here. He was building himself a mythology and he knew that was always going to be the most important weapon he'd ever unleash on anyone.

Forget guns, forget knives, forget casual torture. In the world in which he moved, the most important weapon of all was the doubt he could almost visibly see in the eyes of those arraigned against him. The suspicion that nothing they could do would ever be enough, that he would always somehow prevail.

Yaroslav felt the lights in the small house coming on as darkness started to fall. Soon, as in very soon, they'd have yet another example of that. Soon, another story would start to circulate and this story could prove the most powerful of all.

In the mythological stakes he was about to move into a totally different league.

The message would be simple and clear. No matter where you are, no matter the forces on your side, you are as naked as the day you were born and just as defenceless. The slaughter of the next few hours would stand as testament to that.

And as he stood there, almost statue-like, Yaroslav felt his mouth start to salivate.

Everyone inside that anonymous terraced house, with one exception, felt as if they were living inside some sort of alternative reality. Everything looked normal, the conversations sounded ordinary, the concerns everyday. There were debates on domestic matters, who wanted that type of cereal, who'd ordered that specific low-fat milk. Papers were strewn around the floor. Television programmes were marked up for watching or recording. A couple of computer games were open on the table. The usual defences erected against that most habitually crippling enemy, boredom.

At least it used to be the most crippling of enemies. But that had changed. And that's why everything felt dream-like, felt normal and yet not. That's why Ros felt as if every conversation and each exchange was being filtered as if through a mask.

There was a far more potent enemy out there now. And no matter the precautions they took or the measures that had already been put in place, there was always the possibility that something would go wrong, would go horribly wrong in fact and that the enemy, perhaps even now at the gates, would breach the barricade.

Initial reservations aside, Ros understood the necessity for the subterfuge. Yaroslav had proved impossible to trace in the previous few months. He seemed to have vanished from the face of the earth at the same time as leaving the all-too visible evidence that he was still very much inhabiting it. To tempt him out into the open in this way and in this manner, attempting this sort of direct action against the very body intent on putting him away forever, was simply too good an opportunity to ignore.

But it was undeniably a risk although they still held their trump card of course.

Tyra.

The Trojan horse who was anything but.

Only Yaroslav didn't know that.

Of everyone in the house, Kirino remained unaware anything was amiss. Ros had to admire Tyra as she dealt with her as coolly and calmly as ever. She never once let her guard slip, never once strayed into territory that might give her companion any pause for thought or any reason for concern.

If Tyra had doubts herself of any description, any moment where her customary confidence deserted her, it didn't show. Tyra was either a robot or a consummate actress. Both possibilities worried Ros more than she cared to admit.

Only perhaps she had admitted it in a sense. The night before, in fact. She'd showered, had accepted with a quick smile a towel that had been handed to her as she'd finished by a tall rangy man with a hint of French in his accent. Instinctively she'd checked out his body, noting with approval that he seemed to work out. His upper torso was honed despite the fact he had to be well into middle age. So many of the men that came into the club, particularly on the so-called party nights, had let themselves go to seed.

For a moment she'd contemplated accepting the silent invitation that had come with the towel. It would be a diversion and a diversion was just what she needed.

Then, as she'd put down the towel, she'd seen Oskar.

Through the window, Kirino watched the patrol car disappear. The information they'd all been given had been accurate, as ever. The local force would do a sweep of the area twice in the course of a night. The police officers in question hadn't been told exactly why, some vague reference had just been made to some women living there who'd previously been in one of the refuges in another part of the city.

It was all being kept deliberately low-key so far as the local police were concerned. If there was any real trouble they'd be quickly by-passed as more specialist reinforcements would be summoned. But for that to happen the authorities would have to be aware that trouble had broken out and Yaroslav didn't intend they should be aware.

Not until it was all way, way too late.

Yaroslav knew that the protection officers were still in the house. Again that wasn't unusual. One of them, usually the female, frequently stayed over, particularly lately when Tyra and Kirino had been spending more and more time in each other's company, preparing the case against him. That's what they'd been doing today, going over their respective experiences, cross-checking facts and dates, giving the investigating officers chapter and verse on his activities.

It was all damning stuff, as he had to concede. But it wouldn't mean a thing if they couldn't back up those statements with an appearance from one or other of them in court.

And for not the first time Yaroslav thanked whatever passed for a God these days for the happy accident that had led him to establish his activities in a country obsessed with protecting the rights of its citizens. If he'd committed even half the crimes he'd executed over the last year or so at home, the state would have put a bullet in his head a long time ago with no questions asked and no lawyers consulted or judges canvassed either.

He'd be dead, as were most of those who'd crossed him in that time, as dead as the occupants of that house would be that very night in fact.

With one exception of course.

Always that single exception.

'You didn't return my messages. Didn't acknowledge my texts. I've sent email after email. No reply.'

The night before, across the bar, Ros had watched a woman in a tight-fitting business suit playing with the erect members of two of the regular club attendees. Her husband was at her side the whole time, watching her face and her face only. She was expressionless. The two men she was with were not.

Ros kept watching them, sightlessly. Oskar kept his eyes on her and her alone.

'It was like this once before, wasn't it?'

Ros hesitated, knowing exactly to what he was alluding, not wanting to acknowledge it.

'Nothing for days, weeks even, as if I didn't exist, then all of a sudden you turn up out of the blue. Whatever happened then, it's happening again now, isn't it?'

Ros kept silent.

'I can't do it, Ros. I can't stand to one side all that time and then pick up the pieces again.'

'I didn't ask you to pick up the pieces last time.'

Too late she choked back the rest of the words.

Oskar nodded at her.

'But I did. And you needed me to do.'

Then Oskar paused.

'So what would have happened if I hadn't?'

Across the room a low moan sounded as one of the men climaxed over the fingers of the woman in the tight business suit.

The woman looked down, dispassionate, at the semen seeping over her hands, the second man climaxing at the same time over her other hand.

Ros didn't reply, just kept watching as the woman wiped her hands with the emissions as if she was applying moisturiser.

Oskar nodded at her.

'I guess we'll find out, right?'

Back in the safe house, Ros kept a watching brief on Kirino who was actually a little edgy that evening. Ros didn't know why. They'd all taken such pains to keep everything normal.

But Kirino had lived on her wits for some years now. She was attuned to every small shift in mood and something in the general atmosphere in the house must have registered. Some unconscious memory of some other betrayal perhaps.

The preparations were to peak the following evening. They knew Yaroslav had been keeping watch, planning his hit. Courtesy of Tyra, they knew exactly how he was going to do it too. The back-up was already assembling, ready to slip into place under cover of darkness.

Kirino should be asleep when it all kicked off, and even

though she was unlikely to remain asleep for long, he wouldn't be able to get to within three locked doors of her. Yaroslav had indeed built himself a powerful mythology this last year or so, but not even Yaroslav would be able to force his way past the six armed officers who would be on duty that night to reach his quarry.

Ros had contemplated getting Kirino out of the house completely but they couldn't risk any interruption to the normal routine. All she'd said to Masters had been true. One false step, one over-cautious precaution and everything would be ruined.

Ros checked her watch. She'd been due to meet with Jukes, Kirino and Tyra five minutes ago. Yet another trawl through a legend, a life story, that within a few short hours should be redundant. But it didn't matter, they had to keep rehearsing the story as much for their own sake as anything else.

Ros knew better than anyone that it had to become second nature. It couldn't be a role sloughed the moment someone turned off the lights or it would be useless – which made Jukes's tardy time-keeping all the more surprising. He'd always been the one who'd drummed into her the importance of routine.

Ros wasn't to know that at that moment Jukes had his neck pinned back against the wall of the downstairs toilet by an arm that had apparently materialised out of that wall behind him as he bent to the sink to wash his face. Reflected in the mirror behind him, all Jukes could see was the arm, attached apparently to no body, just protruding from the wall, strong fingers scrabbling for a grip on his throat, squeezing his windpipe.

Jukes lost consciousness and, falling onto the floor, the last thing he saw was that arm again.

Just an arm extended out from the wall behind the toilet, disembodied, floating.

Kirino was taking a bath. Ros said she'd call her when the

conference, which was what they called those extended rehearsals, was due to start.

Tonight they were doing role play. Kirino and Tyra were to take it in turns playing the part of a hostile witness, someone they might come across at some time in the future, a chance encounter with someone who would try and get under their skin.

It could be a passenger on a bus whose seat they'd inadvertently taken, a girl in a bar who thought they were looking at her boyfriend in too predatory a way. The specific scenario didn't matter. What did matter was how they handled it.

When they were put under pressure could they, or more accurately could the person they'd become, cope with it all?

Or would they revert to type, become the person they once were, would the mask slip, the face behind the disguise reveal itself?

Kirino wasn't that good at the role-playing but Tyra was clearly a natural and the more uncomfortable she made Kirino feel the more she seemed to get off on it.

Bitch, was Kirino's verdict.

But not tonight. Kirino stretched out one last time in the water, closed her eyes. Tonight she was going to make a special effort. Tonight she was going to skirt dangerously close to some real-life incidents from both their pasts, things she'd hardly even referred to up to now. Let's see if that wiped the smile off her face.

Kirino opened her eyes and looked up at the ceiling to see a face staring down at her.

Just a face.

Nothing else.

It didn't seem to be attached to a body, it just seemed to float above her, framed in the expanse of white ceiling.

A face she never expected in her life to see again, apart

perhaps from inside a courtroom, but which was now hovering above her head, almost within touching distance.

Looking down at her frozen, naked, body in the water.

Kirino thought she'd been scared at times in the past. She thought, on occasions, she'd even been terrified.

But now she knew what true terror felt like.

Because now she couldn't even scream.

Yaroslav had picked two of the best for this one. Exiles, like himself. Men who weren't simply hired muscle. Men who'd appreciate the savage beauty of it all and who would put in that little extra effort as a result.

It was elaborate, of course. It was, again, almost unnecessarily theatrical. So much of what he'd done lately had been the same. But wasn't that the point of theatre, that it stuck in the mind, lived on in the imagination long after the actors had left the stage?

That's what Yaroslav intended and he knew the two men he'd picked would see that. That's why they'd endure the almost impossible conditions for as long as was required. Inside the very walls of that small house, they too had felt the same mounting excitement he felt, they too had burned, as he had, with the anticipation of it all.

This story, when it did the rounds as it would, as he'd make sure it would, would be one of the best yet.

A protected house, a protected witness, specialist officers in constant attendance and what did he do?

Did he mount a frontal attack using guns, mortars, grenades or rocket launchers?

Did he torch the building and all inside, razing it and its occupants to the ground, reducing everything before him to burning cinders?

He could have done all of that and more, but he didn't. He'd apparently just walked through the walls instead. He'd simply materialised inside. One moment there was no-one in the house, the next moment there was a face, a hand, a strong arm around a neck, choking all life out of the helpless body in its grip.

That last little detail was the neatest touch of all. They'd had a couple of days to study the routine of the house, courtesy of the access provided by the communal roof spaces. They'd been inches from their different and respective quarries all that time. When the moment came it was going to be subtle somehow and therefore more horrifying. Yaroslav knew Tyra would appreciate that last bit particularly. Which should make up for not involving her in every last detail of the plan.

It was the silence. That's what had done it. Once before Ros had experienced that same silence, as if the world was holding its breath. As a small child she'd too held her breath, in the millisecond between a front door opening and an explosion sounding, spraying brains and bone and blood all over the hall and stairway of her old home.

She'd held her breath and waited and that's what she found herself doing now. She became aware of silence, from the downstairs toilet and from the upstairs bathroom, just silence, no sound at all; and she was doing it again, holding her breath.

As a small child she'd done nothing. She could do nothing. She'd just waited and watched. Stood to one side as everything played out before her helpless eyes.

Now, years later, she'd learnt her lesson. Without thinking, Ros hit the panic button.

A moment later the door opened in front of her.

At the bottom of the tiny strip of garden and listening to the ever-present hum of the nearby traffic, Masters felt the alarm sound in his pocket. He paused as he experienced one instant of total disbelief, perhaps as his brain went into denial mode.

Then he turned back towards the house and ran.

Kirino was stretched out in a crucifixion pose, her arms and legs secured with sailing twine. She was still in the bath, which was filling with ever more water. Only the hot tap was running meaning she was being slowly – although it didn't feel that slow to her – scalded to death.

Whether that would kill her or whether she'd drown first was a moot point. Her head had been tipped back so it was at a lower level than her arms and legs. Yaroslav calculated she'd have around three to four minutes before the near-boiling water came up over her mouth and nostrils. After that there'd be another minute or so before she drowned. Three or four minutes of terror followed by a few more of horror accompanied all the time by the smell of simmering flesh.

Yaroslav would have liked time to do more but in the circumstances he was going to have to settle for what he could. Kirino wasn't, after all, the only target that night.

Jukes had been choked to within an inch of his life but hadn't actually been finished off. He'd been dragged from the downstairs toilet in a state of collapse but then brought round by matches inserted under his fingernails, secured in place with fast-drying superglue and then set alight. An old trick. The combination of burning flesh as the flames licked the fingers and the nails disintegrating in the heat, usually brought the victim of a beating back to consciousness and it did so with Jukes.

Like Kirino upstairs, and thanks to the petrol-soaked rag that had been stuffed deep into his mouth which was almost but not quite choking off his airwaves, his screams were only silent no matter how loud they must have been sounding inside his head.

For his part, Masters knew he was walking into a trap. He knew he had to have been monitored all the way from the small garden back into the house and he wasn't destined to be disappointed. The moment he dashed back into the house his arms were pinned behind his back by a pair of the strongest hands he'd ever experienced, clamping them tight.

A swift blow to the kidneys further robbed him of any ability to put up any kind of protest. Next came the sight of Ros, a piece of some kind of twine twisted round her neck, the other end tied to what looked like a butcher's hook in the ceiling. Her feet were perched precariously on a chair. One step from the chair and she'd be swinging in space. There wouldn't be enough of a fall to kill her, meaning her death would be of the slowest possible variety as she turned, uselessly, again and again, choking all the while.

Masters didn't struggle, couldn't struggle, as a similar piece of twine was hooked over his head and as another butcher's hook was slam-bolted into place in one of the ceiling joists above. Expertly, he was patted down, his gun extracted from his pocket and laid on the table. As he was scooped up into position by those same strong arms, the door opened and Conor came back in from outside, a takeaway pizza in hand, eyes widening as he took in the sights before him.

Not that he had too long to take it all in.

Yaroslav appeared behind Masters, picked up the officer's own gun from the table and shot Conor once in the stomach, then once straight through the heart leaving him twitching on the floor. Then his body was slung outside.

Conor was small fry, neither witness nor – really – any sort of effective protection officer if Yaroslav's research, which was usually of the highest order, was correct.

Something to be dismissed.

An irrelevant slab of meat.

Which was when Tyra appeared, although she must have known what was happening from the moment she heard that first, stifled, scream upstairs. Yaroslav had left her alone of course. The longer she stayed out of the way the longer he had to prepare the tableau, to set out the scene. It pleased him that she hadn't had to witness any of the inevitably-messy rehearsals for the main event that was about to play out before her.

Yaroslav nodded across at his two companions. Their part of the job was finished now. He didn't want any distractions for the next. He wanted to be free to do whatever he wished. He was in complete control and he wanted his victims to know that. He was now sole arbiter of what happened to their lives and there was no point in even beginning to consider any sort of appeal to anyone else because there would be no-one around.

Just him and his unwilling disciples dancing to his tune.

His two companions melted away, disappeared into the night. From the ceiling above Ros's head, water began to drip through the ceiling from the bathroom.

From somewhere, the next room perhaps, or from the hallway outside the downstairs toilet, came the smell of burning flesh.

Across the table, Tyra looked at Yaroslav and Yaroslav looked back at her. He felt now as he always felt at moments like this. As if he was not of this world, the mortal world. As if he was superhuman instead. And maybe that's exactly what he'd become.

Because he now watched, disbelieving, as Tyra picked up the gun from the table. He kept watching, ever more disbelieving, as Tyra turned it towards him and pulled the trigger, completely at a loss to understand how this could be part of their plan. But he very definitely saw the flare as the bullets exploded from inside the barrel and he felt them smash into his body, turning his guts inside out.

As the first, then the second and then the third bullet hit him he could still see Tyra and everyone else in the room. It was as if no matter how many times he was shot he remained alive, as if he couldn't be killed no matter what.

Then came the blackness.

3 2

THERE WAS A moment years earlier, driving away from the Kincaids, when Ros had felt it creep over her.

She'd only been in the job a short while, hadn't even begun to understand that she was going to have to rely on instinct for so much of the time. For much of her working life she was going to be in the position of a doctor, trying to delve beneath what she was being told, attempting to burrow beneath the evasions and scared half-truths until she reached the real story.

Or maybe she was more like a vet. Because most of the scared souls she encountered were as mute as cowed animals. It wasn't always fear, sometimes they had no choice. One witness Ros came across in her first full year in her new posting was silent for a particularly good reason. Just before he entered the programme – and with an aggrieved persecutor well aware of what he was about to do – he'd received a late-night visit. During the course of what had been a particularly brutal beating his tongue had been sliced out at the root.

What Ros had felt, driving away that night, was fear. It was generalised, unfocused, there'd been no specific reason for her to feel that way, nothing had happened, which was why she didn't do what she later felt she should have done, turned and gone back.

But why should she? If she'd had a reason, if there'd been some unexplained detail that had begun to bother her then she would have returned, but as her senior officer at the time had pointed out, she would have been killed too because if their attackers weren't going to spare a small boy they certainly weren't going to spare a police officer.

She'd felt the same fear settle over her just before the Yaroslav attack. Only this time there were plenty of reasons to feel afraid. She could almost smell danger on all sides, feel it at every turn. They could plan so much but there was still an element of unpredictability in it all, they could all still be taken by surprise.

As they had been. And even though in operational terms an objective had been achieved, a price had also been paid.

Jukes, his injuries aside, was going to recover.

Kirino would need an extensive period of hospitalisation and no-one was going to persuade her within a million miles of a courtroom now, but she was also going to survive.

Then again no-one needed to persuade her inside a courtroom. The threat had been defused. A madman had been taken off the street and would not now be returning. Whether that justified the death of an officer she'd only just come to know in any meaningful sense – and with whom she'd only very recently connected – she didn't know but that didn't really matter now.

Conor was dead and that was that.

'What do we do?'

Ros remained silent.

'Ros?'

Ros stared out beyond her sister, down towards Penarth and, beyond, to the open sea. The water was angry, the swell surging, the sort of tide where most local residents thanked the gods of good foresight for the barrage.

That's where Ros wanted to be right now. On the sea. Being buffeted by the strongest possible waves. Watching it form valleys, then mountains. Concentrating on one thing and one thing only. Blotting everything else out, not having to make any decisions save one.

How to survive.

'I know it's against the rules. If there are still any rules. But how long do we go on like this? I don't know, but you do or at least you could find out.'

Di hunched closer.

'I can't talk to anyone. If I try they just say the threat is still present, but how can it be after all this time? If anyone was still out there, if anyone was still looking for Emmanuel surely they'd either have got to him or – I don't know – .'

Di struggled, helpless.

' – given up?'

Di hunched, ever closer, on the bench. Behind them fumes wafted from a local eatery, the smell of pizza mixing in with the faint whiff of engine oil from one of the passing water taxis.

From the next, unattended, bench came the sound of a local radio station playing music via an unseen speaker, unnerving the occasional passer-by who suddenly heard a song coming apparently out of nowhere.

Di kept her eyes fixed on her younger sister while Ros kept her eyes fixed on the water, the traffic heavy, the water-taxi throttling back to half-speed to avoid any unnecessary wash.

'We've not actually met. Only talked. He won't meet me, won't come anywhere near me, won't let me anywhere near Mum and Dad even though he says he knows where they are.'

Di nodded at her.

'Not till you say so. He doesn't think there's any danger, not now, but he's not going to risk it, not after everything.'

Ros kept staring out over the water.

'You're the key. You can change all this, all you've got to do is make a few phone calls, do a few checks, make sure everything Emmanuel's saying is true.'

Ros looked back at the beseeching eyes before her.

For a moment doubt and fear clouded those eyes but Ros just stared back at her, level and cool, seemingly as calm as ever.

If only Di knew.

Then Ros gave a slight nod of the head, spoke for the first and only time since they'd sat down.

'OK.'

And then came the faces again.

Always at night.

Always when she was alone.

She'd spent the last few evenings in the club, surfing through various old and new acquaintances, sharing the showers, Jacuzzi and sauna with bodies old and new, not caring who they were, not listening to what was being said, just holding on, moving on, then holding on again.

Somewhere in the middle of that was Oskar. He didn't say anything, but he didn't touch her either. He just left her alone, left her to work it all out herself.

For not the first time she wondered what the hell she was doing. If she had to draw up a shortlist of all the qualities she wanted in a partner, what would be lacking when it came to the young Swede? Not much if the truth be known. So what was holding her back?

But even as she phrased the silent question she knew the answer. It would mean making a commitment. A commitment would mean she had a stake in something – which would mean there was something then to lose. And she didn't want to lose anything else. Better not to have, than to have it and then watch it all run away through her fingers.

She knew what Oskar would say. Why would she inevitably have to lose what the two of them could build together? And she wouldn't be able to answer, couldn't even begin to explain.

She just knew it would vanish the moment she even started

to believe in it because everything always did. Somehow, without ever meaning to, she infected all that was healthy and turned it into something that was not.

Just ask the faces in her nighmares. Ask the Kincaids. The little boy with the blasted knees. He was coming back to her now as he always would, running down a supermarket aisle, kicking his ball against a garden wall.

Only now there was another face and another voice as well. She'd heard it as she came back into the apartment that very evening. Putting down her keys, it came as if out of the ether behind her. A voice she'd only just got to know. A voice she'd wanted to get to know better. And it was here, in her private retreat, a sanctum to which she rarely granted anyone access, but those sorts of voices didn't need any sort of permission to make their presence felt.

It was just two words, a simple greeting of the type she'd heard a hundred times before.

And now there they were again, those same two words, only this time without the former – and deliberate – trademark hesitation before the final address. This time the traditional mark of respect actually sounded genuine.

'Hello Ma'am.'

Tyra strode along the side of Atlantic Wharf, deliberately taking the path closest to the water. It would take her longer than taking a left by the County Hall and heading past the fast-food outlets before coming up to the large glass-fronted building on the edge of the Wharf itself but Tyra didn't care.

Today she wanted to savour each and every moment. She wanted to postpone the inevitable gratification. It was going to be pretty intense as it was. Maybe she was being greedy wanting to milk it even more. But then again that's what she was. She was greedy and always had been and she always would be and for that she saw no reason to apologise. She wanted more than most and so she achieved more than most too.

Take away that hunger and she'd be like the rest of them. Doing their jobs. No more, no less. That had never been her way. As her colleagues had already discovered.

As they were about to discover again.

It wasn't difficult manipulating people. She'd learnt that early on too. One image always stuck in her mind. She couldn't have been more than four or five, she was in a class in her primary school, sitting on her square of carpet. Hers was decorated with the picture of a boat. Other children in the same class had animals and cars. Her teacher was writing some words on the board, a teaching assistant was fussing with a crying child, a harassed nursery nurse who was always harassed so Tyra remembered, was setting up a play area for the next day.

There was a visitor to her left, she didn't know who he was. He might have been the parent of one of the other kids or an inspector of some kind, she didn't really care that much. All she knew was that every time she looked his way and smiled up at him, he smiled back.

And that wasn't just the once, that was every single time. It was almost like some reflex response she could conjure at will. All she had to do was turn her head slightly in his direction and smile up at him, almost shyly, from underneath her fringe and he couldn't seem to help himself, he grinned back, unable so it seemed to take his eyes from her.

Later, she'd wonder about that particular visitor. Later, she'd realise there might have been something else behind that seemingly-instinctive response. Maybe she even recognised it then for what it was.

But that wasn't the point. For the first time she'd understood that it wasn't just children in the class she could bend to her will, there were those in the adult world too. Maybe that's why that memory had been preserved over all the intervening years, why no detail of that classroom scene from so long ago had dimmed; even at that age she could apparently make an adult do as she wished.

The refinements would come later. Most of the experiments in that line would be conducted in her teenage years but even then she was flexing that muscle, extending the boundaries, playing the tune to which others would sing.

Tyra, regretfully, cut up from the water. Now she couldn't delay this any longer. It really was time to walk into that building, take the lift to the top floor, let herself into the apartment overlooking the old docks and the new bay.

Tyra had bagged this for herself. She'd earned it, as she'd made crystal clear to anyone who might have questioned her. After all she'd been through at Yaroslav's hands, she wanted, deserved indeed, the satisfaction of going through his apartment herself. She was open about her motives. She'd been there so many times as a possession. She craved the moment she could walk in there in her true colours, as the persecutor she truly was.

Only she wasn't.

Was she?

Tʏʀᴀ's ɴᴇᴡ ʟᴏᴠᴇʀ watched her as she moved into the building, registering – before he followed her inside – the extra-special spring in her step. He could almost sense the exultation that seemed to illuminate her in some way.

She looked exactly what she was. A woman totally on top of her game and no wonder. It was a game that was nearing its conclusion and she'd played it to perfection. And OK, she was damaged goods, but who wasn't? Everyone was compromised in some way. Everyone had demons. She just knew how to use them, that's all.

But perhaps her greatest strength was her innate instinct for simplicity. Where others might complicate things unnecessarily she would never do that. There might be twists and turns along the way but she always kept her goal in sight.

First, that goal was Yaroslav and she'd set about ensnaring him with a dedication that had left him little choice but to submit.

Then came the next refinement although it was only a logical development in truth. This was a woman who spent her life behind a mask. So now they were all to discover there was a mask beneath the mask.

Was anyone – initial shock aside – really going to be all that surprised?

Jukes had been told to sit on the Conor death for a couple of days. The family would be told of course, but for operational reasons those in positions of power and influence – or at least rather more power and rather more influence than Jukes – wanted time to think, to assess, to plan. As was made clear to anyone who cared to question that decision, the whole protection field was still at an embryonic stage in its development. No-one wanted one tragic lapse to damn the work of an entire department, to compromise it forever in the eyes of fellow officers and, even worse, other potential witnesses.

They'd walked a tightrope with Yaroslav and in one sense it had been justified. In another sense too high a price had been paid with the death of an innocent officer.

Jukes would like to have said he felt sorry. Any department that lost an officer was usually plunged into a period of fairly intensive mourning. Aside from the fact that any officer tended to be part of a tightly-knit unit, there was the PR aspect to it all.

There'd been a slogan doing the rounds of the local schools in the previous few weeks in the wake of a well-publicised failure to care for a vulnerable small boy, a high-profile case that had resulted in his death. Since then it had been drummed into every teacher and care worker, anybody working with any infant at all, vulnerable or non-vulnerable and the slogan was simple.

Every child matters.

It had been the police mantra for years too, with just the one word substituted.

Every officer matters.

Every officer counts.

The life of every police officer was and should be sacrosanct.

Very often the only souls those officers had to count on were other men and women from their own department. It was something steeped deep in the culture, something almost embedded in the very walls and floors of each and every individual station.

So it was odd in a sense that Jukes hadn't even thought about Conor from the moment he heard that gunshot. He almost had to be reminded there'd been a casualty on his watch at all. He'd made all the right noises, had said all the right things in all the right places, had expressed the usual fine-sounding sentiments as he helped plan the story that would be fed to the press and worked out the details of the damage limitation exercise they would now have to put into place.

But Conor had been wiped from his mind the moment those arrangements had been concluded and he knew why.

It wasn't that he was getting cynical or uncaring in his old age. His eyes were just fixed on a rather larger matter than an officer who never wanted to be in his department in the first place.

When he'd first joined them, Jukes had seen Conor as something of a liability and in a sense that had turned out to be true.

In another sense, the only sense indeed that mattered to Jukes right now, Conor coming into the department was the best thing that could possibly have happened.

Masters also hadn't given Conor a single thought and the reason was simple again too.

Conor was dispensable.

Yaroslav was of much more immediate concern.

And now, breathing in the slight salt on the air, watching some nearby seagulls feasting on scraps, he knew he'd have prioritised the events of that day and their immediate aftermath in exactly the same way, irrespective of the outcome.

Everything he'd done that day had made complete and total sense in operational terms.

And everything he was about to do now was going to make total sense too.

Of course, there'd again be those who wouldn't approve and that, as he had the grace to concede, would be putting it mildly.

There were those who would have fifty fits in fact. Renowned for being determinedly unconventional, perhaps this was going to turn the maverick into something completely uncharted, take him down a road hitherto untravelled to a destination as yet unknown.

Masters looked up at the window above. The lights were on, meaning she was inside.

She was inside and the end was in sight.

Tyra had loved the look of total shock on her new lover's face. He'd journeyed through several emotional states that night, from interest to intrigue to frank incredulity at his good fortune. Whatever else he'd expected he hadn't expected the evening to end with the pair of them in bed.

For some reason, indeed for good reasons, he'd always thought of her as out of reach. There'd always been something about her that seemed to repel advances.

Several had tried, of that they were both well aware.

Just look at her.

Who wouldn't?

But she seemed to have chosen him, which seemed inexplicable at first. And even as she undressed him with the lightest of touches he had more than a faint suspicion that there was more to this than a sudden rush of passion for a colleague who, previously, had hardly been acknowledged and an hour or so later he was proved right. And that was when, before her amused gaze, his expression changed out of all recognition.

For a moment she thought he was going to have some kind of heart attack. All this on top of all that severe exertion. A quite literal battering of the senses, both physical and mental.

But then his breathing had slowed as his brain began espying the possibilities. And she started to see that her faith hadn't been misplaced, that she really had seen something in him that reminded her of herself.

And she could also see that something inside him was already finding this idea every bit as extraordinary as she had found it and was already becoming intoxicated with all it offered too.

And so she'd told him more.

'There's this phrase they use in cards. I went out with a poker player once and he used it all the time. Busted flush. To tell the truth that was pretty well him most of the time too. He'd started online and he was OK when he couldn't see the faces he was playing with. But once he was in the same room as any other player something in him froze.'

Tyra tapped out the ash from her cigarette into an ashtray she'd balanced on her flat stomach. He had an arm behind her, cradling her head so she could take drags whenever she wanted. He didn't smoke and had never liked the smell but he didn't tell her that. He had absolutely no idea where this was leading but he didn't want to do anything to break the spell. Something told him this was one of those moments that changed lives and he was right.

'That's what this is. A busted flush. Band-aid over a wound that can never be healed. Everything about it's shit, from the way we go about it to the measures we put in place, the happy accidents when someone actually says what they've agreed to say, the total fuck-ups when it all goes wrong like it does ninety-nine times out of a hundred and we've wasted all that time and all that effort, just pissed it all away.'

'It's a fallible business.'

She turned on him, her eyes seeming to flash sparks.

'It's not a business. Any business has to be built on success or it fails and this has failed time and again. If we get a face into court it's a miracle and even when the miracle happens what happens to them afterwards?'

She shook her head.

'It's time for a clear-out, to start again, think again, dismantle the whole fucking thing.'

He hadn't a clue what she was talking about. He'd even started to wonder if she was just letting off steam. He'd had a girlfriend once who did it now and again after a stressful morning in work. She'd worked in a school with a large immigrant population and while she loved the kids most of the time, negotiating the different cultures, different outlooks and different languages, day-in, day-out, also made her occasionally explode.

Maybe that's what was happening here. Maybe that's what the previous evening had been all about. An explosion of tension. A release. They'd both experienced that several times over as his now-aching balls attested.

And yet she was still talking and she was talking ever faster now too as if she was reaching some sort of climax again.

'So let's blow the house down.'

He stared at her cigarette burning down between her fingers. Red-hot ash was hovering just a centimetre or so from her skin but she didn't even seem to notice. Her eyes, her whole being, were focused on one thing and one thing only right now and that was himself and he felt as if she was almost sucking him inside her, bending his will to her own.

'Sure, we deliver now and again, sure, we take the occasional maniac off the street. But let's take something else out too, let's take that whole bunch of prissy little social workers out at the same time. Let's put all those bleeding hearts out of their misery. They don't even believe in what they're doing themselves. Let's put a great big nail in their coffin.'

He stared at her, rapt. Once again, he had no idea if this was madness or genius. He had no love for the department that seemed to be attracting all her bile right now either, although it had never occurred to him that anything could be done about it They'd just seemed to him like any of the other specialist departments they all hated such as compliance or, the most hated of all, that unit of outcast cops who investigated other cops.

But he was getting more and more swept along in this. The likes of Ros used to be a minor irritant, now they were becoming something much more than that. The number of cases they were being forced to liaise on were increasing year on year. And it wouldn't have been so bad if they were largely innocent victims involved in those cases, but they weren't. The vast majority of the faces they handled were villains who should be buried and the keys to their concrete coffins buried with them, never mind re-settled and cared for throughout the rest of their natural lives.

'And what do they do? Once they've had their day in the sun?'

It was as if she could read his mind.

'Anything they want. All courtesy of a grateful state. You want to go back to your old ways, you do that, we'll just turn a blind eye.'

She hunched closer to him and he knew already that this was going to be impossible to resist.

'So what if we deliver one prize and then destroy another. On the same night in the same fell swoop. And just in case you're wondering, this isn't just a point of principle. One week later, when the dust has settled, when they've realised they can't keep a lid on this, once the rumours start to circulate about the biggest cock-up in the department's history and when everyone who works for them, who's cared for by them, either now or in the future, begins to get this awful sinking feeling about them all, we collect.'

'Collect what? From who?'

She eyed him amused. She had picked right. She could almost see the naked greed in his eyes as he stared back at her.

'To undermine a whole department? Take out the whole

crazy notion of defending the indefensible? Stop protecting people who should be persecuted? Not to mention handing a get-out-of-jail card to a few seriously heavyweight faces along the way? There's one hell of a lot of people out there who'd pay well over the odds for something like that.'

She nodded at him, focusing on the first question, ignoring the second, knowing he wouldn't ask the second question again once he'd heard the answer to the first.

'One mil. In cash.'

She nodded at him again.

'Each.'

Banks stared back at her for a moment.

'But you'll need someone on the inside, won't you? Someone actually inside the department?'

And once again, there it was.

That same, knowing, smile.

TYRA MOVED TO the door as the buzzer sounded. She'd already been alerted by the concierge as to the arrival of her new visitor.

For a moment she caught sight of herself in a full-length mirror. Instinctively she checked her appearance, a smile briefly illuminating her face as she did so. She looked good. Strictly speaking it didn't matter. But it did.

Detail, detail. It was everything.

Behind her on the sofa, Banks shifted, nervous. He hadn't lost an ounce of faith in his companion. She was in total charge as always; but going up against everyone he'd formerly worked for and everyone he'd always worked with, was still a daunting prospect. But the prize on offer put any late attack of nerves into some sort of perspective.

Tyra opened the door and Jukes walked in, taking in the view from the floor to ceiling windows first, as did everyone, before his eyes swept over the room, taking in the only other occupant aside from Tyra who was now moving to fix them all a drink.

Banks nodded at a man who still outranked him, but didn't receive any answering nod or smile in return. Jukes seemed to be telling Banks that no matter what he'd done, no matter how much help he might have rendered them all these last few weeks, he was still small fry.

But Banks didn't care. So he was small fry who was about to have a million quid in the bank.

Poor him.

Still no-one had spoken. Tyra handed his drink to Jukes,

stood for a moment in front of him with her own drink in hand. In one sense everyone knew what they were here for and conversation was superfluous. All the talking, all the negotiating and all the planning had been done. They'd now moved beyond all that and it was time to collect.

Behind Jukes the buzzer sounded once again.

Jukes moved to the floor to ceiling window, looked down onto the water. On a walkway a young girl was moving past carrying a musical instrument in a case. It wasn't the girl on the train, but the girl on the train was all Jukes saw.

Perhaps – sometime – maybe even later that same day – he'd complete what he'd already started. Previously he'd toyed with the idea of making an approach under the guise of some sort of official enquiry. It wouldn't be the first time a police officer had used a warrant card for something that was very definitely not police business. But maybe there was no need for that now. Maybe all he had to do was act on the clear invitation he'd already read in her eyes.

Behind him, Banks still hadn't moved from the sofa and he wasn't going to move either. In this sort of company he didn't want to come across like a nervous schoolboy even if that was actually how he felt. His shirt was sticking to him uncomfortably and he made a mental note not to remove his jacket. He didn't want to expose the two large damp patches he could already feel forming under his arms.

Tyra didn't glance this time at the full-length mirror as she made for the door. She just opened the door, her practised smile freezing on her face as she saw a dead man staring back at her.

With Masters standing behind him.

Banks was the second person in that room to realise something was badly wrong. The pair of strong hands gripping his neck told him there'd been more than a slight hiccup in the plans for that particular meeting. A pair of eyes staring at him as he was dragged towards the balcony told much the same sort of tale as well.

Banks just about managed to jam a leg against one of the sliding doors of the patio window as it was hurled back, but it was only a temporary halt in his inexorable progress outside.

Masters lashed down with the heel of his boot catching Banks just below the knee, fracturing the bone, sending a crack echoing around the walls of the apartment before the now-unresisting Banks was dragged outside.

For a moment Banks didn't make a sound, he couldn't, the sudden and lacerating pain obliterated everything else, but a scream was building, he could feel it inside, it would only be a moment before it was released, across the water, across the whole of the city, rolling up into the distant hills.

But it didn't come out. As Masters dragged Banks out onto the balcony, Jukes handed him a cloth napkin draped around a bottle of what was clearly intended to be celebratory champagne, now quite clearly destined not to be opened.

Masters took the white napkin, stuffed it deep into Banks's mouth, twisting and turning it so it blocked any attempt at a scream, blocked indeed his initial attempts to even draw breath. Then Masters nodded at the grim-faced Jukes as he slid the patio door shut behind him.

He always had approved of teamwork and that had been of the slickest variety.

Back in the apartment, Tyra just stared at the gun that had been trained on her since she'd opened the door but it wasn't the gun that was really claiming all her attention right now.

It was more the dead man who was holding it.

Tyra kept staring at Conor, Ros now appearing behind him in turn. And – ever the consummate chess player, even now, even in these circumstances – Tyra was already trying to work it out, running through the various options to explain all that had suddenly happened in the last couple of minutes, trying to understand how she seemed to have got everything so horribly and unexpectedly wrong.

If Conor was alive then what had happened back in that house had been a charade. If that had been a charade then all that had happened – or all she believed had happened – to Yaroslav must have been the same.

Tyra looked at the gun trained on her and then, in her mind's eye, she saw another gun.

The gun left by Masters on that kitchen table.

And all of a sudden Tyra began to understand.

Out on the balcony, Masters released his grip. The only escape route was behind him through the now-closed patio door. The only other option was over the side of the balcony down a ten-storey drop.

Banks looked back inside the apartment. Instantly the realisation hit him that he hadn't been dragged out here to allow his co-conspirator space and time to be interviewed inside. He'd been dragged out here for a quite different purpose, and while Banks was occasionally a little slow on the uptake he really didn't need to be any sort of genius to work out what was about to happen next.

With a strength that totally belied his wiry frame, Masters hoisted Banks up on the guardrail and held him there, suspended over a sheer drop.

Banks didn't even dare open his mouth. The wind from the water below whipped into him, the buffeting sensation only increasing his current and keen sense of imminent jeopardy.

He felt his scrotum tighten, jamming his balls up deep inside his crotch.

It was his one and only phobia. His recurring nightmare from childhood had always been something like this, suspended over a high drop, peering down into an abyss, caught between safety and terrifying, dizzying, danger.

In his nightmares he'd always wake up. But now Banks looked back into the same pair of eyes that had tracked him for the last few moments and was unsure if he was going to extricate himself quite so easily this time.

Then all of a sudden Masters smiled. For a moment warmth flecked his eyes as he contemplated Banks, tottering on the edge of the drop, kept safe only by his hands. And in that moment Banks felt a deep sense of relief course through his body.

He'd seen Masters in similar situations before. He'd seen him hand out similar lessons in the past to those – like himself as he'd have to be the first to now concede – who'd crossed him. He'd witnessed the same sort of softening up meted out to others and it always worked too with those self-same souls talking long and volubly later.

Banks nodded at Masters, a clear signal or so he fervently hoped, from a subordinate to a senior officer. Banks understood. He understood and he surrendered. And Banks was already beginning to wonder what kind of spin he could put on this, how much of the blame he could off-load onto that bitch inside. He wasn't exactly going to get away completely free on this one and he knew that, but it was possible he could rescue something from the wreckage.

Then Banks looked down, an involuntary response, the last thing he wanted to do right now, but Masters had looked down and Banks couldn't help it, his eyes mimicking those of his captor.

Banks became aware of a family, a father, mother, a small child or possibly two, he couldn't quite make them out, moving away towards the water, one of the children skipping now after the family had paused to let the mother re-tie his shoelaces. There was now nothing underneath him, no people passing by.

Banks looked back at Masters again. That same smile still illuminated his face. But it wasn't a smile that held within it any sign of forgiveness, Banks could see that now. There was something else in there instead, something which in his desperation he'd mistaken for salvation.

There was anticipation. There was relish. Masters was savouring a treat about to be experienced. He'd been playing it out in his mind as he'd waited for that innocent family to move away from under that balcony, for the coast to become clear again.

Masters reached into Banks's mouth, dragged out the cloth that had been blocking his airwaves.

'Who?'

Banks gasped.

'I don't know.'

'Names.'

Banks gasped again.

'I don't know any fucking names, she never told me.'

Inspiration suddenly struck him.

'Jukes. Ask Jukes.'

Then Banks stopped. The memory of that napkin handed by Jukes to Masters just a few moments earlier flashed through his mind.

Obviously he'd misread Jukes.

Obviously Tyra had too.

Much as they'd misread so much else.

Masters looked down at the concrete walkway. There were

several balconies between the top-floor apartment and the ground but the balcony on that apartment jutted out a metre or so beyond the balconies and guardrails of those below. Banks could almost see Masters make the quick mental calculation, satisfy himself that his captive couldn't possibly reach out as he plunged downwards, couldn't grab hold of some passing guardrail to break his fall in a desperate attempt to mitigate at least any potential injuries. Banks would fall clean all the way to the ground if he went over at that point.

Maybe he shouldn't have squirmed in his grip like that. Maybe if he hadn't, Masters would have kept hold of him, would have returned him back to safety once he'd satisfied himself that Banks really didn't have any answers to any of his questions.

But Banks couldn't help it, he did squirm and, as he now went over the side, arms and legs scrabbling for a grip that would never materialise, another part of his childhood nightmare flashed through his brain. It was always the part that would wake him, sweating, screaming sometimes before crying into the shoulder of his mother who'd have come in when she first heard him whimpering and who would now be holding him, reassuring him, soothing him as she told him that everything was fine, that it was just a silly nightmare, that it wasn't real.

How would it feel?

The mere question was enough to wake him because the answer terrified him so much. How would it feel to hit the ground, perhaps head first, still conscious, feeling your head crack, your bones smash as the rest of your body hit a millisecond later?

Would death be instant or would there be a few moments of the most agonising pain imaginable as his body literally split open, as his organs poured out onto the ground?

Would there be a second or so when his eyes actually took it all in, saw everything that had happened to him before darkness cut in?

Two seconds later, Banks found out.

As Banks went over the side – and as the strangled scream sounded from out on the balcony – Tyra took her chance.

Tyra only had a fraction of a second and she knew it. But she knew there'd be that moment when the eyes of those in that apartment would flicker, almost involuntarily, towards the window as that scream sounded and that would be her opportunity and she intended to take it.

The scream came, at the same moment there was indeed that sideways flicker of the eyes and Tyra lashed out with her hand, snatching a knife from the table, a knife Jukes had himself used just a few moments earlier to peel an apple from the impressive display replenished daily by the concierge, before slashing it across his treacherous throat – treacherous in her eyes anyway – digging it deep into his windpipe.

Blood sprayed out, geyser-like, Conor recoiling, instinctively as it did so. Conor was now between Ros and Tyra and that turned a moment into something fractionally longer and that was very definitely all Tyra needed.

She was out of the door and heading down the stairs before Ros's warning yell had even left her mouth.

Tyra came out on the next floor down. She knew it would be madness to keep going down the stairs like that, she had to keep them second-guessing. At the far end of the corridor a door had opened, another of the residents emerging from inside, a young man dressed to go out, his mobile in his hand, about to check on some meeting or other perhaps, a meeting he was now destined never to make.

The young man smiled, another instinctive reaction as Tyra approached. She was a young woman walking along the carpeted corridor of an expensive apartment block with access strictly controlled by a highly-trained concierge. Why should he even begin to imagine there might be danger in such an encounter and among such surroundings?

Five seconds later he'd been dragged back into his own apartment and was lying on the floor of his inner hall, drowning in his own blood as his slashed throat poured blood back into his lungs.

A second or so later he was in one of the small cupboards that ran off the hall, the cupboard secured and locked, nothing to alert anyone to the contents inside.

Tyra came into the kitchen, used a chair leg to lever up the hatch leading to the refuse chute. Tyra hesitated for a moment even though in truth she had little option. But it was going to be a tight squeeze even for her ultra-skinny frame.

Then Tyra fed herself inside, feet first, twisting herself into a human cylinder, her arms crossed and pinned at her side. Then she began to lower herself inch by inch down the chute, taking her time. She knew by now her pursuers would be spilling out onto the street before doubling back and beginning the inevitably lengthy task of checking first all the corridors, then the walkways and then, finally, the apartments. In a sense it didn't matter how long it took, the longer the better almost. She'd no particular wish to spend the next hour or so in close proximity to trails of refuse but there were worse ways to spend that next hour or so. Being in close proximity to Masters would very definitely be a less attractive option.

With luck, by the time she'd finally inched her way down the shaft, Masters and his fellow-officers would have completed their initial search and be on their way outside, blocking off all the surrounding streets, checking all cars and taxis leaving Tyra some much-needed time and space to work out a next move she really thought was going to be denied her just a few moments earlier.

Then Tyra tensed. For a moment something flashed across her mind, a thought so appalling she dismissed it instantly.

Then back it came again and this time it wouldn't be dismissed quite so quickly.

Because now Tyra smelt something too.

Just metres away, Masters reflected on Bella, the beautiful Bella.

What happened to Bella, her husband and her child wasn't strictly speaking down to Tyra. She didn't play any part in the planning or execution of that particular horror. Not even Masters at his most evil-minded could lay that at her door. Yet there was a sense in which she shared at least some measure of culpability.

Yaroslav must have known Tyra was holding something back. Masters had sensed it himself, but he'd just written her off as a more than usually unbalanced example of an officer fast-tracked beyond her emotional maturity.

Or maybe she was simply and generally fucked-up in some other way. He didn't really care that much. She seemed to be doing her job and doing it well and that was all he needed to know.

Only she wasn't doing her job at all. She was playing each of them off against the other and the wily Ukrainian must have sensed something amiss as well. He couldn't have known what. She wouldn't have survived if he had. But sense it he did and Masters now strongly suspected that was behind his ever more elaborate attempts to demonstrate his power.

He wasn't just sending out a message. He was a young

boy in a playground trying to piss higher than any of his companions, hoping the girl passing by would notice.

So while she didn't participate directly in the torture of one of his officers and his wife – or the extraction of her unborn baby from her protesting womb – she still played her part in it all every bit as much as the prime tormenter that day. And that justified everything in Masters's mind.

It justified the rags being stuffed into the bottom of the refuse chute, it justified the lighter fuel being sprayed onto those self-same rags, although not too much, he didn't want an inferno, he wanted this to last some time, at least as long as Scott and the beautiful Bella would have taken to die.

And then, when he was satisfied that his preparations would achieve the end he desired, it justified leaning close to those tightly-packed rags and lighting that match.

Fulfilling his promise to Scott's mother along the way.

Tyra smelt it again. The first time her brain hadn't allowed the sensation that had suddenly assaulted her nostrils to translate into anything like a coherent response. Her conscious mind simply closed it down. Some defence mechanism kicked in, a reflex action over which she had no control.

The second time something else, simple fear perhaps, cracked her mind wide open.

The third time her slight, slim body felt the coldest chill she'd ever experienced in her life, a chill which seemed to begin in the very centre of her stomach and was now spreading outwards.

This time she couldn't even begin to fool herself this was all in her imagination. She never permitted herself such indulgences anyway. Tyra had survived so far by dealing in certainties and facts. She dealt with what was before her and if there was nothing then she never allowed it to trouble her.

What was before her now was something she'd never even come close to experiencing before.

How could she?

Who else but the dead – or the walking dead – had ever known what it was like to be burnt alive?

Now Tyra saw the first few wisps of smoke wafting past her and now too she heard the first crackle as the flames, still thirty metres or so below, licked at the remnants of the detritus flung down from the various apartments in the complex, still clinging obstinately to the sides of the shaft, destined not to do so for too much longer.

It was all about to be well and truly purged in a cleansing more complete than anything that could be achieved by the occasional blast of bleaching agent emptied down the shaft by its maintenance staff.

This shaft was about to become white-hot clean. Nothing that previously clung to the sides was going to remain.

And neither was she.

Tyra looked up as suddenly a small shaft of light opened above her. Instinctively she closed her eyes as a sudden deluge descended, some liquid, a pasta sauce by the smell of it, vegetables too, splattering down on her head, some sticking, some rushing past her, heading on down the shaft.

A second or so later she heard the sound of the discarded food beginning to sizzle as the growing fire fed itself with a new source of fuel.

Above her head the same shaft of light appeared again but this time no food was flung down and as the refuse shaft remained open Tyra understood why.

Whoever was standing there had caught the first faint whiff of something burning.

And whoever was standing there, in front of the now-open shaft, was allowing air to rush into the confined space, feeding the flames below more efficiently than even the figure at the bottom of the shaft had managed with his lighter fuel and rags, turning a still-relatively modest fire into something that was going, within a very few moments, to indeed resemble an inferno.

Masters had regrets in his life. Who didn't? You didn't get to his exalted rank without the occasional twinge of conscience regarding the steps that had occasionally been taken to get there.

As for a failed marriage and a now-troubled relationship with his offspring there was plenty of cause for regret in those failures too.

Occasionally he let his mind drift back, play on other sins and omissions. Such instances were rare but not unknown. None of them troubled him to the extent that they kept him awake at night. They were simply there, on the edge of awareness, waiting to give him occasional pause for thought.

All of which meant that up to that point in his life he'd survived remarkably untrammelled by the sorts of regrets that seriously troubled the vast majority of his contemporaries, but all that was now about to change.

Because as he stood at the bottom of that refuse chute, as he heard, first, the whimpering from inside and then the gagging and retching and then finally the agonised screaming reverberating up and down a chute that had become a furnace, he knew he was going to be tormented from that moment to the day he died that the death of the woman he'd known as Tyra wasn't more prolonged or more excruciatingly painful.

ROS DROVE, ONLY too conscious of the presence beside her.

Ros was used to car journeys of the strictly solo variety. When he'd been with her, Oskar thought that was down to her fear of parallel parking. At some point during the trip she might have to make some sort of half-complicated manoeuvre and didn't want any sort of audience. Ros had simply smiled under the gentle teasing and hadn't enlightened him.

When she was small it was the car journeys she'd always dreaded the most. When they were in the house, or rather more accurately in the succession of houses in which they were placed before the one where they finally settled, they could fill the space, punctuate the silence.

They could move and they did, from room to room, checking on this, doing that, tidying this or that item away. In the house and outside in a usually-small garden they could always find something to do.

But there was nothing they could do in the car. They couldn't move anywhere or do anything, even though the shrill voice of her mother tried to compete with the deafening silence that always descended the moment those car doors slammed shut.

They simply had nowhere to hide. There was nothing between them and the knowledge that there used to be three children in the back of that car, squabbling, singing, giggling, whispering some innocent confidence, one to the other and now there was just the one child there, a child who wasn't singing or giggling and who quite clearly wouldn't be whispering confidences, innocent or otherwise, to anyone from that point on.

As soon as she'd passed her driving test, Ros made herself a promise. From that point on all car journeys she made, so far as was humanly possible, would be by herself.

But today she had a companion.

Sitting alongside her sister, Di stared up at the small house before them, smoke curling from its chimney. From years earlier she had a memory of her father chopping logs, stacking them by the open fire he always lit at Christmas and sometimes on other occasions too, for a family birthday or a visit from some long-lost relative. She remembered the spit and crackle of the wood as it burnt and the sparks that danced in the chimney.

By her side, Ros was looking at her as if she knew what she was thinking right now. Maybe Ros had those same memories. And maybe all she was thinking about on coming up to this place, this house, was all that had been lost as well.

Something they could now finally start putting behind them.

Ros also looked up at the smoke curling from the side of the house but she wasn't thinking of former homes no longer occupied by any of her former family or open fires that blazed no more.

Tyra was much more on her mind.

All that happened had been hushed up of course. It was always going to be. Of the actual witnesses, Banks had, somewhat incredibly, survived but was in no fit state to make any sort of testimony – and the word of a crippled ex-cop invalided out of the force with the equivalent of a dishonourable discharge was hardly going to mean all that much anyway.

Masters had retreated into his usual impenetrable shell. The investigating authorities were going to get nowhere with him and they knew it.

Ros had also taken the Fifth Amendment, but even the most cursory of enquiries revealed that she was up in the apartment all the time Tyra was being rendered into something non-human, her flesh bubbling into liquid, her bones melting in the furnace of that refuse chute.

Jukes was being hospitalised even as all that was taking place – and while some of the flat residents did hear screams that seemed oddly close, but distant at the same time, they clearly didn't have too much to add to the general pool of knowledge.

Besides, most of them were rather more concerned with the chute itself which didn't seem to be working and which emitted the strangest odour whenever they attempted to access it, but a specialist cleaning company sent in by the local police along with several barrels of a powerful cleaning solution soon dealt with that.

Ros didn't want to think about Tyra and her last moments. She also didn't want to do anything to avenge her end. Like Masters before her, she was still haunted by another picture and this one didn't owe anything to the final agonised moments of a human being turned into something else.

Like Masters, every time Ros thought of Tyra she thought of Bella, the beautiful Bella, and Scott, and their unborn child.

And as soon as that grotesque tableau came into vision, Tyra well and truly faded from view.

She'd been so close to pulling it off. The last twist, the final refinement. She'd presented one face to Yaroslav, one face to her colleagues on the force and another to the paymasters she was meant to meet that day. She'd inveigled Banks into the subterfuge and had believed she'd inveigled Jukes into it all too. It was just the one miscalculation, but it was to prove costly.

Ros led Di to the door.

Inside the house, Elsha looked at the policeman who'd taken up position, you couldn't call it sitting exactly, on the very edge of her sofa. He seemed to perch rather than anything else, as if ready to spring up at a moment's notice.

They'd endured the company of so many officers over the years. She really should have become used to them by now but this one seemed different somehow. He didn't seem like a policeman for one thing. He didn't talk like one, hadn't made the usual tired-sounding speeches about procedures and ground rules and things they were and were not allowed to do.

This officer – called Masters, according to Ros – also hadn't made the usual half-apologetic references to this all being for their own general welfare and protection. He'd simply been introduced by Ros as a colleague, as someone who was there as some kind of back-up, but back-up for what she didn't actually say.

Elsha also couldn't work out the relationship between this new arrival and her youngest daughter. They were clearly colleagues and equally clearly knew each other well. But was there anything more to it than that? Elsha had no idea. Then again she'd never had the faintest clue what was going on in Ros's private life.

And anyway, something told Elsha she really didn't want to pry too deeply into it all.

Macklyn didn't know what to expect either. He didn't mean from the upcoming encounter, he'd been told what that was all about and it was simple enough. Apparently he was about to be reunited with a daughter he'd last seen some twenty years earlier, a daughter he never expected in his lifetime to see again.

He was also to meet a man who'd precipitated the total destruction of his former life and family, rupturing all associations with friends and former colleagues, casting him and what remained of those nearest and dearest to him into some kind of purgatory from which there would be no escape.

That much was clear and it said something about the torpor into which he'd settled in the intervening years that the fact of this much-delayed reunion – or confrontation – didn't really impinge on him too much.

He was aware of it, he knew when it would take place, but that was it. It should have blown his life apart but it didn't. Macklyn had waited for some sudden surge of emotion to rip through him but so far it hadn't come. He too looked at the tense copper across the room and wondered if it would come at all.

Or whether they'd just spend a more or less anodyne afternoon, drinking tea, making small talk before his daughter and her one-time partner left and he and his wife would settle down as they did every evening these days to watch television.

There was a moment, just a single moment before the doorbell sounded, when the light suddenly faded outside.

It was a simple cloud movement. A momentary eclipse of part of the sun, nothing more. Elsha wasn't even sure if anyone else noticed it. The tense-looking policeman didn't seem to. And Macklyn didn't move either although it would perhaps have been remarkable if he had. What he was like in his school she had no idea, but at home she sometimes wondered if she'd married an amoeba.

Then she'd hear him, late at night, small sobs escaping from his mouth as he slept and she knew that somewhere deep down he was still the man she'd fallen in love with and married. Then he'd wake and become unrecognisable again.

But Elsha had tensed. She always did. She hated the moment

the light started to fade anyway and today she could really have done without this passing of the clouds outside. The doorbell sounding a second or so later made her heart race. The police officer, who'd risen to answer the door, glanced at her as he passed, registering her agitation, putting it down to the reunion that was about to take place no doubt.

How could he think otherwise? He hadn't been there that day when the sun also went behind a cloud and a shattered head had emerged from the other side.

But this time there was no clap of what sounded like thunder fracturing the silence. This time there was just a slight scrape as the front door caught on the warped wood of the hall floor as it always did. Then there were the sound of voices from the other side of the sitting room door, the voice of the policeman first and then Ros answering him.

Then the sitting room door swung back open and, for the first time in twenty years, Elsha was suddenly face to face with the second of her daughters, the middle child, the one they'd decided almost from birth was going to be the troublemaker of the family, she just seemed to have that mischievous quality in her from the very beginning.

A scamp, her doting grandmother had called her without living, thankfully, to see her fond prophecy come all-too true.

For a moment no-one seemed to know what to do. No-one moved or spoke. Ros just watched as she always seemed to do, waiting for others to make the first move. The police officer moved back to the sofa where he perched once again.

Elsha looked at her husband but he hadn't moved, in fact she couldn't be sure he'd even looked at Di at all.

Elsha hesitated again, then and for want of anything else to do, held out her arms. Di, her Di, moved into them which was when, for the second time in as many moments, the sun went behind a cloud again but this time Elsha hardly noticed.

She was holding a lost daughter in her arms for one thing.

And Ros had told her, had told her father, had told Di presumably, that everything was now OK, that they were all now safe.

Then came the second ring on the bell.

Masters moved to open the door. His presence was all part of the larger, unspoken, agreement made in the aftermath of the butchery in Yaroslav's apartment. Ros wasn't going to do anything to nail Masters for the Banks incident. In return Masters was going to help out Ros. He didn't quite understand what this family meeting was all about and his attempts to find out even a little more had been met with the usual stone-wall. It wasn't his business and if he didn't want to be there he didn't have to be.

But for the first time Masters felt as if he was on the brink of some sort of breakthrough with the young protection officer. And so here he was.

For now it seemed to be a totally ordinary domestic scene. Some sort of family reunion was taking place from what he could gather. The father seemed fairly well out of things but the mother, even if she didn't seem too mobile, was a bag of nerves. The other daughter, Ros's sister, seemed rather more cool and collected, although as he passed her on his way to answer the door he could see she was trembling.

Ros just looked on, every inch the detached observer which he knew she was not. What she did to release all that pent-up energy and suppressed emotion he had no idea. Part of him didn't want to know. Part of him suspected he wouldn't rest till he'd found out.

Masters opened the door and looked out at a man, middle-aged but still clearly fit, slightly greying hair cropped short. Masters took one step back as the door swung open, the man standing slightly too close to it as if he was hugging the safety of the doorway, crouching close.

As Masters did so some instinct awoke. He literally smelt the onset of danger much as Tyra must have smelt the onset of that smoke in that cramped refuse chute.

For that second he looked into the visitor's eyes, searching for clues, knowing even as he did so that this wasn't the source of the danger he could now sense all around them.

The man looked back at him, which was when Masters saw the blood beginning to stain the front of his coat. Then the buttons on the coat gave way and blood, skin tissue and internal organs began to spill out onto the front step. The man half-turned and Masters could see that sometime in the last few seconds he'd been hit in the back by what appeared to be a flat-nosed bullet, its tip designed to explode just after impact. The bullet had entered his body in the middle of his back and had then exploded deep inside his stomach, forcing his intestines, liver and kidneys out from beneath the ruptured skin.

Back in the sitting room, Ros was the first to hear the dull thud as what sounded like an object landed on the front step outside but she wasn't the first to react. Masters had been right, Di was trembling but it was nothing to do with this reunion with a mother and father she'd never expected to see again.

For years all she'd thought about was her lost lover, a lover she craved, even after all he'd cost her, perhaps because of all he'd cost her, the only one in the world who could possibly understand all she'd endured and the only one who could begin to put it even halfway right.

And today was the day she'd see him again, touch him, hold him and every time she thought about it she felt like her whole body was in the grip of some unendurable fever.

Di was at the door before Ros could do anything, before

Masters had time to press the alarm sensor strapped to his belt to alert the back-up waiting all around the small house to the unfolding emergency.

Di came into the hall, stopping as she saw the slumped figure at Masters's feet, tried and failed to take in the mass of blood and internal body organs that had spilled out on the floor.

Then she looked up and saw the figure standing just across the small street.

And this time there was to be no mistake. This one had done his homework rather more thoroughly than the last hired hand dispatched to complete this assignment. This one knew exactly who he was looking for and who he was now looking at. This time there was no possibility of any sort of error in identification.

Di just had time to realise that the crumpled figure on the doorstep was Emmanuel, her Emmanuel, just had time to take in the unalterable fact that he'd never hold her again, never look into her eyes, never talk to her, when her world exploded for the second time in as many seconds. The bullet followed the same trajectory as the one that had killed her sister some twenty years earlier, the one that had been meant for her, a bullet that was finally delivered to its intended target. The bullet was of the same type as the one that had just killed her former lover, meaning it exploded as it entered her brain, forcing shattered fragments of that brain out through her smashed skull.

For the second time in her life, Ros – coming into the hallway behind – watched the world through the prism of an exploding body, only this time she didn't stand and stare in mute disbelief, this time she acted.

The gunman had already turned, was running back down the road. Ros knew that back-up was at hand, that the most sensible course of action was to wait, to remain inside, to let the specialist marksman Masters had seconded to this most unusual of details get a fix on the fleeing figure and bring him down, but Ros was beyond those sort of considerations right now.

Once again it was simple. All those years earlier she could do nothing. All those years earlier she simply had to stand and watch as everything fell apart around her. But this time she could do something and this time she would and now she didn't care if that meant she too would fall. Perhaps she'd fallen years earlier anyway.

Then, suddenly, the gunman stopped and turned back. He'd seen the marksmen for himself now. He'd seen the guns trained on him. He knew that no matter how fast he now ran he was never going to out-run them. He also knew that he was going to be disabled, not killed, brought down but not finished off. Then he'd be bundled into a police van to begin the lengthiest of interrogations followed by the most savage of incarcerations.

The people he worked for knew it might come to this and they – and he – knew they wouldn't allow it to happen, but that wasn't the reason he stopped at that moment, on that road, still within sight of the house. For what he now had to do, to bring all this to its pre-agreed end, he could have dived into the garden of one of the adjoining houses, bought himself the few moments he needed.

But he had something else to do. He wanted an image imprinted on his eyes, an image to take with him to the grave. The other sister meant nothing, she was just a quarry, a mark and there'd been a fair few of those over the years, names he couldn't now recall, faces only dimly recollected.

But this name he knew. This face he recalled only too well and he wanted her to look into his eyes, he wanted to see that flash of recognition and of realisation. It was a cold and lonely place he was about to go to and he wanted company. If he was going to hell he wanted the last person he saw on earth to be dispatched there too.

Ros stopped as Oskar looked back at her. She didn't move as he nodded, almost imperceptibly. And she kept watching as he put his gun in his mouth, a gun with just one last bullet in the chamber and pulled the trigger.

And Ros kept watching as his head also now disintegrated leaving a body standing, almost comically for a moment, as if she was suddenly watching some giant cartoon, before his body fell, as if it was dissolving, onto the road.

Ros went back to work a month later. She could have taken longer but what was she supposed to do? She'd gone to the club a few times, had even taken the advice of the department doctor and gone on a holiday to the sun.

Not that Ros had any real idea where to go. She'd never been one for holidays in the past. In the end she decided by taking the train to London, standing on Paddington station and watching as destinations flashed before her on an airline self-service check-in on the concourse.

A day or so later she found herself back a hundred years or more as her plane touched down in Bermuda. She was driven past pastel-shaded cottages in impossibly beautiful bays. She walked down main streets in a small capital where passers-by wished her good morning. It seemed like paradise, which made her feel – ever more acutely – that she shouldn't be there. And after a couple more days she paid the airline the extra required to bring forward her departure date and had returned home.

Nothing much had changed in her absence. Her private history remained known only to herself and a very select few, none of whom were in her department, so the double shooting a few weeks earlier in a small town many miles away hadn't excited any particular interest or attention.

The official reason for her absence was a family bereavement which was true enough, only she had to attend two funerals not one. Her mother had finally decided she'd had enough of the life she was living in the aftermath of the shooting and had slipped away in her sleep. That wasn't due to any outbreak of grief at the loss of another daughter. It was simply a recognition that there was no way out for any of them any more.

No matter what they did, no matter where they went the past was always going to catch up with them, no matter how carefully they reinvented themselves. And she was tired of it.

And in the end she did hold the trump card. You can't, after all, kill a dead woman.

Conor nodded at Ros, cautiously, very cautiously, as she came into the office. Then he fell silent. For a moment Ros imagined he was displaying a rare sensitivity in treading carefully around her but a few moments later she realised that Conor was unusually quiet because he simply didn't know what to say and that was nothing to do with dead officers in refuse chutes or respect for her recent family loss.

Conor was out of his depth and she was about to feel exactly the same way.

Ros wanted to get back to work to forget the events of the last few weeks, to get back to what she was actually very good at, perhaps with good reason, preparing clients for a life to be lived from that moment on as a lie.

And she had, it seemed, a new client to look after, a client admitted onto the programme that very morning in fact, which was the good news. And this particular client was in a good position to blow the lid on many others in the criminal food chain which should have been even better news.

Conor handed Ros a file. The downside was that this particular client was also a known cop-killer and cop-torturer. Ros stared at Yaroslav's name, written on the front.

Ros kept staring at the file for a long, long moment, but they had no choice and she knew it. They had to take him in and offer him the usual protection. But from that moment on she and her department would be regarded even more as outcasts by the rest of the force and she knew that too.

Ros took a cup of coffee from the machine, went to the window and looked out over the car park, a few pool cars parked under the Mega-Bed Sale sign which was still missing its B.

At the far end of the small yard, Masters stood with Jukes. Maybe he'd called to talk about Yaroslav, maybe he'd called to talk about the hundred and one other cases currently littering just about each and every drawer, desk and floor right now.

As Ros kept watching, Masters tensed slightly, as if he knew she was looking down at him. Then he looked up, at the same time as the sun partially disappeared behind a cloud.

Ros kept watching Masters, now half-concealed in shadows. Across the yard, Masters kept looking up at Ros, half-hidden on the other side of an opaque divide.